FINAL BOW AT THE BIJOU
AN EVIE HARRIS MYSTERY
Amy E. Lilly

Library of Congress Control Number: 2022915746
ISBN-13: 979-8-218-06104-3

To my Sisters in Crime.

Chapter One

"No one has seen my sister since she stepped into the cabinet."

Evie stopped mid-step in the hallway outside her father's study. She had returned from her morning walk to the corner grocer to buy coffee and was making her way toward the kitchen when she heard men's voices. She pulled the hat pin from her dark blue cloche and set them both on the side table. Easing across the oak floors, she leaned in to listen at the partially closed door.

"I don't know what I can do to help you, Jack. I retired from the police force after my wife and son..." Her father's voice faltered. He cleared his throat and continued, "I'm not the chief anymore."

"I was sorry to hear about their deaths, George," another man said. "We hoped you might make inquiries on our behalf. So far, the police don't appear too concerned about his sister's disappearance. They visited the theater and asked a few questions. That was it."

There was a moment of silence. Evie slowly opened the door to peer in.

"If the great Harry Houdini can't make headway with the Richmond police, I doubt if I'll fare much better," George said.

Evie gasped and dropped the bag of coffee. *Harry Houdini!* Backing quickly away from the door, she hoped her father wouldn't realize she'd been eavesdropping.

"Evie, why don't you join us rather than peep around doorways?"

Evie straightened her skirt and smoothed her hair before walking into the study. Two men stood up to greet her. "Gentlemen, my daughter, Evelyn. Evie, Harry Houdini and Jack Thompson."

The younger man inclined his head. An angry red and purple scar puckered the side of his face near his left eye. The rest of his face was unmarked. "Pleased to make your acquaintance, Miss Harris."

Her stomach somersaulted. Even with the scar, if she were a woman looking for a man, Jack Thompson would catch her eye.

"Evie, you've turned into a picture of your mother," Harry Houdini stepped forward and clasped Evie's hands in his. "I haven't seen you since you were a small child. Now, here you are, a beautiful young lady."

"A pleasure to meet you, Mr. Houdini," Evie stammered. "I apologize, but I don't remember you."

Houdini smiled. "Perfectly understandable. You were about three years old on my last visit."

The world's greatest escape artist was in her father's house. A shiver of excitement coursed through her. It was reminiscent of a night years ago. Evie recalled she had watched Houdini perform on stage with her family. At the time, she thought her father was joking when he said he knew the performer. She couldn't wait to tell her friend, Maeve, about her famous visitor.

"Have a seat." George motioned his daughter to the brown barrel-shaped chair that sat by the fireplace. "You might as well join us. You'll just eavesdrop if I send you away."

Her cheeks blazed, but she didn't care. Evie scurried to the chair, trying hard to school her face, but she barely suppressed a small grin. Houdini was in her house! Was it too much to ask him to sign the latest copy of *Adventure* magazine featuring his milk can escape act?

Her father cleared his throat. "If you can't make headway, I suppose I can ask questions of the old team. Tell me about your sister."

"Flora is a good girl, but I don't think she possesses an ounce of fear," Jack said. "When I was away during the war, my parents tried to shelter her, but Flora wanted to taste every bit of life. She would go to the theater by herself and sneak out to parties, but she's also generous. She would give the shoes on her feet to any poor gal with a sob story. She's no Dumb Dora, but she thinks everyone navigates through the world like she does. Honest and free-spirited."

Jack paused and lit a cigarette. He exhaled, and his eyes followed the smoke as it drifted toward the ceiling. After a moment's silence, he continued. "Flora and I have always been close. It's why I can't believe she wouldn't stay in touch with me. She met Felix Croucher. He's a charlatan and a scoundrel." Jack slammed his fist on the top of the desk which caused Evie to jump. "He and his brother run a two-bit vaudeville show. Felix is the magic act. Flora fell in love with the idea of becoming an entertainer. She went to every performance while they were in Pittsburgh, and her head was full of wild ideas. She said Croucher was going to take his show to Hollywood one day and she could try to get a part in a film. Flora believed his lies."

"It's difficult to get a part in the movies. I should know," Houdini said with a wry smile.

"I tried to tell her that vaudeville wasn't the life for her, but she wouldn't listen. Two weeks later, Flora didn't come home. She left a note to say she'd joined Croucher's act on the vaudeville circuit and would be in touch," Jack said.

"Your parents should have called the police. They might have brought her home," George said. "If that was my Evie, it's what I would have done."

Although she bristled at the idea of her father dragging her home from anywhere, Evie remained silent. If she said a word, her father would banish her from his study, and she wanted to hear the rest of Jack's tale.

"Flora is twenty-one. She's an adult as far as the police are concerned. They don't seem to care she hasn't been seen since last Saturday," Jack said. "By the time I arrived at the theater, the show was long gone. I followed them to Youngstown, but Flora refused to come back with me. She truly believes that Croucher is her key to becoming the next Hollywood star."

"Why do you think she's missing?" George asked. "She may have run off with a beau and made her way west to try her fate with the moving pictures. She'll come home in a week or two and beg forgiveness."

"Normally I'd agree with you, George, but Flora promised to write every day so my parents wouldn't worry. Not that it helped much, but it eased my mother's nerves." Jack ground his cigarette out in the cut crystal ashtray in front of him. "She was excited to be on stage, but she hinted in one letter that she'd return home when the show closed here in Richmond. After we missed letters this past week, Mother asked me to come here."

"The show is part of the Wells Theatrical Circuit. They came here from Baltimore two weeks ago. The only reason they're still here is that Wells is installing new seats and extended their contract," Harry said. "I used to know people on the east coast circuit, but my contacts haven't been able to tell me much. The only thing we've learned is that the Croucher brothers are shady operators."

Jack pulled a photograph from his coat's breast pocket and placed it on the desk. "This is Flora. She was on stage for the final trick with Croucher last Saturday. He did his disappearing cabinet illusion. When the curtain fell, she didn't take a bow with the rest of the show. No one has seen her."

Evie leaned forward and looked at the picture. She stifled a gasp. She knew this girl, but she couldn't tell these men, or it might reveal her own secret. Instead, she chewed her lip and studied the picture. Flora appeared younger in this photograph than when Evie had met her. Petite with dark hair, Flora's eyes were rimmed lightly with kohl. With her similar coloring and slight frame, Evie could pass for Flora's sister. On the night they'd met, Flora's long hair was bobbed, and she had burgundy wine-colored lips. Her slim body had looked phenomenal in the short sequined dress with a fringe. Evie remembered feeling dowdy next to Flora's glamour.

"I contacted Marco Croucher, Felix's brother, and he sent me around Robin's roost. I still don't know where she stayed after the show. A boarding house? A hotel? Who knows? As far as Croucher is concerned, Flora ran off with a man or went back home. My mother is beside herself with worry. The show is here in Richmond for two more weeks. Once they leave, I may never find Flora," Jack said.

"If we get someone with the show to talk to us, maybe I could find out what happened to her. It's a close-mouthed bunch though. Even I can't crack their silence," Houdini added.

Someone on the inside could find out where Flora is, Evie thought.

"It would be the best way to find out information," Mr. Harris agreed. "The cops make folks skittish and less likely to talk."

Not knowing what possessed her, Evie piped up. "I can go undercover. If I pretend to be interested in joining the show, I could look around. Ask questions about Flora."

"Absolutely not." Her father came up out of his chair. "No daughter of mine will consort with folks in show business."

Harry stood up, his face a mottled red, and crushed his hat onto his head. "Sorry to have bothered you. We'll show ourselves to the door."

"Now, Harry, that's not what I meant." Her father's tone was contrite. "Evie's just a girl, and no match for these vaudeville characters. Not everyone is as upstanding as you."

Houdini considered George's words for a moment before he gave a conciliatory nod. "Your father's right, Evie. It may be dangerous, and the theater is no place for an inexperienced girl."

Evie clenched her hands in her lap to keep from blurting out that she wasn't a girl, but a twenty-two-year-old woman. Old enough to marry, have a job, or even go to the theater to find a missing girl. Her protest would fall on deaf ears. It was an old argument she had exhausted with her father long ago. Attitudes were changing about women across the country, but here in the Harris household, they remained the same.

Jack stood up and shook her father's hand. "I appreciate your time, Chief. I'll be staying at the Jefferson Hotel if you learn anything."

"I'll be in touch. Harry, good to see you again." George shook his hand.

Her father walked the men to the front door. Evie waited in the study, thinking about Flora Thompson. When Evie crossed paths with Flora at The Black Cat, an underground booze joint, Flora had been laughing and chatting with a group of men and women, a gin and tonic in her hands. That night, the booze flowed heavily in the room. Evie had spotted Flora dancing on a table as a man sitting in the shadows watched her. The friends Flora had arrived with were gone. What night had that been? A week ago? Two? For the past four years, Evie's days and nights blurred together in a haze of gray, and it was hard to remember one day from another. Her only bit of color were her visits to the gin joints. The tinkle of glasses, the heavy smoke in the air, and the anonymity of the crowd until she stepped on the stage. She was no warbler, but she could belt out enough of a tune to hold the audience's attention. When she was done singing, she stepped off the stage and became Evie Harris once again. Evie remembered wishing she could change places with Flora and have a taste of a life of happiness and fun. A reprieve from the life she lived for the past four years.

After Harry and Jack left, Evie waited for her father to speak. He sat in his large leather chair and packed his pipe with tobacco. Striking a wooden match against the top of his desk, he sucked the fire into the pipe bowl. Within moments, the peaty smell of tobacco filled the study.

"Evie, I know you want to help, but some people in show business aren't decent folks. They don't have the same scruples, and this girl, Flora, fell in with shady folks."

"But Daddy, I wouldn't be in any danger."

"Evelyn Jane Harris, I won't visit this conversation with you again. I'll talk to Sergeant Foster tomorrow and put a flea in his ear to send a man back to the theater. I guarantee that young lady went chasing after a man. Now, go. I have letters to write. Please shut the door behind you."

Disappointment and anger washed over her, but Evie knew better than to argue with her father. She wanted to discover more about Houdini's relationship with her family. How did her father know him? However, her questions would have to wait. Once her father banished her from his study, all chance to chat about Houdini evaporated. At one time, she and her father had been close, but now they were miles apart. In her father's eyes, Evie was still a child. The day her mother had died, time had stopped moving and Evie remained eighteen to him. They were like strangers sharing the same space. Their days no different from their nights. She saw no way for them to come together as a family again.

She shut his door then picked up the coffee she had dropped earlier. Her boots echoed down the hallway as she walked to the kitchen. When the door swung shut behind her, Mittens darted from his warm spot by the stove and weaved his body between her legs. He meowed his displeasure at the absence of milk in his dish.

"Mittens, if I were a cat, I'd spend my life exploring the city and going places I'm not allowed to go to now." Evie grabbed a bottle of milk from the icebox and poured a small splash into the cat's dish. "You, my dear cat, are wasting your feline freedom."

She grabbed an apron from a peg by the door and put it on. Mrs. Fortune normally cooked and cleaned for the family, but she had gone to spend three weeks with her sister who had just given birth to her fifth child. Cleaning the house and cooking dinner was up to Evie in her absence. She pulled out a large stoneware bowl to make bread. In the pantry, she scooped flour out of the bin and cut yeast off the cake stored in the dark corner. She pinched salt from the small cellar kept on the counter, adding it to the bowl away from the yeast, then she added water.

She loved the scent of the yeast as it bubbled and mixed with the flour and water. As her hands stretched and pulled the dough into shape, she recalled the mornings spent with her mother watching her hands perform these same actions. A tear trickled down her cheek, then fell into the bowl.

Leaving the dough to rise, Evie slipped her apron over her head and hung it back on the peg by the door. She needed to call on Maeve to tell her about the morning's visitors. She grabbed a shawl and walked out the back door. The Harris's yard adjoined the Clement family's yard. The children had spent years running back and forth between the homes. Evie's mother, Rose, had been close friends with Maeve's mother, Helen. When Evie's mother had died four years ago, Helen had stepped in to help. If not for her caring words and support, Evie felt she would have died from the grief of losing her brother during the war followed a short time later by her mother. Influenza had managed to invade their house of mourning and added to their pain.

Evie knocked on the Clement's back door before opening it and calling out. "Maeve? Are you home?"

Shoes clattered on the back stairs, and a moment later, Maeve burst through the kitchen door. "I was hoping you'd visit. Who were those fellas I saw leaving? One of them was swell."

"You wouldn't believe me even if I told you," Evie said with a sly grin.

"Well, if you want to keep it a secret, that's fine by me," Maeve said. Evie knew better. Maeve loved a good story. She planned on being a reporter if she ever convinced her parents to let her leave the typing pool at the paper where she worked a few days a week.

"It was Harry Houdini."

"Bull feathers."

"Would I pull your leg? It really was him. I guess he knows my father from back when Daddy was on the force. Harry said he remembered me from when I was little."

"It's Harry, is it? Aren't we the bee's knees now?"

Evie waved Maeve's comment away. "That's not the only thing. *Mr.*

Houdini came to ask Daddy's help. The gentleman with him, Jack Thompson, has a sister who's gone missing."

"That's nothing new. A bunch of dumb bunnies go chasing after any flash fella with a car. They come back home and tell everyone they visited an aunt in the country."

"It's not that kind of missing. Flora Thompson had a gig with a traveling magic show. She stepped into a cabinet that makes people disappear, and nobody saw her after that."

"I saw that trick during a magic show at the Bijou last year," Maeve said, nodding. "The girl walked into the cabinet. The magician and his men twirled it around and said the magic words. When they opened the cabinet, the girl had disappeared, and—"

"I want to help find Mr. Thompson's sister," Evie said, interrupting Maeve before she could continue her tale.

"How are you going to do that?"

"I'll get a job with the show," Evie announced, "and you're going to help me."

Evie outlined her plan as they walked upstairs to Maeve's bedroom. "I'll go to the theater and ask if they need any girls to work the magic show or sing between acts. I'll poke around and see if I hear any news of Flora."

Maeve laughed. "You won't get a job looking like that, Evie."

Evie scowled. "What do you mean? What's wrong with the way I look?"

"Nothing's wrong with your looks except you're more of a wholesome Mary Pickford when you should be a glamorous Gloria Swanson."

"The guys didn't complain about my looks at The Black Cat," Evie said.

Maeve rolled her eyes. "A few local boys with liquor in their bellies don't count. What they know about show business would fill a thimble. You need to cut your hair and put on some glad rags and lip color, so they don't think you're a country girl fresh off the wagon."

"I can't cut it." Evie grabbed her chocolate-colored twist of hair.

"You'll have to if you want to pass as a woman who stays up late and travels with a show. If you ever want to break into show biz, Evie, you need to quit being such a Milquetoast."

"I'm not," Evie protested. "Get the scissors."

After she settled herself on a chair, she closed her eyes, waiting for Maeve to cut. When Evie felt the cold steel of the sewing scissors against her nape and heard the *snick snick* of them slicing through her hair, she thought for a moment that she might faint. She opened her eyes and glanced down at the long tendrils of her hair scattered across the floor.

Maeve grabbed her head and straightened it. "Hold still or it will be crooked."

Evie squeezed her eyes shut and sent a small prayer upward that she hadn't made a mistake. She couldn't imagine what her father would say. "We saw the missing girl that night we went to The Black Cat for me to sing."

"We did?" Maeve gave Evie's chin a nudge upward. "Stop moving."

"She was the pretty girl dancing on the table right before we left. Remember?" Evie blew a stray hair from her bottom lip where it clung.

"Maybe. I was chatting with Constance and her beau, so I wasn't paying attention. Done. Don't look in the mirror yet," Maeve admonished her. "I need to comb and style it with gel first."

Evie surrendered her hair and her future to Maeve's quick fingers as she pulled and curled her shorn locks into submission. "Now for a bit of lipstick and a touch of kohl around the eyes and you, my dear girl, are the epitome of high fashion," Maeve declared. A moment later, she thrust her hand mirror into Evie's hand. "There."

Evie opened one eye and peeked at her reflection. She looked like a different person. Gone was the girl who could still plait her long hair into pigtails at night. In her place was a fashionable woman. Maeve had created kiss curls around her forehead, and the kohl on her eyes made her resemble a movie star or the missing Flora Thompson. Evie loved it.

"I'm a new person."

"You belong on stage singing at a nightclub in New York, not a cheap speakeasy in the Fan." Maeve moved to her wardrobe and opened it. "I have the perfect outfit for you to wear to the theater." She flicked through her dresses and pulled out a drop waist shift dress in lovely robin's egg blue.

Evie slipped off her plain gingham everyday dress and pulled the new one on over her slim hips. She twirled. "How do I look?"

"Lovely. You can keep the dress. It turns me into a blueberry with my curves. Daddy complained it was too short and threatened to take my clothes and replace them with men's trousers if I wore it. Can you imagine me wearing pants? I would die of embarrassment. It's the perfect length for you though with your short legs."

Evie reached over and hugged Maeve. "You're the best girl in the world." Evie put her own clothes back on and folded the blue dress. "I'd better get back home and get Daddy's supper ready. Mrs. Fortune won't be back until tomorrow, so we're surviving on my cooking until then."

"You're welcome to come to dinner here. Mama is making chicken and dumplings tonight."

"Maybe another time. I have a feeling he'll be livid when he sees my hair. Daddy thinks women who have short hair are loose and riding a handbasket straight to hell."

"You can always drive the handbasket and make it a cracking good journey. I'll ride with you to hell and help you steer." Maeve tugged open a dresser drawer. "Take this scarf and cover it. Tell him I put a tonic on your hair, and it has to sit on your head overnight."

"That takes care of this evening, but eventually he'll find out. If Mama were still alive, she would have cut her hair just to shush him." Sadness tinged Evie's words as she thought of her mother.

"When are you going to the theater?" Maeve asked.

"Tomorrow morning when Daddy goes to the stockyard. Mr. Hardesty purchased land out in the county and plans to buy cattle. They are going to a livestock auction. It will take hours."

"I'll go downtown with you and wait at the five and dime. I don't understand why you want to find Flora, but I'll go with you."

Maeve leaned over close to Evie and looked in the mirror. Although they were best friends, they couldn't appear more different. Maeve's pale hair seemed to glow next to Evie's dark bob. Evie wished she could explain to her best friend, but some feelings were too private to share. During that brief encounter, Evie wanted to look like Flora. Act like Flora. *Be* Flora. If she were honest, she wanted to be anyone and anywhere but here. If she said how she felt aloud, Maeve would be hurt, and Evie couldn't do that to her best friend.

"Nine o'clock?" Evie asked.

"You'd better make it eleven. Theater folks don't strike me as early risers," Maeve said.

Evie headed back home with her short hair tucked under the scarf. She spent the rest of the afternoon finishing her loaves of bread and preparing a simple supper of smothered beef with green beans. At dinner time, her father glanced at her headscarf but didn't comment.

"Mrs. Fortune back tomorrow?"

"Yes, sir. You don't care for my cooking, Daddy?"

Her father took a long drink of water. "It's on the salty side, Evie. You should spend more time with Mrs. Fortune in the kitchen and less time mooning over those silly magazines. A husband wants a wife who can cook more than beans on toast."

"I may not even marry. I might just stay a spinster and join the police force." Evie waited for a sputter of indignation from her father, but he disappointed her when he failed to glance up from his dinner plate. "I said I could become a police officer and carry a gun."

Her father reached up and removed his spectacles. He pinched the bridge of his nose and finally looked at her. "Evelyn Jane, women cannot and should not be police officers. There are shiftless characters in the world, and a skirt is ill-equipped to handle them."

"But Daddy," Evie said, "Richmond just hired two women this year. It was in all the papers."

Her father snorted and ignored her comment. "Your Aunt Dorcas telephoned earlier. She's injured her ankle."

"How did she do that?"

"She was at Kitty Hawk for some fool air show. She tripped as she stepped out of a hot air balloon." Her father shook his head. "If she weren't my little sister and your mother's best friend... well, enough said. She asked if you could come stay at her house while she recuperates."

Evie's spirits lifted. "I'm happy to help her."

"Her train arrives back here on Tuesday. You'll need to help her for a few weeks." He speared a green bean with his fork and pointed it at her. "Do not let her talk you into any of her hare-brained shenanigans."

They finished the meal in silence. Evie pictured herself wearing the gray uniform of the female officers with their sharp collars and black ties. She imagined cracking her first big case, and her father saying he had encouraged her right from the beginning. She sighed. It was no use. Everybody expected her to find a husband and marry. It's what nice girls did. She would have children as her future, not a career. Her stomach rolled in protest of such a humdrum life.

After supper, her father retired to his study. Evie washed the dishes and cleaned the kitchen. She hummed *Jazz Baby* as she worked, and soon the kitchen was spotless and ready for Mrs. Fortune's return. Once upstairs in her bedroom, she pulled the scarf off her head. Gazing in her vanity mirror, she looked for a hint of her mother's beauty that Houdini had seen, but the reflection left her wanting. She wiped cold cream across her face. Her fingertips traced slow circles across her cheekbones and forehead as she thought about her mother. Sighing, she stood and pulled a nightgown from her bureau. Four years ago, the pink silk had seemed glamorous and mature when she had picked it out on a rare shopping trip to Washington, D.C. Her mother had splurged on several new outfits for Evie to celebrate her acceptance to college. Rose Harris had rarely defied her husband, but she had stood firm about Evie getting a higher education. Now the dusky rose pink had faded to a pale blush, and its hem was frayed and worn. Evie wouldn't replace it. It was a bright memory from her past that she held onto and savored at night before going to sleep.

Lost in her nostalgia, Evie reached under her bed and pulled out a small cedar wood box. Hidden beneath her mother's embroidered handkerchiefs was a packet of letters from her brother tied up with a small bit of blue ribbon. She untied the bow and pulled the last letter she had received from the small stack.

Dear Evie,

It's freezing cold here in France. Everyone talks about spring in Paris, but I would be content never laying eyes upon this place again.

I got your letter. I wish I could have been there to see you graduate. When I get home, I'll take you to the grandest restaurant in Richmond and buy you the most expensive dessert on the menu to celebrate. I'll even let you taste champagne. After that, it's back to egg salad sandwiches at the Woolworth's once I'm on a policeman's pay.

I can't believe my little sister will be off to Sweet Briar College soon. Try to remember Daddy's still stuck in the nineteenth century. I'm happy Mama could convince him to let you attend. He'll stop blustering once you begin and boast to anyone who will listen about his brilliant daughter.

I've got to go on patrol. The Krauts are active tonight, and I see little sleep in the coming days. Give my love to Mama and Daddy. Tell Mama not to worry.

Peter

A tear slid down Evie's cheek. Peter had enlisted as soon as he was eligible. He had talked nonstop for months about patriotism and duty. What did a nineteen-year-old understand about war and life? Nothing. Evie wiped away her bitter tears and shoved the letters back into the box.

Peter hadn't lived to see twenty. Evie was angry at everything death took away–her brother, her mother, and her own chance at a life. She had come home from college only months after she left home to take care of her mother. She had never returned to finish her education. Now, it was she and her father rattling around in the too-quiet house. She suffocated from the grief that choked the air.

She slid the box back into its hiding place and climbed into bed. Sleep didn't come easy to her. Her mind raced with memories of what had been and with plans for what could be. She thought of the moment with Flora as they had fixed their lipstick in the mirror at The Black Cat. Later, Evie had stepped onto the makeshift stage, and the bright young girl she had shared a mirror with slipped from her mind. Drifting off to sleep, Evie vowed she would find out what happened to Flora Thompson. She would prove to her father she was a capable woman ready for adventure, not a fragile girl in need of a husband.

Chapter Two

Evie heard the front door close before the sun was full in the sky. She peered out her window and saw her father striding down the street. She slipped out of bed and padded barefoot down the stairs to the kitchen. She lit the stove and placed the coffeepot on the ring. Evie cut a thick slice from the loaf she had baked the day before and smeared it with peach preserves. Her father had left the newspaper on the kitchen table. She perused the pages, waiting for the coffee to boil.

She found what she was looking for buried halfway through the paper—an advertisement in the lower left corner. Phenomenal Felix's Traveling Troupe was scheduled to perform the coming weekend at the Bijou Theatre with a short film shown before the performance.

Evie finished her breakfast and had a wash at the sink before styling her hair. She put on the blue dress and picked out a pair of bone-colored shoes. She sat at her dressing table and applied kohl lightly around her eyes and dabbed some color on her lips and cheeks. Evie rarely wore makeup, but on the few nights she went out with Maeve, she always added a hint of color to her cheeks and lips. She touched some drops of *Le Jade* behind her ears and on her wrists, then with a critical eye, she peered closely at her reflection in the mirror. It would have to do.

Shortly after ten o'clock, Evie went to the front door of Maeve's home. Helen answered the door. When she saw Evie's short hair, she let out a small cry. "Your beautiful hair! What have you done?"

"I wanted something different," Evie said. "It's so humid in the summer. I wanted a head start on the weather, so I lopped it off."

"What did your father say?" Helen reached forward and touched Evie's hair.

"Nothing. I waited and not a word." Evie told herself that it wasn't a fib since her father *really* hadn't said a word last night. Since he hadn't seen her hair, it was only a tiny lie of omission.

Helen tilted her head back and forth like a small bird. "It suits you with your fine features, like a fairy creature."

Evie grinned. "Thank you. Is Maeve upstairs?"

"I'm coming, Evie!" Maeve's voice rang out from the nether regions of the house. A moment later, she flew out from behind her mother. She pecked Helen on the cheek. "We'll be back before supper, Mama."

"Do you have pocket change?" Helen called after the girls.

Maeve grabbed Evie's hand and dragged her down the sidewalk. "Yes," she called over her shoulder.

Evie struggled to keep up with her taller friend's long strides. "Slow down. The trolley's not due for five minutes."

"Sorry." Maeve slowed her marathon pace to a trot. "I forget you have short legs."

They arrived at the stop as the trolley clanged around the corner towards them. After they found a seat, Evie turned to Maeve. "What if I find out someone kidnapped Flora, or she's held captive in the theater?"

Maeve arched an eyebrow. "Isn't that the whole reason we're doing this? You want to find something to help the dashing Jack Thompson."

"I'm not remotely interested in Mr. Thompson. Somebody needs to find his sister, and it may as well be me. What I meant to say is what if I discover something horrid has happened to Flora?" Now that they were on their way downtown, Evie felt her earlier bravado evaporating like the fog leaving the James River as the morning sun rose.

"You excuse yourself politely and leave," Maeve said. Life was very black and white in Maeve's world. She would make an excellent reporter one day if she ever got her chance. Just the facts were what she wanted, and just the facts were what she gave.

"I'm talking about afterward. If I find something, I can't tell Daddy. He'll be livid. Skirts have no business poking their noses into crime." Evie dropped her voice down into a rumble as she imitated her father's stern voice.

"If you find something, you and I shall go to Mr. Thompson and let him take the information to the police. Your father will be none the wiser. Chances are you won't discover anything so stop being so nervous. This girl probably ran off with a fella."

Evie knew Maeve was right, but the heavy lump forming in her stomach wouldn't go away. Before she could give any more thought to her plan, the trolley slowed and stopped. They hurried down the steps, skirting around a stray patch of ice on the street. A moment later, they stood in front of the theater and stared at it in silence.

Suddenly, Maeve grabbed Evie by her shoulders and turned to face her. "You are the smartest gal I know. I'll be across the street waiting for you. If you don't come out in an hour, I'll go in and rescue you."

"Okay." Evie took a deep breath. "Wish me luck."

A sign tacked to the door said the theater was closed until Friday, February 24th. She grabbed the ornately carved door and pulled it open. As it eased slowly shut behind her, the hubbub of the street died away, and the eerie silence of the theater embraced her. There was no one in the ticket booth, and the lobby was empty. Evie walked across the grand expanse of the marble entry and peeked through the heavy red velvet drapes. It was dark except for the stage.

"No! How many times must I go through the routine with you?" A black-haired man with a cape tied around his shoulders threw his hands up in the air and stalked off the stage.

The woman he had shouted at stood and glared at his retreating back before she bent to pick up a silver hoop that lay on the floor. A bit of dust puffed from the curtains, and Evie sneezed. The woman squinted her eyes against the stage lights, trying to see up the unlit aisles. "Hello? The theater is closed to the public until Friday."

Evie stepped through the velvet curtains and walked down the aisle to the stage. "I'm Evie. Evie Shaw." She hesitated for just a moment before giving a false name. "I'm not here to see a show. Actually, I'd like a job."

"What's your talent, doll? Singing? Acting?" The red-haired woman wore a green dress that emphasized her curves. She had a jade pendant on a silver chain that drew the eye to her ample cleavage. She had appeared younger at a distance, but under the harsh lights of the theater, Evie could see the faint beginnings of lines creasing the skin by her close-set eyes. Evie thought she was attractive in a hardened way that promised her beauty would beat a fast retreat as the woman grew older. Evie wasn't sure, but she looked like one of the women who had been out at the speakeasy with Flora.

"I can sing, but my friend told me you might have an opening in the magic act."

The woman appraised her. Evie ignored the urge to show the woman her teeth like a horse on the auction block.

"You're the right size and look."

"Pardon?" Evie asked.

"For the magic show. Ain't that what you just said? You have to be tiny to fit into Felix's crazy contraptions. You're the same size as the last girl, too, so her costumes should fit you. I'd be happy not to fill in anymore. It's not my bag. You ever been on the stage before?"

"I–uh–I was in a play at school." She felt the heat rise in her face. What on earth made her say that? She really was a rube if she thought a silly school performance qualified as stage experience. "And I sing for folks now and then."

Her shame amplified when the woman snorted. "That ain't stage experience, darlin'. You go back to your school plays and let the professionals get back to work."

Knowing she was losing ground, Evie blurted, "I'm a fast learner. If the show doesn't open again until this weekend, I'll do whatever it takes to learn the routine."

"We don't have time for a little girl looking for a lark. Our show opens on time. Felix and Marco can't coddle the likes of you. I suggest singing in your church choir if you want eyes on you."

"Let me have one day, and I'll show you what I can do," Evie begged. She felt her chance slipping away.

"I'd like to see what this little chickadee can do, Annie," a male voice drawled. A tall man emerged from the shadows of the stage and strolled toward Evie. He was wiry with his dark hair slicked back. Etched above his lip was a trace of a mustache. He looked to be in his mid-thirties, but Evie was a terrible judge of age. The rolled sleeves of his white shirt revealed powerful forearms corded with veins. His brown eyes raked over her, then he held out his hand. "Marco Croucher, and you are?"

"Evie Shaw." She placed her small hand in his. His skin felt rough and warm against hers.

"Well, Evie Shaw, why do you want to come work for Felix's magic show? Fame? Fortune? Escaping a bad love affair?" His dark brown eyes flashed amusement as Evie flushed again. "We've had several girls with the same problem on our stage begging for a chance. What makes you different?"

"I'm smart, not afraid of the stage, and I know I can do this if you give me a shot. I've always wanted to be on the stage, but my father would never allow it."

"It appears the chickadee doesn't like to have her wings clipped." He let his thumb trace lightly on the back of the hand he still held. "Be here at ten tomorrow morning, and we'll see how you do."

Evie shivered away from his bold touch and withdrew her hand from his grip. She swallowed hard. "What about Felix Croucher? Do I get to meet him today?"

"Oh, don't worry about him," Marco drawled. "My brother does what I tell him. I keep him… focused."

Marco turned and hopped back on the stage. Evie was dismissed. He put his arm around Annie, who leaned against him.

"Thank you, Mr. Croucher," Evie said.

"Please call me Marco. In show business, we're family."

Evie gave a nervous wave goodbye and hurried out of the theater. When she left the dark confines of the building and stepped onto the sidewalk, her eyes blurred momentarily from the sun's glare. Evie felt the cold, nervous fear that had tinged her encounter with Marco Croucher leaving her body. She had done it. She would be on the job tomorrow and see behind the velvet curtain.

"What happened?"

Evie jumped and clasped her hands to her chest. "Goodness! You frightened me, Maeve. I thought you were heading to the five and dime?"

"I was too nervous for you, so I hung around at the edge of the alley. Was it that horrible?"

A huge grin cracked Evie's face. "I report to the theater tomorrow at ten o'clock. I have a day to prove I can be a magician's assistant. I'm on the case." Evie ushered Maeve down the sidewalk to Miller & Rhoads. "Let's get some lunch, my treat, and I'll tell you everything."

An older gentleman held the door for them as they entered the department store walking arm-in-arm a few minutes later. They had to wait in line before it was their turn to order at the crowded lunch counter. They carried their egg salad sandwiches and glasses of sweet tea to a small Formica table in the corner.

"I don't know what happened. One minute I was introducing myself, and the next minute, I was begging them to give me a day to prove I could do it. It was like I became the kind of woman I read about in my adventure stories. My heart's still beating fast." Evie put her hand to her chest and laughed.

"Did you poke around at all?"

"I didn't get a chance. I met a bulldog of a woman who was ready to send me back to high school. Marco Croucher, Felix's brother, came out and told me he'd give me a shot. Something about him made me uncomfortable. It was like I was a little goldfish with a hungry shark circling me."

"Golly, are you sure it's safe? I'm all for having a bit of fun, but not if you're in real danger." Maeve frowned. "What will you tell your father? If you're gone every day, he'll wonder what you're doing."

The minute she had walked into the Bijou Theatre, the thought of performing in the show took hold of her, and all thoughts of consequences had left Evie's mind. The big stage was so different from the tiny one she sang from in The Black Cat. She sipped her tea and thought for a moment. "I need a few days to investigate. I'm not officially joining the show. I'll find out what I can about Flora's disappearance, turn the information over to Mr. Thompson, and Daddy will be none the wiser." She bit into her sandwich.

Maeve gave Evie a baleful look. "If you say so, Evie, but your father didn't become chief of the Richmond Police Department by ignoring what's going on around him. He's going to find out."

"Didn't I tell you? I'm going to stay at Aunt Dorcas's."

"How'd you manage that? Your father hates your aunt."

"He doesn't hate her. He disapproves of her. Anyway, she's broken her ankle, which is why I'll be at her house for the foreseeable future," Evie said.

"Excellent! Not that she's broken her ankle, but that you get to stay with her. I love your aunt." Her blue eyes twinkled. "I must find an excuse to come visit you."

"You know Aunt Dorcas loves to see you."

"I'll bring some of her favorite molasses cookies."

They finished their lunch and spent the next hour shopping for fabric and sewing notions. With her fashionable modern bob, Evie wanted to make a new dress, too. Although she could buy one straight off the rack, Evie enjoyed sewing. It reminded her of when she was a child sitting by the fire watching her mother's quick fingers sew buttons on a dress or mend a tear in Peter's trousers.

Once they finished shopping, they took the trolley to the stop on their street. After a quick chat with Maeve's mother, Evie went home. When she walked in the front door, the sound of humming greeted her. Mrs. Fortune was home from her sister's. Evie found her in the dining room waxing the sideboard.

"I'm glad you're back," Evie greeted her.

"Lord, child, what did you do to your hair?" Mrs. Fortune's hazel eyes widened in shock. "Mr. Harris must a had himself a heart attack because you sure are a sight."

Evie's hand tucked her short hair behind her ears. "The stars in Hollywood have their hair like this."

"I don't know about no Hollywood stars. Your daddy won't be likin' your hair lookin' like a boy's."

"Daddy hasn't seen it yet. He might like it."

"Humph. I best be making his favorite roast for dinner then. Maybe a full belly will keep him from lockin' you in your bedroom until you're safely married." She flicked the feather duster across the sideboard and squinted at Evie. "What kind of trouble are you getting yourself into?"

Evie raised her eyes and batted her eyelashes in her best portrayal of innocence. "Why whatever do you mean?"

Mrs. Fortune placed her hands on her wide hips and stared at her. After a long silence, Evie relented. "Harry Houdini came to the house yesterday."

"Mr. Harry was here? I haven't seen him in a month of Sundays."

"You know Harry Houdini?"

"Yes, Miss Evie. Last time I laid eyes upon him, you were a little one just out of your nappies. If I recall correctly, he loved my peach cobbler." She tucked the duster into the large pocket of her apron and headed through the swinging door to the kitchen. "It's too early for peaches, but I got sweet potatoes in the pantry. Mr. Harry might enjoy my sweet potato pie."

"He might not visit again," Evie protested. "He came with a gentleman named Jack Thompson, whose sister, Flora, is missing. Mr. Houdini thought Daddy might help him."

"Your father was the best police officer in his day. Straight and honest as an oak tree your daddy was when it came to workin' cases. Not like some of those men they got on the force with one hand out for a dollar while their heads turned the opposite direction. If Mr. Harris is on the case, I guarantee he'll find her."

"Actually, *Miss* Harris is on the case."

Mrs. Fortune stopped what she was doing and put her hand on Evie's forehead. "No. You ain't got a fever. Did you eat today? Are you lightheaded?"

Evie laughed, then told her about the events of the day. When she finished, Mrs. Fortune sat down on a wooden chair at the table. "Lord, that's a mighty big lie to tell your daddy, Miss Evie."

"Just a few days," Evie promised. "Then I'm finished."

Mrs. Fortune harrumphed again, stood, and pulled out a mixing bowl from a cabinet. Without another word to Evie, she began to pull the ingredients from the ice box for supper. Evie swore she heard her mutter under her breath, but she ignored it. She left the kitchen and waited for her father to arrive home. She paced like a caged cat from the front parlor to the kitchen until Mrs. Fortune had shooed her away with threats of breadcrumbs and water for dinner if she didn't leave her be. Evie finally settled into a chair in the parlor by the fire with a magazine that failed to hold her attention. An hour later, ten-year-old Charlie ran up the street to deliver the message that Mr. Hardesty and her father were dining in town following the auction. Evie ate supper with Mrs. Fortune in the kitchen before retiring for the evening to her room to read a novel.

The next morning, she waited to descend the stairs. When she heard her father leave the house to purchase his daily newspaper, she slipped into the kitchen and found Mrs. Fortune rolling out a crust for a pie. Evie poured a cup of coffee and drizzled honey over a slice of bread.

"You be careful down at the theater. You don't come home by dinner, I'm gonna tell your daddy what's going on, you hear me?" Mrs. Fortune fixed Evie with a stern glare.

"I'll be careful."

Evie didn't have on a stylish outfit like the day before, but she felt her tailored blue plaid skirt with a blouse still made her look sharp. She didn't know what Felix Croucher might expect of her today, and its sporty style allowed her legs to move freely. She tucked her hair under her new cloche she had purchased with Maeve the day before and added a heavy wool cape to guard against the dampness and cold that still lingered from the recent snowstorm.

Her father was returning with his paper when she walked back downstairs. He removed his brown homburg and hung it on the hall tree by the front door. "Good morning, Evie. Where are you off to this morning?"

"Good morning, Daddy." She pecked her father on the cheek, hoping he wouldn't notice her hair safely hidden under her hat. "I'm going downtown with Maeve this morning. I'll be back for dinner before I go to Aunt Dorcas's this evening."

The headlines from the newspaper he held in his hands already distracted her father. He opened his study door, barely giving her another glance. "Hmm… oh, yes, yes. Excellent idea. You girls have fun."

Evie walked down to the corner to wait for Maeve. They had planned to meet at nine thirty and ride the trolley. Maeve would spend the morning shopping. The two had agreed they would meet back at a diner at two o'clock if Evie finished rehearing. If not, they would meet at Maeve's house no later than five o'clock.

Maeve dashed to the corner as the trolley jingled its way to a stop. Out of breath, she hopped on board and slid onto the seat next to Evie. "That was a close call."

"What happened?"

"Mama knows we're up to something. She always knows when any of us are doing something we shouldn't. She's a female Sherlock Holmes. I told her we were going to the early matinee but wanted to visit the shops beforehand."

"Did she believe you?"

"I'm here, aren't I? The look she gave me as I walked out the door guaranteed I'll face an interrogation when I return home."

The trolley lurched to a stop at the corner of 8th and Broad Street. Maeve hugged Evie and wished her luck. Maeve would stay on the trolley until its next stop further downtown. In her nervous haste,

Evie tripped her way down the steps. The wind whipped the cloche from her head and sent it tumbling down the sidewalk. She darted after it. Just before it rolled into the street, she swooped down and grabbed it.

She backed away from the road to avoid a vegetable cart pulled by an old nag and felt a hand on her shoulder. Startled, she let out a yelp and turned to see Jack Thompson.

"Miss Harris, a pleasure to see you again." Jack tipped his hat in greeting.

Evie felt a blush rush up her neck to her cheeks. "Evie, please." She glanced at her watch and noted she had ten minutes before they expected her at the theater.

"Would you like to join me for coffee?" Jack asked. He motioned toward the diner at the end of the block.

She experienced a small twinge of regret, but she quickly squashed it. Her eyes went to her watch again. "I'm sorry. I've got an appointment in a few minutes. Perhaps another time, Mr. Thompson."

"Do me the courtesy of calling me Jack. Another time, Evie." Jack tipped his hat again and strolled down the street.

Evie rushed to the theater entrance and jerked the doors open. She stepped into the dim interior and took a deep breath. Her hand shook as she parted the curtains and stepped through them.

A young man wheeled a tall black box onto the stage. He straightened and pulled a dingy white handkerchief from his rear pocket and wiped his face. He reminded Evie of a badly formed statue with its bits and pieces slightly off kilter and the clay of the face smeared towards the left. He dropped his handkerchief. When he stooped to pick it up, he spied Evie. "Hello?"

Evie stepped out of the unlit recesses at the top of the aisle and walked down to the stage. "Hello. I'm Evie Shaw. I'm the new assistant. Marco Croucher told me to come today. Are you Felix Croucher?"

The man barked a laugh. He sat on the edge of the stage and slid carefully down next to her. "Not me. I'm Will Mason, props man. Felix should be out in a minute. Follow me and I'll get you up on stage. Performers usually come in through the alley entrance."

"I'm sorry. I didn't know."

Evie followed him as they skirted the orchestra pit and made their way to a black curtain on the right side of the stage. He pulled it back and revealed a plain wooden door. He opened it and motioned her through. She climbed the narrow steps to the side stage. Her heart fluttered in her chest. She walked out to the stage with Will trailing behind her. She turned and looked up at the empty balconies and imagined what it must be like with the orchestra playing and every seat filled. She smiled.

"Who are you?" A man strode across the stage, his oiled black hair glistening under the lights. He halted a few feet from her and stared. He had hooded black eyes that pinned Evie in place like a butterfly on display.

She fumbled for words. "Evie H–Evie. Evie Shaw. I'm the new assistant. Well, I'm here to try out to be the assistant."

He continued to stare at her, and then his mouth lifted at the corner in a small smirk before giving her a wide smile. "Apologies. For a minute, you reminded me of someone else. In fact, you could be her twin. Wishful thinking, I suppose. I am the Phenomenal Felix Croucher." His eyes twinkled as he winked at her and bowed deeply. His smile changed his persona from frightening to congenial, and Evie felt her nervousness depart.

Evie couldn't help but grin back at him. She gave a small curtsy. "Glad to meet you, Mr. Croucher. I'm excited to get started."

"First, call me Felix. Mr. Croucher is my brother. Second, let's get you changed," He placed a hand on the small of her back and guided her towards the wings of the stage. Evie slid away from his touch. Were all show biz men so forward?

She glanced back at Will and saw him staring at Felix. The hint of anger she caught on his face disappeared when he caught her looking at him. Will shrugged and turned away. Evie hurried to keep up with Felix. He led her down a narrow hallway which ended in a large open room with roughly built wooden alcoves against one wall. There were several people in the space, including the woman from yesterday. Felix stopped and knocked on the entrance to a back room. "Mary? This is Evie Shaw. She's my new assistant. Get her a costume. Evie, I'll see you out front in fifteen minutes."

A large woman lumbered to her feet from her seat behind a rack of clothes. She was raw-boned with frizzy gray hair that framed her florid face. Her smile revealed gapped gray teeth. "C'mon and I'll get you fixed right up, love. I'm Mary Mason. I'm in charge of costumes." Her accent wasn't the slow drawl of Virginia.

"Mason? I met a Mister Will Mason," Evie said.

"Aye. That's my son."

"Are you English?"

Mary's fleshy lips split into a smile again. "From London. Been in America a long time though." Her beefy hands flipped through the array of skirts and jackets. She pulled a dress out with a royal blue and silver-striped bodice and a flounced skirt and thrust it at Evie. "I think this one will do. You best get changed. Don't want to keep Mr. Felix waiting."

Evie looked at the scrap of fabric in her hand and wondered where the rest of it was. Surely this was only half of it. The Bijou was family friendly, but what she held in her hand was more of a bawdy burlesque costume. She looked around the large space for a dressing room. She didn't see anywhere to change from her street clothes into a stage costume.

"Bit shy, are you?" Mary asked. She laughed and pointed to a row of alcoves. "Over there, love. It's where all the girls do costume changes between acts. Pull the curtain. This is a ladies' only space, so no one will bother you."

Evie took the costume and rushed to a nearby alcove. She tugged a dirty white sheet which served as a curtain across the space. A three-legged stool sat in the corner, and a few nails hammered into the wall served as clothes pegs. Glancing nervously around the small space, she slowly unbuttoned her blouse. She hung it up and then stepped out of her skirt. She quickly pulled the costume over her head and buttoned it. One of the small crystal buttons at the bottom of the bodice was missing.

With no mirror, she had no way to measure her appearance. She tugged at the short skirt to cover her knees. The act of tugging at the bottom caused the top to reveal more of her already bare cleavage. Not that she had much to show. Her lithe body was only now coming into fashion after years of causing her no amount of embarrassment in school.

She sat down on the stool. *What in the world was I thinking? I'm not a policeman.* How foolish was she to think she could find a missing girl? She was in the soup now, though, and there was nothing for her to do but try to get through the day. Perhaps she should just throw in the towel. She could put on her clothes and politely excuse herself and go home.

She shook her head. Evelyn Jane Harris was not a quitter. If her father saw her now, he would never let her out of the house again. But if she found Flora, it would all be worth it. She stood up, squared her shoulders, and walked out of the alcove.

She stopped at the edge of the stage. Felix was talking to a petite woman dressed in a costume like hers. The conversation appeared heated, so Evie waited and listened.

"I'm going to say something to him. This can't continue, Betsy," Felix said. He put his hand on the woman's shoulder and pulled her into his arms. "You don't have to stay with him, you know. I can help you leave."

Betsy pulled herself from his embrace and looked up at him. "And go where? I have no money. Family doesn't want to take care of me. All I have is right here." She swept her arm around. "No. Leave it be, Felix. For my sake, I'm begging you."

"It's for your sake that I need to say something."

Betsy shook her head and walked off the stage. Felix gazed after her.

Evie waited a moment before stepping out. "I'm ready."

Felix's grim expression immediately brightened. He walked towards her with his arms open wide. "Ah, Evie, you are a gorgeous butterfly in that costume. You'll help me dazzle the audience, for sure."

Evie blushed. "I haven't performed on a proper stage, but I've always dreamed of being in show business."

As the words came out of her mouth, Evie realized that they were true. She loved singing on the occasional Friday nights at The Black Cat, even if she had to tell a lie to do it. She dreamed of performing on a big stage. She would save her pocket money and rush to the newsstand to purchase *Screenland*, and she followed all the stars. A typing pool and a husband couldn't be all there was in her future, could it?

"It's fine. I can teach you everything you need to know to assist me on stage. We're going to start with the disappearing cabinet act today. It's the highlight of my show, so the trick must be flawless." Felix nodded at the large wooden box centered on the stage. "Before we start, promise you won't reveal my secrets. Can you promise me that,

Evie?"

"Yes, sir." Evie couldn't imagine who she would tell about today besides Maeve and perhaps, Jack. "Your secrets are safe with me."

Evie prayed her face wouldn't betray her fear. She would step into the same cabinet as Flora. She worried Felix could hear her knees knocking.

He smiled. "Excellent. Step over here to the cabinet, and I will walk you through the trick."

Evie went over to the wooden box. Upon closer inspection, she could see it had small wheels on the bottom that were hidden by a blue curtain that covered the box and touched the floor. This was the magic trick that Maeve had described, and the last place Flora had been seen. Her stomach flip-flopped.

"The biggest part of magic is showmanship. I could put you in the box, make you disappear, and it's still magic, but does it entertain?" Felix gave her a probing look.

"No," Evie said. She didn't know where he was going with this, but she felt that it was the answer he expected.

"Exactly. To entertain the audience, they need a performance. An extravaganza." He turned from Evie towards the empty auditorium. "Ladies and gentlemen. Welcome to the Phenomenal Felix's magic act. What you see here tonight will astound and amaze you. The magic the spirits give me will make you scratch your head and believe the unbelievable. Tonight, I will make my beautiful assistant disappear." He stretched out his hand to Evie and twirled her around toward him. She tripped over her own feet and would have fallen except Felix had a tight hold on her.

Felix stopped and laughed. "You must be quicker than that, my dear Evie. Let's try it again."

He reached out his hand to her and this time, Evie twirled gracefully across the stage until she stood by his side. Felix pulled back the cabinet's curtains. "Look around the cabinet. What do you see?"

Evie looked around the box. "Nothing."

Felix shook his head. "Wrong. Look down. What do you see?"

Evie leaned down and saw a small hole in the floor. "A hole. I see a small hole."

"Good. Now the trick is for you to step into the box, move to the side, then insert your finger into that hole and lift. Try it."

Evie did as he instructed. She felt awkward and worried she might fall face first out of the box. She reached down and discovered that when she pulled, part of the stage lifted and revealed a wooden ladder that disappeared into the murky bowels beneath the stage. "It's a trapdoor."

"Exactly. The key to the disappearing cabinet is to place it exactly on top of the trapdoor. An inch or two to the left or right and the trick fails."

"Where do the stairs go?" Evie asked, intrigued by the ingeniously simple nature of the trick.

"Under the stage. When you are through the trapdoor, you must reach up and quietly close it. The audience must never discover its presence. There is a set of stairs that will take you back into the dressing area. Usually, I make this trick my finale, but I'm thinking of having you reappear on stage in a new trick. I'm still working out the details, but it promises to be a showstopper. The spirits haven't revealed all to me yet."

Evie's brows furrowed. "Spirits? Is this theater haunted?"

Felix became serious. "Not the theater. Me. I'm haunted."

Chapter Three

Evie stayed silent. Was Felix serious? She knew a number of people believed in the afterlife, including Mrs. Fortune. It was Harry Houdini himself who demonstrated spiritualists were frauds by revealing the tricks of their trade. Like Harry, she wasn't gullible enough to fall for a spiritualist's tricks. She didn't voice her thoughts. Instead, she asked, "Ghosts haunt you?"

"Spirits," Felix intoned. "Lost souls who want to help me bring comfort to their loved ones through my magic. I've seen things..." His voice trailed off and a fevered look came over him.

Evie glanced around. No one else was near them, although she heard voices backstage. She hadn't come prepared for this. A missing girl was more than enough. She couldn't cope with a man who believed in the dead rather than the living. She had enough focus on the dead in her own home. She hadn't expected it to follow her here to the Bijou.

She coughed. "I'm going to climb down the ladder to finish the trick."

Her voice broke his trance. "What? Sorry. My mind seems to wander more often these days." He poured a glass of water from a metal pitcher placed on a small table at the front of the stage. "Go ahead. Then meet me back on stage. Afterward, we'll run through the entire trick, so you can practice your timing."

Evie climbed down, her feet careful to find each rung as she clutched the edge of the ladder. Ten rungs later, she found solid ground beneath her. She looked around the space. There were no electric lights under the stage. Instead, the space was lit with a few small lanterns. She spotted the steps leading up, but she hesitated. She was here to investigate Flora's disappearance. The girl had stepped into the same cabinet as she herself just had, climbed down that ladder, and then no one saw her again.

Evie glanced around. Cobwebs covered the large wooden beams above her head. The floor beneath her was brick and mortar. It was too dark. She grabbed a lantern from its hook, but it did little to illuminate the space. Spiders and other crawling creatures that Evie couldn't bear to think of skittered away from her as she explored. She knew that Felix would expect her back on stage any minute. Despite her fear, she had to be quick. As the pale glow from the lantern broke the blackness in one corner, something glinted amongst some stacked wooden boxes. She squatted down and placed the lantern on the floor. Nestled in a crack was a crystal button like the ones on her costume. She used her fingernails to pick it up. She noticed a dark stain on the corner of one box. It continued in a splatter onto the bricks below. She shivered and gripped the button. Evie realized Flora had worn the same outfit she now wore. Had she lost the button the night she disappeared?

"Evie!" Felix's voice echoed against the walls as he called down to her. "Are you in trouble? Can you not find the stairs? Do I need to come and get you?"

Evie stood up and brushed the cobwebs and dust from the bottom of her skirt. "I'm coming."

She hung the lantern back on its hook. As she rushed across the floor, her foot caught on a loose brick. She caught herself on a nearby box, then hurried up the set of steep steps. She pushed through the curtains at the top and breathed. The dark and damp of the cellar seemed to follow her into the light of the theater. She stopped by the alcove where her clothes hung and dropped the button into her pocketbook.

"Are you leaving already?"

Evie jumped. Will stood across the room by a rack of costumes watching her. The intensity of his gaze flustered her. "No. I dropped my trolley money when I changed earlier, and I just spotted it. Need to make sure I can get home. I'm sorry, but I thought this was the ladies only area."

He had the courtesy to lower his eyes. "I was bringing my mother a bolt of fabric she needed. Almost everyone's gone out for the afternoon. The singers and other stage acts don't rehearse until after two. Felix has the house for now."

"How many other acts are there?"

"Five, including the magic show. Felix's act is the top billing." He shifted and looked like he wanted to say something else. "You'd better get back on stage. Mr. Croucher doesn't like to wait for his assistant."

Evie hurried. Felix paced around the box, mumbling to himself. Impatience flitted across his face before he gave her a tight smile. "Evie, if you are going to be my assistant, you must be quick. Now let's take it from the top, and I want you to make it through the trapdoor with the curtain closed. It will be pitch-black, but you must be as quiet as a church mouse. The audience has to believe that you have disappeared into the heavens."

"No lights?" Evie squeaked.

Felix shook his head. "Only on this side of the stage. Will always leaves a light by the steps that lead up to the backstage. You'll be able to see well enough to traverse the space."

She would have to go under the stage again where the brown spot stained the red brick. A trail of drops and spatter that resembled blood. Ignoring the *frisson* of fear that traveled up her spine, Evie nodded her understanding, not trusting herself to speak.

"Ready?" Felix motioned for her to take her place. He looked serious for a moment as he raised his eyes to the rafters, but then he nodded his head as if agreeing with some unseen entity. He smiled and held his hand out to her. She hesitated for a fraction of a second before grasping his hand. This time, she found herself running beneath the stage, not willing to linger in the eerie dark.

For the next hour, they practiced her disappearance before Felix decided she might be ready to perform it in front of an audience. Evie had mastered not making the curtain move when she lifted the trap door. Her only flaw in the trick was lowering the door without making a sound, but Felix reassured her that she would master it.

"Tomorrow, I will cut you in half," Felix said.

Evie's eyes widened and her jaw dropped. "Pardon?"

He laughed. "Wait and see. My sister-in-law, Betsy, is also one of my assistants. You'll work with her. It's fortunate that you're the perfect size for this trick. It's difficult for me to find someone tiny enough to fit into some of my contraptions, but you are the exact girl I need."

"Does that mean I have the job?" Evie couldn't keep the excitement from her voice.

"Fifteen dollars a week, and you cover your own expenses. If you work out, Marco will increase it. Deal?" He held out his hand.

Evie grasped his hand and shook it. "Deal. Guess I'm lucky you had an opening in the act."

"Yes," Felix said, not looking at her.

"May I ask what happened to the previous assistant?"

Felix wrinkled his brow. "Why do you want to know?"

Evie shrugged. "Curiosity. If I'm going to go on the road with the show, I'd like to know what made someone leave. Poor pay? Bad food?"

Felix didn't answer for a moment. He bent down and straightened the cuff of his pants. "She disappeared."

"We've been practicing the same trick for the past two hours," Evie said, her voice nonchalant.

"No. She disappeared and didn't return to the show."

"Goodness! What happened to her?" She pretended shock.

"She may have had enough of theater life. It's not for everyone. Our parents raised Marco and me in the theater, but not everyone cares for the nomadic lifestyle. The last time I saw her, she stepped into that cabinet there and disappeared. It was the final performance of the night. I didn't see Flora–her name was Flora–again. I thought… well, never mind what I thought. She decided this wasn't the life she wanted and ran back home." He smiled, but it didn't reach his eyes. "No matter. You're here now, and we'll be magical on stage together."

"I'm sorry to hear she didn't work out, but I appreciate you giving me a chance. I'll see you tomorrow then."

"Until then." He gave her a slight bow.

In the dressing alcove, Evie slipped out of her costume and back into her regular clothes. She reached to pin up her hair before she realized she didn't need to anymore. She glanced at her watch. It was half-past two o'clock. She walked down the block to the small diner where she and Maeve had agreed to meet before going to the show at the Lyric. Maeve was sitting at a corner table with a few shopping bags by her feet drinking a glass of tea while reading a newspaper.

The diner had been a favorite of the two friends when they were younger. They often stopped and ate lunch there after a trip to the shops. The stainless-steel counter with its diamond pattern and bright red leather stools remained, but the booths had received a much-needed update. Instead of uncomfortable wooden seats, it now had booths with matching red leather cushions.

Maeve leaned forward and whispered. "I ran into Mama at the store. She asked where you were, and I told her you had walked down to the pharmacy for some headache powders. I hated lying to her."

"You're giving me a headache with your fast thinking," Evie said. "Thank you for not telling her. She would feel obligated to tell Daddy. I hate lying, too, but he wouldn't understand. I'm suffocating under his expectations."

"I understand," Maeve said. "Did you find anything?"

Evie dug around in her pocketbook and pulled out the small button. "I found this. Mary, the costume mistress, told me I'm the same size as the previous assistant. She must be talking about Flora. My costume was missing a button."

"It's a missing button." Maeve shrugged. "Poor mending, but that's not a crime."

"I'm not finished with my story. I found it underneath the stage. It was in a crack next to what looked liked dried blood."

"That's a clue." Maeve took the button from Evie's hands and peered at it. "It's got a bit of fabric attached. Maybe someone ripped it off, but it may have caught on the corner of something and torn off. You can tell Mr. Thompson what you've discovered, and perhaps he can convince the police to search under the stage."

"That's not enough to convince them. The police will want hard evidence, and I'm going to find it for them. I'm going back to the theater tomorrow."

Maeve's mouth dropped open for a moment before she spoke. "You're going back? Why?"

Evie shrugged. "I enjoyed performing on the stage with Felix."

"And? This could be dangerous. It was a lark to go for a day or two, but to work there?"

Evie struggled to find words to explain the thrill when she completed the disappearing cabinet trick without missing a beat. When she looked out from the stage, the audience appeared in her mind, and it made her heart beat faster–not from fear, but from excitement. Would Maeve understand? "I felt alive and excited for the first time in four years."

Maeve's blue eyes filled with tears. "Oh, honey." She moved in for a hug.

Evie stopped her. "I'm okay. At least, I feel like I'm going to be okay."

"I understand." Maeve squeezed Evie's hand. "I have a question. How are you going to keep your father from finding out?"

"I'm going to tell him," Evie declared.

"Golly! Since this might be the last time I set eyes on you for the next few years, perhaps I should borrow those pearl earrings you promised me."

Evie rolled her eyes. "He won't lock me in my room. Once I explain to him it's the only way to find out what's going on, he'll understand."

"Your father? Are we talking about the same George Harris?"

Evie laughed. "He'll yell and bluster about the house, but I'm not a child. I can take care of myself."

Maeve stood up. "Let's go watch Hope Hampton in *Star Dust* at the Lyric theater before you go to meet your maker. You shouldn't go back to the theater, and I really don't think you should tell your father."

***

After the movie, they went to Maeve's house for a cup of tea and some butter cookies. Evie continued to tell Maeve about her rehearsal and the enigmatic Felix Croucher. She drank her last sip of tea and prepared to go home before Mrs. Fortune sent out the promised search party. "Mr. Thompson was outside the theater this morning. He invited me to coffee, but I would have been late. I said no."

"Why didn't you tell me earlier?" Maeve leaned forward, hungry to hear more. "Did you tell him you were on the case?"

"Of course not! He'd be sure to stop me. I'm going to present him with all my evidence as a *fait accompli*."

"He sure is swell looking." Maeve sighed. "You couldn't go wrong accepting an invitation to coffee from a handsome gentleman like him."

Evie laughed at her boy crazy friend. Maeve was going steady with Harold Sumner, but she wasn't ready to settle down and get married. Harold was a great guy. Maeve's promise to be promised kept him content.

Was Jack Thompson handsome? Evie recalled his face with its puckered scar by the eye. She hesitated. "I wouldn't call his face handsome. It's interesting."

Maeve gave her a shrewd look. "You like him."

"I just met the man. He was polite, and he's not unattractive, but I'm not interested. I'm not ready to step out with anyone."

Maeve regarded her for a moment before standing up. "I suppose I believe you. Do you want me to go downtown with you tomorrow? Well, if you're allowed out of your house again."

"No. I'll be fine. I need to go home and pack a few things to take to Aunt Dorcas's house."

Evie walked through Maeve's backyard to her own. She gasped when her foot slipped into a patch of icy mud. The lights were on in the kitchen, and she could see the large form of Mrs. Fortune through the window. She slowed her steps as she thought of what she should tell her father. Would he keep her from going back? Should she tell him about the blood in the basement? If it was from a workman or a mouse, she would appear a fool and have wasted everyone's time. No, she was better off not saying anything.

The bite of the late winter wind drove her to quicken her pace up the steps to the kitchen door. The scent of apples and cinnamon filled the kitchen, and Evie sniffed in appreciation as she walked inside. Mrs. Fortune was singing a hymn so loudly that she didn't hear Evie. When the wind caught the door and slammed it shut, she screamed and dropped the potato she had been peeling.

Clasping her hands to her chest, Mrs. Fortune said, "Lord, child. Give a body a heart attack comin' in here like that."

"Sorry. The wind is getting stronger. I think a storm's brewing tonight." Evie took her cloak off and draped it on the back of a kitchen chair. "My shoes got muddy walking through the yard. I need to go upstairs to change them."

"Your father's in his study. I guess he ain't seen your hair yet because he's in a good mood." Mrs. Fortune leaned over and picked up the errant potato and peeled it. "I've got a pork butt in the oven and after I boil these potatoes, supper's ready. Why don't you go on in there and get it over with? Maybe the apple pie I got cooling on the table will sweeten him back up."

"I doubt it," Evie said in a sour voice. She ignored her wet stockings and picked up a potato. She grabbed a knife to help Mrs. Fortune with dinner.

"I don't need help. You go on." Mrs. Fortune shooed her.

Evie sighed and picked up her hat and cloak to hang them by the front door. Her footsteps echoed on the oak floors. To Evie's ears, each step sounded like thunder in the empty hall. The study door was closed. Evie considered slipping upstairs to her bedroom and pleading a headache.

"Evie? Is that you?" Her father's deep voice stopped her.

"Yes, Daddy."

"Good. I'll drive you to your aunt's house after supper. You can take some of Mrs. Fortune's apple pie to her."

The door to the study opened, and her father stood before her. The smile that appeared on his face drooped. He stared at her, and his mouth turned down further. "What in God's good name did you do to yourself?"

"I cut my hair," Evie said, her voice small.

"Why in the hell would you do a fool thing like that?" her father roared, and Evie cringed. She hated when he raised his voice.

She screwed up her courage and lifted her chin. "All the women are doing it. It's fashionable."

"Of all the silly things that girls get up to, cutting their hair to look like a man's is the most incredibly st–foolish thing I've ever seen. Evelyn Jane Harris, I never thought I would see the day that my daughter would act in such an unladylike fashion. If every girl in Richmond went swimming in the James River in December, would you do it, too?" he bellowed. "If your mother–"

"If Mama were here, she would let me cut my hair. She would let me get a job. She'd be proud of me. I'm twenty-two, Daddy, not twelve. It's time you realized it." Evie's voice shook with anger. She spun on her heel to go to her room.

"Evie, I don't–" Her father reached out his hand to stop her.

She whirled back around. "It's time you let me go, Daddy. You can't keep me a child anymore. Every day that I'm stuck here, I fade a little more."

Before he could respond, Evie ran up the stairs to her room. She locked her bedroom door behind her. Her hands trembled as she unbuckled and removed her shoes. After unrolling her stockings and hanging them to dry, she flopped back on her bed and stared at the ceiling.

He's never going to see me as anything but a little girl. She wouldn't tell him she was investigating Flora's disappearance now. She put her hands on her hot cheeks. Evie closed her eyes and tried to calm down.

Twenty minutes later, a soft tapping at her door, pulled Evie from her reverie. "Miss Evie? Open the door."

Evie considered ignoring Mrs. Fortune, but it wasn't the housekeeper's fault. She slid off the bed and unlocked the door. "I'm not going downstairs."

Pushing the door open with her elbow, Mrs. Fortune bustled in with a plate filled with a hot roast pork sandwich and a slice of apple pie. Mittens trailed after her and hopped onto Evie's bed. "You need to eat. I figured on you not wanting to eat supper with your daddy, but if you're going to stay up here in your bedroom and pout, you might as well eat." She set the plate down on Evie's writing desk.

"I'm not pouting," Evie protested.

Mrs. Fortune put her hands on her ample hips and stared down at Evie. "You're up here in your room with your bottom lip poked out so far it could catch rain. If that ain't pouting, I don't know what is."

Evie sighed, then sat down on her desk chair. She picked up the top slice of bread. Mrs. Fortune had put the farmer's cheese she liked so much on top of the thick slice of pork. "He thinks I'm still a little girl. I'm old enough to marry and start a family. Not that I want to ever marry."

She cocked her eyebrow at Evie. "And you stomping your way up the steps and pouting is gonna make your daddy realize you're grown?"

"I suppose not." Mrs. Fortune had known her since she was born. She had taken care of her mother while she lay in her bedroom dying from influenza. Evie didn't dare lie to this woman who was like her second mother. "I'm tired of being treated like a child. I need a life outside of this mausoleum. I miss Peter. I miss Mama. But I feel like I died with them."

Mrs. Fortune sighed and sat down on Evie's bed. Her large body caused the bed frame to squeak in protest. "Your daddy is like an old mule who's worked its whole life at a grist mill. He knows the circle he's got to walk, and he doesn't stray from the circle. You can unhitch that old mule, but until you lead it away with a rope, it ain't gonna go nowhere but 'round and 'round. It's what it knows. Your daddy knows what he knows about women from your mama. Your mama was a fine woman. Proper and graceful. Her entire world was your father, you, and Peter. It's what everyone expected, and she loved it. Your daddy doesn't understand that someone would want anything different from what Rose wanted."

"So, you're saying, I need to let him stay like an old mule stuck in his circle?"

Mrs. Fortune smiled. "You know what makes that old mule leave his circle? A lump of sugar. You put a lump of sugar in front of a mule, and he'll follow you anywhere. You could try being sweet and talking to your daddy. It takes longer for menfolk to figure things out. It's up to us women to guide them. Why did I make your daddy's favorite apple pie tonight? I knew he'd spot that hair of yours and turn into an old mule at the mill. After I feed him that slice of pie, you come on down and talk to him."

Evie thought a piece of pie was unlikely to calm her father down especially if he heard about her investigations at the Bijou Theatre. It might work on his anger over her hair though. "I'll consider it."

Mrs. Fortune harrumphed. She stood and walked out of Evie's bedroom, pulling the door shut behind her.

Evie picked up the sandwich and nibbled at the crust. She didn't want to talk to her father this evening, but Mrs. Fortune was right. They only had each other now. She wished her father would understand that she had a brain in her head and knew how to use it. She took a bite of her sandwich. The appetite that had left because of her anger returned. A few minutes later, she was scraping the plate with her fork to get the last trace of the apple pie.

She carried her plate downstairs. Her father's study door was open. On her return from the kitchen, she knocked on the doorjamb.

Her father looked up. He removed the pipe from his mouth and motioned for her to come in and sit down.

"Daddy, I'm—"

He put up his hand to stop her. "Evie, I don't know what's going on with you, but you're my daughter. If there is something you want to discuss, you can always come to me. I'm not your mother, and I won't pretend to understand your feminine ideas of style. If you want to have short hair, then have short hair. I don't like it. I'm hearing many tales of young girls cutting their hair and wearing clothes that belong on a harlot, not nice young ladies. I don't want folks saying that I'm not doing right by your mama's memory."

Evie opened her mouth to protest, but her father continued before she got a word out. "Let me finish. Your mother and I raised you to do the right thing, and I'm trusting you. You won't disappoint me."

Evie knew then that she couldn't tell her father what she was doing at the Bijou Theatre. "Thank you, Daddy. It's just that all the girls are bobbing their hair. If I don't like it, I can grow it long again."

"I suppose you're right." He puffed on his pipe.

"I'm off to Aunt Dorcas's. I suppose I'll be gone at least a fortnight."

At the mention of his sister's name, her father's face soured. "Dorcas is the oddest bird. Like night and day, she and your mother. All that traveling around to dangerous places without a chaperone and a lick of sense. Just don't let her talk you into anything so foolish."

"Yes, sir. Thank you, Daddy." Evie didn't dare look at her father for fear he would sense her deception.

"Go on into the kitchen and get a big slice of pie for her. If the old Buick will start in this cold, I can drive you to her house." He stuck his pipe back in his mouth and returned to his stack of papers. Without looking up, her father said in a gruff voice, "I love you, Evie Jane."

"I love you, too, Daddy." Evie fled from the room before she blurted out the truth. She went to the kitchen and prepared a basket of food to take to Aunt Dorcas. The task kept her mind busy and away from the thought that she continued to build a web of lies and deceit in order to have any kind of life.

Chapter Four

An hour later, her father stopped in front of his sister's house. He came
around and opened Evie's door and helped her out. "I won't go in. It's
getting late, and I'm sure Dorcas doesn't want visitors." Her father
gave her an affectionate peck on the cheek before returning to the
Buick. It sputtered its way down the road with its headlamps making
little difference in the dark winter night.

Evie hurried down the brick walkway to Aunt Dorcas's house. The
evening had turned colder, and small pellets of sleet struck her bare
cheeks. It relieved her to see the lights on in the front parlor. Evie
made her way up the icy brick steps and used the heavy brass knocker
to announce her arrival.

"Evie! So good of you to come and take care of me. Come on in out
of the cold. I've just opened a fresh bottle of my special medicine. It's
guaranteed to take the chill out of your bones." Aunt Dorcas leaned on
a black cane with a silver fox head on the top. She motioned her inside.
"Go on into the front parlor. I'll be there in two shakes of a lamb's tail.
This old ankle of mine slows me down."

Evie dropped her bags inside the door and moved to help her aunt,
but Dorcas shooed her away. "Don't fuss. I'm injured, not infirm.
You're here to keep me company so I don't go crazy waiting for my
ankle to heal."

Evie hung her damp coat on the rack next to the door and removed
her wet boots. She took her ice-coated hat into the front parlor and
placed it on the hearth near the fire. Her frozen toes uncurled as the
fire slowly warmed them. Once her chills had eased, she sat down on

the settee and looked around the room. Aunt Dorcas had added a few pieces since Evie's last visit. There was a footstool covered in zebra hide. A carved wooden statue of a man and woman intertwined in a position that Evie could not imagine being possible stood on a pedestal in the corner. There was a precariously balanced stack of newspapers and magazines next to a lady's writing desk. A peacock feather pen stood in an inkwell next to Aunt Dorcas's leather-bound journal. Despite the clutter, the house was dust-free and filled with the scent of lemon verbena.

"Ah, here we are, Evie. I adore your new hairdo. It's very fetching. Now, this is just what the doctor ordered–a nice glass of medicine made from some fox grapes I picked this summer." Aunt Dorcas indicated a large silver tray on a side table by the settee. She nudged her chunky black cat named Sabine out of the way with her cane. Her aunt's own steel gray hair was cut in a razor-sharp bob that brushed her wrinkled cheeks. She settled her thin frame next to Evie and poured a healthy dose of dark red liquid into two crystal goblets. "Here's mud in your eye."

Evie picked up the glass and sniffed it. She hesitated, then took a tentative sip. It had the sweet wildness of summer. "I like it, but you'd best not let the temperance ladies catch you with this alcohol. You'll find them protesting outside of your door."

Aunt Dorcas turned the bottle around. *Doctor D. Cooper's Health Elixir—Cures Arthritis, Weak Blood and the Common Cold.* "I still had some of your granddaddy's empty elixir bottles in the basement. They come in handy every summer." Aunt Dorcas put her foot on the zebra skin footstool. She was clad in a pair of men's black trousers, a red blouse, and her big toe peeked out of a dark red wool sock.

"I need a favor," Evie said, then quickly added, "If you don't want to do it, I'll understand."

"How much?" Aunt Dorcas pulled a silver case from her pants pocket and pulled out a cigarette. She silently offered one to Evie.

"No, thank you. I don't need money, Aunt Dorcas. I need information."

"On men? Honey, I thought you learned all about that years ago when you were stepping out with that handsome Johnathan. It's just like your daddy to put a kibosh on young love. Your mama and I used to–"

"No, it's not a man," Evie interrupted, keeping her impatience tamped down. Aunt Dorcas could chat for hours on many subjects but love and sex were two of her favorite topics. She liked to shock and discomfit those around her. "I'm working undercover at the Bijou Theatre. A girl's gone missing."

Aunt Dorcas spilled a small amount of the wine from her glass as she abruptly set it down on the side table. "What? Does George know what you're doing?"

"Of course not, but I'm a grown woman. I'm tired of everyone acting like I'm still a pigtailed little girl!"

Aunt Dorcas chortled and hugged Evie to her. "It's about damn time you found your backbone. Good for you! I'm glad to see you finally got some spirit in you. I worried you would turn out like my stick in the mud brother. No offense."

Evie let out the breath she'd been holding after her outburst. The breath turned into a sob. "Aunt Dorcas, I feel like I can't breathe for want of some freedom. I miss Mama and Peter, but I can't take much more of sitting around the house waiting for my life to happen. I can't break Daddy's heart. I'm all he's got now, and I'm afraid if I have a job or go to school, he'll wither away in that house without me."

When Evie's sobs turned into hiccups, Aunt Dorcas handed her a silk handkerchief to dry her eyes. "You cannot stop living your life. Rose wouldn't have wanted you to stay at home. I understand why you left college to come home and take care of your mother, but you could have gone back. You are too smart and too beautiful to waste your life in a mausoleum of your own making."

"Who would take care of Daddy? He'd be all by himself." She took a drink of the wine. It eased the chill from her body.

"Mrs. Fortune is there. He has friends. He has me for what it's worth. Your staying at home has enabled your father to keep you wrapped in cotton and treat you like a child. It's time you struck out on your own." Aunt Dorcas refilled Evie's glass without asking.

"A vaudeville show is definitely a big step towards striking out on my own," Evie said. "I'm not ready to tell Daddy though."

"Well, I know George well enough to obfuscate, distract, and dismay him if he asks me about you. By the time I'm done, he'll forget what he asked. You just leave him to me. Now, how can I help?"

Evie told her all about Flora and her disappearance from the cabinet and her decision to go undercover as a magician's assistant.

"Felix believes the spirit world is helping his performance."

Aunt Dorcas didn't hide her grimace of distaste. "Hogwash and foolishness. They are charlatans and con men. Dead is dead. If everyone who died came back as a ghost, this big old world would be mighty crowded. I'd be bumping into an ex-lover on every street corner."

"Doesn't Sir Arthur Conan Doyle believe that spirits are real?"

Her aunt's eyes went misty for a minute. "Oh, poor Arthur. I met him one evening at a gentleman's club in London. It shocked him I had the audacity to come to the club to begin with and to wear trousers. We later became friends. But he has a tendency towards romantic and far-fetched notions. It's his grief that has clouded his good judgment." Aunt Dorcas waved the memory away and turned her small, dark eyes to Evie. "I have quite a collection of books on the subject. You are welcome to borrow them but use caution when you're with Felix. Men who come back from battle have minds that can be fragile. It also makes them unpredictable and possibly dangerous."

"I'll be careful," Evie said. "You should write your life story. I'm positive it would be a bestseller."

"I would love to write my memoirs, but not now. I'm packing up and traveling to Paris as soon as this ankle is healed. I have a certain poet who owes me a bottle of wine, and I plan to collect the debt in person."

Evie took a sip of the illegal elixir and smiled at her aunt. She couldn't fathom how her father could be so different from his free-spirited sister. Aunt Dorcas had never married, at least that she could recall. There was her trip to a tropical island which involved rum and a ceremony which may have been a marriage ceremony or a harvest blessing. Aunt Dorcas was never quite sure. Evie's mother, Rose, had been her best friend. Her mother and Aunt Dorcas had planned to travel the world together, but when Rose had met Dorcas's brother, George, love overruled adventure. Her solo status hadn't hindered Dorcas. She had spent the past thirty years traveling, writing, and leaving a string of broken-hearted men in her wake.

The wine had taken effect, and Evie relaxed. She stared into the fireplace watching the flames as she thought about Felix and his revelation about the spirits. "During rehearsal, Felix would pause and stare off into space like he's listening to someone. It's eerie. I never believed in spirits. If they were real, surely Mama would have visited me after she died."

Aunt Dorcas laid a gentle hand on Evie's knee and patted it. "Your mother was the best friend I ever had and every day, I miss her. She had a way of brightening my day, even when I was in a foul temper. You know, I never begrudged Rose her happiness with my brother. Our plans may have changed, but our friendship remained the same."

Evie wiped away a tear. "Am I selfish for wishing for a moment more with her and Peter? I have so much to tell them both, then I feel guilty for not wanting to share the same thoughts with Daddy."

"No, you're not selfish. A girl needs her mother. It isn't a poor reflection on your father at all, so you have nothing to feel guilty about."

The two of them sat in silence in front of the fire, lost in their own memories. Ten minutes later, Evie heard a soft snore coming from her aunt. She covered her with an old Navajo blanket her aunt had brought back with her after a train trip to Arizona a few years ago. Walking out of the parlor, Evie went into the library. Fortunately, her aunt was meticulous with her books. She insisted on shelving them in the same order as one would find in a public library. Evie traced the leather spines. Psychology books by Freud nestled next to books by Plato. Farther down on the shelf, Evie found books on the occult. One book, *Conjuring Made Easy*, had a pentagram on the front that made Evie shiver. She hadn't been to church since her mother had died, but a lifetime of being preached to on the evils of witchcraft and sorcery remained in her mind. She found a slim volume on spirits and the afterlife and slid it from the shelf. In an upholstered chair near the window, Evie cracked open the book and read.

An hour later, she closed the book. Her neck was stiff, and she rotated it left and right to remove the kinks that had taken up residence while she had huddled over the tiny type on the cheaply printed yellow pages. She had learned a great deal about how to contact the dead via spirit boards, spirit guides, and apports, which from what she could tell involved spirits producing objects. Nothing in the book, however, convinced her that spirits were real.

"Did you find what you were looking for?" Aunt Dorcas asked. She stood in the doorway leaning on her cane. Her mussed hair made her resemble a hedgehog coming out of its burrow.

"I don't think so. I learned how spiritualists claim to contact the dead, but nothing tells me why the dead would linger here on earth." Evie stood up and stretched. "I do have a better understanding of the 'how' of clairvoyance."

"You should talk to Harry. He knows more about spiritualism and fraudsters than anyone else," Aunt Dorcas said. "I'm surprised you haven't asked him already."

Evie put the book back on the shelf. "I didn't want to be presumptuous. I'm not even sure he's still in Richmond."

"Harry would be delighted at the chance to educate you on the topic. It's a hobby of his, and with his movie making career in shambles, he might welcome the opportunity of a distraction."

"I suppose it wouldn't hurt to ask," Evie said. "Maybe he can tell me why so many people cling to the idea that spirits communicate with us. Reverend Willett would froth at the mouth at such nonsense."

Aunt Dorcas snorted. "He preaches nothing but sin and damnation. I can't believe my brother converted so he could buy into such horse manure. Personally, I walked away from religion a long time ago and never looked back. Makes it much easier to do the things one wants to do with no need to Hail Mary or ask forgiveness in a box."

Evie would never say it aloud, but she had the same ideas floating in her head. Daddy converted from Catholicism when he married Evie's mother. He embraced the strict Southern Baptist rules and said he enjoyed Reverend Willett's fiery tirades from the pulpit.

"You can tell he's a good preacher if he keeps you awake," her father always said.

Evie found Reverend Willett's sermons frightening. As a child, she had fretted over every minor infraction and would lay awake wondering how hot the fires of hell really were. She wondered if there was even a God at all. If he existed, she wanted answers to what she had done to deserve so much grief in her life.

Shaking thoughts of the upright Reverend Willett from her mind, she stood. "I should get to sleep. Do you need my help with anything before I go to bed?"

"Do you want to help me uncrate my latest acquisition from Egypt?"

Evie's eyes widened. "You have a crate from Egypt? You should have led with that, Aunt Dorcas. I wouldn't have wasted my time reading that dry explanation on the occult. Is it a mummy?"

Aunt Dorcas chuckled. "I wish. I think you'll find this somewhat related to your current interest in the afterlife. Follow me. It's outside in the garden shed."

After slipping her shoes back on and grabbing her coat, Evie trotted after her aunt, who was quick despite the cane and injured ankle. The garden shed door had a large lock, but Aunt Dorcas produced a key from her coat pocket and in a moment, the two of them were inside. Evie used a match to light the lantern hanging from a hook by the door. A crate covered in stamped letters and strange squiggles sat amid the metal rakes and garden shears.

"Hand me that hammer." Her aunt pointed to a claw hammer laying among some other metal tools Evie didn't recognize.

Aunt Dorcas struggled to pry up the wooden lid. Evie hurried over and taking the hammer, she cracked the lid. A faint whiff of the grave filled Evie's nostrils. She shivered. Aunt Dorcas rummaged around amongst the tools and found a metal pry bar. With Evie's help, she wiggled the bar between the box and the lid and together they pressed down. With a resounding squeal, the nails on one side gave up their grip. They moved to the other side, and ten minutes later, the lid pried loose. The two women lifted it off and set it aside. Evie stood on her tiptoes to peer inside and gasped. A jackal head peeked out from the shavings.

Aunt Dorcas reached down and slowly lifted the statue from its wooden coffin. After wiping away stray bits of sawdust, Aunt Dorcas turned it towards Evie. "Recently arrived from Egypt via parts unknown, may I present to you, Anubis, guide to the dead."

Chapter Five

Evie awoke before the sun had cracked the city's skyline. Aunt Dorcas had put her in the Peacock Room — a beautiful bedroom on the second floor decorated in blues and greens on the walls and bed with radium silk curtains of silver adorning the windows. She had fallen asleep shortly after her head hit the pillow, aided by the elixir of fox grape wine, but her sleep had been restless. She splashed her face with water and combed her hair before slipping on a calico dress. Evie could hear Aunt Dorcas's light snoring through her closed bedroom door. She tiptoed down the steps with her shoes in her hand, so as not to wake her aunt, and went into the kitchen.

The basket with the slices of apple pie sat on the counter. Evie cut a small sliver and slid it onto a plate. She buckled her shoes before taking a bite of the pie. The taste of apples and cinnamon filled her mouth. Mrs. Fortune's pies were the envy of all the other women on the block. She didn't have time to linger and enjoy the sweet treat, though. She scribbled a note telling Aunt Dorcas she was out for the morning for rehearsal and would return home this afternoon to help her. Donning her coat and hat, she opened the kitchen door and left.

Evie trotted down the sidewalk. The street was empty except for Mr. Crabtree's milk truck making its rounds through the neighborhood. It was too early for the trolley, but the walk would give her time to think. *If it was blood on the floor, was it Flora's? How could she find out?*

The closer to downtown Richmond Evie got, the busier the streets. She glanced at her watch. It was barely seven o'clock. She needed to find something to occupy her morning before rehearsal at ten o'clock.

She spotted a newsstand and purchased the *Richmond News Leader*. There was a small coffee shop on theater row where she could sit and wait for her day to begin.

A half hour later, Evie wondered if she should have stayed home and delved into more of the books on the occult. The coffee was bitter despite her liberal additions of cream and sugar. She waved the waiter away when he attempted to top off her cup. She tried to focus on the article regarding the new construction in the surrounding counties, but she found her attention wandering.

"Is this seat taken?"

Startled, Evie looked up to find Jack smiling down at her. "Oh! Um… you're welcome to join me."

Jack removed his hat and sat down. He motioned for the waiter to bring him a cup of coffee before turning his gaze to Evie. "How are you this morning, Evie?"

"I'm fine. Any word on your sister?"

Jack shook his head. The waiter placed a cup of coffee in front of him. He took a sip and grimaced. "This could clean paint off a battleship."

Evie showed him her half full cup of lukewarm coffee. "Or keep you up for three days straight." When he smiled at her, she noticed the scar at the corner of his eye lifted. "I hope you don't mind me asking, but were you injured in the war?"

Jack rubbed at the puckered tissue. When he did, she noticed scars that traveled up beneath his jacket cuff on the back of his hand. "I got into an argument with the wrong end of a Kraut's weapon. I won but earned these." His voice was calm and matter of fact.

"I'm sorry. It's just… I lost my brother in France." She shook her head.

"It's okay. I can talk about it now. I'm one of the lucky ones. We lost a quarter of our battalion by the end of the war." He picked up his cup of coffee and took a small sip. "What brings you downtown this early in the morning?"

Evie considered lying to him, but Jack, more than anyone, had a right to know her plan. "I'm undercover."

Jack's eyes widened. "Pardon?"

"I'm investigating your sister's disappearance."

Jack set his cup down with a loud clatter, which drew a

disapproving look from their waiter. "I must have misunderstood. Did you say you're investigating Flora's disappearance?"

"Yes."

"I'm surprised your father changed his mind. When Harry and I left your home the other day, I thought he made himself perfectly clear on his views of theater folks."

"He doesn't know." At his sound of protest, she hurried to explain. "I'm not in any danger. I'm working as Felix's assistant. As far as he and his brother know, I'm just another girl with stars in her eyes."

"Evie, I appreciate your attempt to help me, but your father's right. This is not something a lady should do."

In a pique of anger, Evie stood up. She pulled a coin out of her purse and placed it on the table. She tugged her coat on and squashed her cloche onto her head. "If a man can do it, a woman can, too. I am not a child. You may not appreciate my efforts, but I'm determined to find your sister!"

Jack stood and placed a restraining hand on her arm. "Please sit back down, Evie. I'm sorry."

Evie reluctantly returned to her seat. She stared defiantly at him, too angry to speak at first. "Are you able to get into the theater and look around?" she asked, her jaw jutting forward.

"I--no." He sighed. "I tried to, but when I went backstage, Marco Croucher tossed me out."

"Well, I'm your gal on the inside," Evie said. She leaned forward. "I'm only looking around to see if I can find anything of your sister's that might indicate where she is. What better way to do that than to work for the magic show? You said so yourself."

Jack stood up. "I can see you're determined, and I can't stop you. If you're going to do this, then you need to come with me."

She followed him as he strode out of the diner. "Where are we going?"

He held the door open for her. "To see a man about magic."

Fifteen minutes later, Evie stood in the lobby of the Jefferson Hotel. Jack had excused himself while he used the house phone to call Harry Houdini's room. She stared at the ornate columns which surrounded the lobby like golden soldiers waiting for commands. The grand staircase made her wonder if royalty would appear soon. She spotted what appeared to be a rough piece of wood near a marble pool further into the lobby. Intrigued, she moved closer. Evie had read about some of the new modern art that incorporated the natural world. Here was her chance to see it.

"I wouldn't do that if I were you, Miss." A porter in a burgundy uniform with gold epaulets held out a gloved white hand to stop her.

"Is there something wrong?" Evie asked, trying to peer around the man. She just wanted a glimpse. It wasn't as if she were going to touch any of the artwork.

The porter stepped aside but still held up a restraining arm. "Meet our more permanent hotel guests."

Evie gasped. There in the pool were several alligators. One even had his snout open to reveal an intimidating row of jagged teeth. "Oh my!"

"Indeed, Miss. They sometimes wander out of the pool and startle some of the guests. I do my best to keep it from happening, but… "

Evie took a hurried step backwards. "I think I'll wait over here in one of these comfortable chairs. Far, far away from the alligators."

When Jack returned, Evie said, "Did you know there are reptiles in this hotel?"

Jack chuckled. "It wasn't the reason I booked a room here, but it has proved entertaining to see guests' faces when they first spot the brutes."

He led Evie to a table in the dining room. The tables were covered with snowy white tablecloths accented with burgundy napkins. Bud vases containing single roses graced the top of each one. Evie sighed with delight at the sheer elegance of it.

"Let me buy you a cup of coffee while we wait for Harry," Jack said.

"I'm dying for a decent coffee," Evie admitted. "I left the house this morning before seven."

"Then let me buy you breakfast. If you're looking into my sister's disappearance, a meal is a small price to pay."

A small man with a shiny, bald head appeared next to their table. Jack ordered two cups of coffee. Evie looked over the menu. She goggled over the prices. Although her family wasn't poor, the price of two eggs and toast was more than she spent in a month on trolleys and lunches with Maeve.

"I'm not very hungry. Perhaps just a slice of toast." Her empty stomach growled its objection to her words. She flushed. "I must be hungrier than I thought. Two scrambled eggs and toast, please."

When the waiter had departed, Jack leaned across the table. "I want to apologize. I realize I might have been overbearing earlier. I appreciate your help with locating Flora. I'm at a loss on where she could be. Yesterday, I spoke to a gentleman named Mr. Mason at the stage door when he was taking a smoke break. He told me Flora had headed home to Pennsylvania."

"Will Mason. He works props. His mother, Mary, works as the costume mistress. I've met them, but I haven't questioned either of them." Evie described her first day at the theater. She left out the stain on the box and floor, not sure what to say. "I've learned nothing of value yet. Rehearsal starts at ten o'clock this morning. I'll see if I can ask him why he thinks Flora returned home."

"Ah, Evie Harris, what brings you to visit us this morning?" Harry Houdini sat down on the seat next to her. He wore a coat of navy-blue wool, which made his eyes appear pale sky blue instead of gray. "I'm surprised your father let you lower yourself to meet with a showman like myself and in a hotel, no less. The moral and upright folks of Richmond will wag their tongues."

"Daddy meant nothing with his words. He's protective of me since Mama passed." Evie surprised herself by how quickly she rose to her father's defense.

"Mr. Harris doesn't know she's here, Harry. It seems Evie has taken it upon herself to investigate Flora's disappearance. She's gone to work at the theater as Felix Croucher's new assistant."

Harry let out a bark of laughter. "You, my dear girl, are your mother's daughter."

"Did you know my mother well?" Evie asked. She ached to gather more memories of her mother and brother before they faded away. Evie would never forget the sound of her mother's voice or the dimple that would appear in one cheek when her brother smiled. She guarded those memories for fear of losing them. She added each new story someone told about them to the memory chest in her mind to be taken out and savored on nights when she longed for their company.

"I met your mother when your father was just a sergeant, and your brother was a baby. She had spirit and would brook no argument from anyone, including your father. She made me handcuff her to the radiator in your house and insisted on learning how to uncuff herself with just her teeth! After that, I visited your home whenever I traveled through Virginia. Unfortunately, it's been some time since my last visit, and I missed seeing your dear mother before she passed."

"I never realized my parents knew you. Mama never said."

"That's my fault, I'm afraid." He lit a cigarette and inhaled deeply. He blew a large smoke ring that floated lazily up towards the ceiling. "I asked my friends in law enforcement to keep my relationship with them a secret. It wouldn't do to give the public too much insight into my magic tricks. Enough of me, tell me about your trip to the Bijou."

Evie then retold the men everything that transpired.

"There's something else." She hesitated, weighing her words. "There was a reddish-brown stain under the stage, and a button from one of the assistant's costumes on the ground next to it. I think the stain might be blood."

Jack's olive complexion paled. He stood up abruptly, causing his chair to tip and crash to the floor. "I'll thrash the truth out of Croucher!"

"Sit down, Jack. It won't do to go over there half-cocked. Evie might be mistaken," Harry said.

"I couldn't be sure because Felix interrupted and told me to hurry back onto the stage. I'll try to look at it closer today," Evie said.

Jack hesitated, then sat back at the table. He turned to Evie. "I don't like you going back there. I'll go to the police and insist they look closer at Croucher."

Evie appreciated Jack's concern, but she knew the police would take no notice of a missing girl who had run off with a vaudeville show. They were more concerned with Bolsheviks and riots at factories, than a girl who had run away from family. "I have to go back. I've only been there a day and haven't asked the right questions. I spent so much time yesterday learning one trick that I didn't have much time to look around."

"I don't know. My sister is missing. Now, I worry you'll disappear, too. Something isn't right with that show. I believe Flora discovered something and wanted to leave."

"I'll find out. I need a few more days, and I'll be careful."

"You'll check in with me or Harry every day?" Jack insisted.

"Yes," Evie promised.

"Well, now that we have that settled," Harry said, "I think I can help with your learning. Finish eating your breakfast, and we'll get started."

Evie and Jack ate their breakfast while Harry sipped a cup of coffee. The eggs and toast stopped Evie's stomach rumbles, and the coffee erased the bitter aftertaste from the cup at the diner. Once the waiter had cleared their plates, Harry pushed his cup to the side. He reached into his pocket and pulled out a box of safety matches.

"I will use my magnetic personality to keep these matches from falling to the table." Harry showed Evie and Jack the box of matches and demonstrated that the box was full. He held the matchbox with one hand and removed the lid with the other. He dropped the lid onto the table, then turned over the full box of matches. The matches failed to fall.

"How did you—" Evie said in amazement.

Harry held up his hand to silence her. "I command the matches to drop."

The matches tumbled out of the box onto the table. Evie clapped her hands in delight. "That was amazing!"

"Not amazing," Harry said. "It was a simple sleight of hand. Watch me."

Harry picked up the matches and placed them back in the box. He showed the box to Evie and Jack. On top of the matches was a broken half match wedged above and holding them in place.

"But I saw the full box of matches and didn't see the broken one," Evie said in protest.

"Ah, but did you?" Harry waggled his finger at her. "I showed you the box was full, but I didn't remove the cover completely until after I had let you have a glimpse. A simple misdirection by me and a small assumption on your part. This is at the heart of all magic shows."

"Felix said the biggest part of magic was the showmanship," Evie said.

"To a certain extent, he is correct. While the audience is busy watching a beautiful girl dance across the stage or the magician patters away to the audience, it misdirects their eyes away from the trick long enough to conceal a wire or change a card. There's nothing mystical about magic, my dear Evie. It's entertainment."

Harry showed them several more tricks, including the best way to pick a lock. He astounded Evie when he pulled a set of lock picks from his pocket and presented them to her. He showed trick after trick, each time repeating them and explaining to Evie how he performed them. She realized that when he spoke faster, she should watch his hands closely. Soon, she caught his attempts to misdirect her eyes.

Laughing when she spotted him slipping a coin up his shirt sleeve, she glanced at her watch. "Oh, my goodness. I'd better hurry if I'm to make it to the theater by ten o'clock."

"Yes, you'd better be off," Harry said. "Evie, it's been such a pleasure to see you. You've grown into a delightful young lady. Your mother would be proud, I'm sure."

Evie blushed with pleasure. She bade him goodbye and stood to leave. "Thank you for teaching me the magic tricks. It's sure to help me appear more confident when I go to rehearsal today."

Jack stood up and helped Evie on with her coat. "I'll have the concierge call a taxicab, and I'll see you to the theater."

Fifteen minutes later, the taxi skidded to a stop on the icy road two blocks from the theater. Evie was early, despite lingering over breakfast with Jack and Harry.

"I'll let you off here. It wouldn't do to have Croucher spot you with me," Jack said.

"He'd wonder how a girl who is skint can afford a taxicab downtown and how I know Flora's brother," Evie agreed.

Jack hopped out and came around to her side to open the door. "I'll meet you at the end of the block and take you home this evening."

Evie hesitated. If any of the people from the show spotted her with Jack, the gig would be up. "Perhaps it would be best if I went home on the trolley."

"I'll be discreet," Jack said. "I'll feel better seeing you safely home. It's the least I can do after the risk you're undertaking."

The front entrance was locked, and she remembered Will's words about the entertainers' entrance. She made her way through the snowdrifts formed from last night's storm to the alleyway and the side entrance.

Will leaned against the brick exterior, a cigarette in his mouth. "Good morning, miss. You're here early," Will dropped the cigarette, and it hissed as the hot cherry hit the snow. He ground the cigarette beneath the heel of one of his well-worn boots, then held the door open for her.

"I wanted to make sure I wasn't late for rehearsal. I love show business. I'm hoping to make it to Hollywood one day!" Evie tried to make herself gush like a star-struck girl.

Will grimaced, making his twisted features a caricature of a man. "It ain't for me to say nothing bad, but plenty of girls get themselves in trouble thinking they're going to make it big."

"I won't get in trouble." Evie stepped into the theater and stomped the bits of snow off her shoes.

Will hovered close behind her. "Just keep an eye out for those smooth-talking Johnnies who hang out in the alleyway sometimes after the show."

Evie's eyes widened. "Men hang out in the alleyway?"

Will laughed. "You really are green, aren't you? There are men who make it a habit to step out with girls from each show as it hits the town. And they aren't looking for a wife, if you get me. How about I make sure you get on the trolley in the evenings to keep you safe?"

Evie looked at Will. His face, pale and pock-marked underneath his shock of red hair, appeared sincere. He gave her a reassuring grin, and she felt herself warm to him. "I'm sure I'll be safe. I appreciate your offer though."

"Can't lose our new assistant before opening night now, can we?" Will stepped closer to her.

"What happened to the girl who worked here before me? Did she run off with one of those Johnnies or head off to Hollywood?" Evie asked, hoping her voice sounded nonchalant. She stepped away from him and removed her coat in an attempt to disguise her discomfort with his nearness.

Will shrugged. "Flora? She never walked by herself, so the Johnnies didn't trouble her. I guess she went back home. I believe she was from Pennsylvania. She came from good people. Don't know why she took up with the likes of us to begin with. We were a lark, and when she was done with her bit of fun, she left."

"Why? Didn't she like working with Mr. Croucher?"

"I suppose she did. I didn't ask her. She was a nice girl, like yourself. Maybe she got homesick. I never got a chance to ask her or tell her goodbye. I was supposed to run errands for Marco the evening she left. Funny thing. I ended up stuck at the boarding house with Ma because someone took off with the truck. I'd have given her a ride to the train if she'd asked and said my farewells."

Evie pondered his words. Will seemed saddened by Flora's sudden departure. Evie considered asking him about Flora's relationship with Felix, but she didn't want to seem too pushy.

"Will!" Mary's voice echoed in the space. "Quit gabbing and get over to the boarding house and bring me my valise. I left my best thread, and I need to finish sewing Mr. Felix's new jacket."

Will turned his head away, but not before Evie saw the scowl cross his face. "Yes, Ma."

Evie strode across the wooden floor. She removed her cloche and hung it with her coat on the peg in the dressing area she had used the previous day. "Good morning, Mary. How are you this morning?"

"Morning," Mary mumbled. Her gray hair frizzed out of its bun. Evie noticed a smear of mud on the bottom of the woman's skirt.

The change in manner from the pleasant woman from the day before to this tired creature who failed to meet her gaze surprised Evie. "Is everything all right?"

"Oh, it's nothing. Just a spot of rheumatism and no sleep. This cold weather's going to be the death of me. To top it all off, I went and fell on a patch of ice."

"I'm sorry. Is there a hot plate or something where I can make you a bit of tea or coffee? I could use something myself. It's chilly in here." Evie glanced around the cavernous room. She spied a small hot plate on a wooden table with an enamel coffeepot.

"I could surely do with a spot of tea. Thank you, love." Mary groaned as she settled into the wooden chair. She picked up a pair of tights and darned the heel. "I hope that Mr. Marco books some shows farther south. My old bones could use some sun. Come sit and chat with me a bit before everyone arrives."

Evie poured the boiling water from the kettle into a reasonably clean teacup she had found next to the hot plate. She pulled a tea bag from a tin and plopped it into the hot water. Brown tea tinged the water and swirled tendrils across the cup. Evie swirled the bag a few times, and then she grabbed a bowl of sugar cubes and carried them both over to Mary.

"I hope I make it through opening night without a hitch." She handed Mary the cup of tea. After making a second cup, Evie settled herself onto an upturned wooden box. "Does the show travel all over?"

"Just up and down the eastern seaboard. Felix wants to head west to California and take a chance in Hollywood, but Mr. Croucher keeps us in the east. Besides, it's hard to get on with the top-notch theaters in Chicago, New York, and Denver. This show performs in all of Mr. Wells's theaters."

"Mr. Wells? Who is he?"

"Jake Wells. You haven't heard of him?" She narrowed her eyes. "You don't know much about theater if you haven't heard of him."

"Didn't he used to play baseball?" Evie searched her memory of all she had read about vaudeville in the entertainment magazines.

"Yes. That's him. Now he owns a bunch of theaters. You may meet him. I heard he was in the area this week. He likes to keep tight control over his investments. Now that the new theater seats are installed, I'm sure he'll stop and inspect them." Mary's nimble fingers tied a knot, and then she bit the thread in half. She looked up at Evie. "You got dreams of heading to Hollywood to star in the movies?"

Evie nodded. "I would love to be on a Hollywood set with Rudolph Valentino. Could you imagine it? Staring into those dreamy eyes?"

Mary snorted. "A young girl would be better served to find herself a husband and settle down. Show business ain't easy, Evie, but you listen to Felix, and you'll be fine. He and Marco grew up in the business. My mother was a seamstress in London, so I got to hobnob with some entertainers myself when I was younger. If not for meeting Mr. Mason, I could have been a famous magician like Felix."

"Felix said something about spirits talking to him. Does he really believe in ghosts?" Evie asked.

Mary gave Evie a wary look and picked up a spool to thread her needle before speaking. "He saw things during the war that a body like me might scarce imagine. I'm not saying the spirits are real or not. If Mr. Felix believes he sees them, then who am I to disagree? I don't entirely believe myself, but some of these theaters can be spooky late at night."

Evie didn't know what to say. She would love to speak to her mother and brother one last time, but she knew that wasn't possible. The preacher on Sunday morning sermons had promised they would all see their loved ones again, but Evie believed that if God were truly merciful, the war wouldn't have existed. Felix wouldn't have seen the horrors on the battlefield and her brother wouldn't have died. Shaking away these morbid thoughts, she said, "Felix told me the last girl went back home."

"Flora was a girl who should have stayed home with her own kind. Buzzing around Mr. Croucher like a mosquito. I reckon she finally realized that he didn't have time for the likes of her. Making herself a fool over— well, I shouldn't gossip."

"What do you mean?" Before she could finish, however, Evie heard Felix calling her name from the stage. She put her teacup down and hurried to slip into her costume. Five minutes later, she stepped onto the stage to begin rehearsal.

"Ah, Evie, there you are. You ready to learn a new trick?" Felix wheeled a long, coffin-shaped box to the center of the stage.

"Yes." Evie hoped she sounded more confident than she felt.

"Today, I'm going to saw you in half," Felix announced. He lifted the lid of the box and motioned Evie over. "Come closer and look inside."

Evie glanced into the box. Divided into two compartments by two thin pieces of wood, there were holes for a head and arms in the top compartment with a small rectangle cut near the divider. In the second half were two holes for legs. Her forehead furrowed as she tried to determine how Felix would saw her in half. "How does it work?"

"This is where Betsy comes in." He made a beckoning motion, and the young woman with whom Felix had been arguing with yesterday stepped out of the shadows. "Betsy, this is our new assistant, Evie. My sister-in-law Betsy."

"Nice to meet you."

Betsy gave Evie a thin smile and nodded her head. "Felix, do we really have time to train someone new? It's two days until opening night."

"Evie is a natural, Bets. Don't worry your pretty little head. Give the gal a chance. I gave you one."

Betsy snorted. "Fine. Can we get started? I still need to practice with my batons for the opening number."

Felix held his hand out to Betsy to help her into the end of the box. As she climbed up, her shoe caught on the edge, and she fell backwards. Felix grabbed her upper arm and Betsy gave a gasp of pain. She steadied herself and wrenched her arm from his grasp. "I'm fine."

Felix gave her an enigmatic look and opened his mouth to speak, but he thought better of it because he turned to Evie. "You get to be the top of the torso, lucky girl."

Evie allowed Felix to help her climb into the box.

"This trick is why we need petite girls in the act. You must bend your legs and fit them through the gap in the box's bottom. Then your head and arms fit through the holes on the top and side."

Evie laid down and found the box to be a perfect fit. Felix leaned over and closed the lid. Evie turned her head and saw Annie sitting in the orchestra pit watching them.

Felix bowed to the imaginary audience. "Ladies and gentlemen, tonight I shall do the unthinkable. I will saw my lovely assistant in two. Evie, can you move your arms and legs to show our guests that all your limbs are real?"

Evie waved her arms and smiled at the nonexistent audience. Felix grabbed the box near Evie's head and moved it clockwise. She looked up and saw the catwalk above her turn, and for a moment, she had a sense of vertigo. Felix finally stopped moving.

"Ladies, hold tight to your man because this trick is not for the faint of heart. With the sharp teeth of my saw, I will make the beautiful Evie half the gal she was before."

Evie couldn't see Felix, but a moment later, she felt the box vibrate as he sawed through it. He kept up his stage patter while he worked. Evie squeezed her eyes shut at the grating noise of metal on wood. When she opened them, a momentary glint from the front caught her eye. Someone had entered the theater. A sliver of sunlight from the glass-fronted lobby illuminated their visitor. It was Marco.

Was he keeping an eye on his brother? Or on me?

Felix stopped sawing and came to stand by Evie's head. "Tell the audience how you're feeling, Evie."

Evie hammed it up. "I feel swell, Felix. How do I look?" She waved her hands around.

Felix laughed and winked at her. "Gorgeous, darling. Let's see if you're even half the girl I think you are." He grabbed her end of the box and twirled it around. "Wiggle your toes. As you can see, Evie is magically split in two. I need my assistant in one piece, so I must reverse the process. I just hope I can put her back together again before my next trick."

"Gosh, Felix! I do, too!" Evie exclaimed.

He twirled her around and around, then he slid her box back to the center of the stage. Felix covered the box, including Evie's face, with a heavy red cloth. "I will now make her whole again. Abracadabra! Spirits make her one."

Felix whipped the cloth away from the box, then he opened the top. He lifted Evie out, and she leaped gracefully to the stage. Although her legs wobbled after her odd position, she didn't let it show. She turned to the nonexistent audience and gave a deep curtsy. As she did, she saw Annie, the singer who hadn't want to give her a chance to audition, walking to the door leading to the backstage area.

"Well done, Evie," Felix said.

Evie grinned. "I loved it."

"While you two are gabbing, I'm still locked in a wooden box. Can someone let me out of here, please?" Betsy's muffled voice called.

"Gosh. Sorry, Betsy." Evie hurried over to the end of the box and unhooked the latch to release her.

Betsy stood up inside of the box. "Are you going to stand there or are you going to help me out of this contraption, Felix?"

Felix's smile faltered. He rushed over to help the petite Betsy from the box. "Uh, sorry, Bets. I didn't mean to forget about you."

As he lifted her, her hands snaked around his shoulders. Betsy gave a husky laugh. "Like you could ever forget a woman like me, Felix." She released him. She gave Evie a long, hard stare, then sauntered off the stage.

Evie turned towards the front of the house and saw that Marco had disappeared. She wondered if he had heard his wife's flirtatious tone. Feeling awkward, Evie watched Felix stare after Betsy. When he didn't turn back around, she cleared her throat. "What trick shall we work on next, Mr. Croucher?"

For a moment, Felix still didn't turn around, and when he did, Evie glimpsed a man who appeared to be in pain. The look disappeared so fast Evie might have imagined it. "I told you to call me Felix. Mr. Croucher is my brother. I think we should attempt to do the Flame and Fountain illusion tomorrow. In the meantime, you can practice handing me equipment with panache."

They spent the next two hours working on Evie's entrances and exits from the wings. She also learned how to hand him decks of cards, large rings, and other magic equipment with a theatrical flair. When Felix finally told her they were done for the day, Evie felt like her face might become permanently glued into a stage smile.

"You did well, Evie," Felix said. "I think you have genuine talent. Are you sure you haven't performed on stage?"

Evie's cheeks warmed at the unexpected compliment. "No. Only sang onstage a time or two, but nothing really professional."

Felix picked up the black silk cloth he had used to perform his multiplying egg illusion. "Would you like to go to dinner with me tonight, Evie? Strictly for professional reasons, of course." He continued, "I like to know the person I'm working and trusting with my trade secrets."

Evie hesitated. She wondered what Jack would think if she went to dinner with Felix. She mentally shook herself. She was a single woman and didn't need the permission of a man she barely knew to accept a dinner invitation. "Thank you. I'd be delighted to go to dinner with you. Strictly business, of course."

"Shall I pick you up around seven o'clock?"

"That would be fine," Evie said. She gave him Aunt Dorcas's address.

Evie scurried off stage. She would have to hurry if she wanted to convince Maeve to come with her this evening. Business or not, Felix was one of her suspects. She changed back into her street clothes. She waved a quick goodbye to Mary, then she left through the alley door. She nearly knocked over a young woman who was carrying a small Scottie dog in her arms. Her eyes widened when she looked at Evie's face and she took a step backward.

"Sorry," Evie said. "What a cute little dog." She reached out and scratched behind its ear.

"You startled me. I thought you were someone else. Are you the new girl?" The girl holding the dog couldn't have been over sixteen years old. Freckles sprinkled her face, and her small, upturned nose made her face look even younger. "I'm Julia McAlrony. This is Sammy."

"Evie Shaw. Yes, I'm the new assistant for the magic act."

"I wish I could work with Felix, but I'm a bit too tall for what he needs. Wrong coloring, too." She pointed to her flame red hair. "You resemble Betsy. That makes it easier."

Until Julia said it, Evie hadn't realized how much she and Betsy were alike in coloring and looks. "I suppose. Are you part of the show?"

"Sure am. Me and Sammy do tricks on the stage." She looked down at her watch. "Oops. I've got to go. I don't want to be late for rehearsal. Marco and Felix can be sticklers for rules. Nice to meet you, Evie."

Evie said goodbye and hurried down the sidewalk. She arrived at her trolley stop as it pulled away from the curb. She heaved a sigh of frustration. She could walk the distance home in the time she would stand and wait, but her feet were ever so tired after her stage rehearsal.

A car pulled up next to her and stopped. "May I give you a ride home, Evie?"

Seated behind the wheel of a black Ferris sedan was Jack Thompson. Evie looked at the slush-covered sidewalk in front of her and decided that following propriety wouldn't give her the window of time she needed to be back in time to meet Felix at seven. "I would be grateful. I missed the trolley and there won't be another by for ages. I'm staying with my Aunt Dorcas on East Grace Street"

Jack came around and opened the passenger door for her. Once seated, he handed her a heavy wool lap rug for her legs. "It seems it slipped your mind that I would see you home. I borrowed this fancy new automobile from Harry. How did the investigation go today?"

Evie felt a pang of guilt. After the excitement of the day, she had forgotten about her promise to meet Jack. "Very well. Felix, I mean Mr. Croucher, said that the last time he saw Flora was when she stepped into the cabinet. He believes that she didn't enjoy traveling with the show. Will Mason, and his mother, Mary, think Flora went back home. So far, they all have the same story."

Jack's eyes stayed on the icy roads in front of him, but his mouth tightened. "They told me the same thing. If it's true, why didn't Flora return home? Or get in touch with us to let us know she was safe?"

"Mary hinted that Flora was star-struck and wanted to go to Hollywood. Is it at all possible she headed west and was scared to tell you her plans?"

"No. Flora knows that although I may not agree with her choices, I would never stop her from going after what she wanted. My father would shout and complain, but Flora is his favorite child. He and my mother would have paid for her travel there and insured she had a place to live. Money isn't an issue, and my parents are very indulgent with Flora. My sister has always had a generous allowance."

Evie thought about what he said. Her own father would never react like the Thompsons. He would probably lock her in the Richmond City Jail to keep her from flitting off to become a movie star. Nice girls didn't want silly things like careers, stardom, or freedom.

"Evie? Did you hear me?"

Evie hadn't. "Sorry, no. I was thinking about what you said."

"I asked if you talked to Marco Croucher." Jack's hands tightened on the wheel as he said Marco's name.

"No. He wasn't there today. At least, not so I could speak with him. He came into the theater while I was on stage, but he didn't stay. One of the other girls in the act said he was very strict on rules. Maybe Flora didn't like the constraints of the show and joined another act, but that still doesn't explain why she hasn't written home."

"You need to watch Croucher. He has a reputation," Jack said. "He can be very charming, but his charm hides a snake ready to strike when the moment is right."

Evie believed him. Something about the way Marco had looked at her the first day had made the hairs on her arm stand up. He felt dangerous. "I'm going to dinner with Felix tonight. Strictly business." She hurried to add.

The car skidded as Jack's foot pressed down on the brake. He pulled off the street and parked. "Is that a good idea?"

Evie bristled. "I'm not a child. If I didn't think it was safe, I wouldn't go. He's picking me up at seven. We're just going to dinner. It will give me the opportunity to ask him more about Flora. Isn't that what you wanted?"

"I don't like it." Jack looked at her. "You're playing a dangerous game that you're ill-prepared for. I didn't stop you when you said you were going to the theater to investigate, but going out to dinner with Felix–"

"Didn't stop me?" Evie felt angry tears well up in her eyes. She threw the rug down on the floor of the sedan and grabbed the door handle. "Let me tell you one thing, Mr. Thompson. You are not my father, and even if you were, I am not a child to shut up in her room and told to be quiet and not disturb the adults. *I* decide with whom I will have dinner and where I want to spend my days. Not you. It's

1922 and women are no longer chattel!"

Evie wrenched the door open. Jack grabbed her arm to stop her, but she gave him a disdainful look. "You might like to think you would have let Flora go to Hollywood, but really, Mr. Thompson, you're just like all the other men. You think women have no dreams but to cook and clean for you and bear your children."

She stepped out of the car before he could speak. Her foot landed in an icy puddle, but she didn't care. She walked the remaining three blocks, staring straight ahead, refusing to look back at Jack as he drove his automobile slowly behind her. When she arrived at Aunt Dorcas's, she stomped up the front steps to the porch and entered the house without a backward glance.

Chapter Six

Evie walked down the hallway and called for Aunt Dorcas. When there was no response, she went into the kitchen. On the table was a tin of chocolates with a note from her aunt informing her she had gone to a late lunch with a neighbor, and she would be back later. Despite the damp and cold, Evie walked the fifteen blocks to Maeve's house. Maybe the winter temperature would cool her hot cheeks. As she walked, she couldn't contain the tears she had fought so hard to control for the past ten minutes. They fell on her wind-nipped cheeks, and she let out a sob. *Damn you, Jack Thompson, for being like every other man.*

She didn't want Mrs. Clement to see her crying and ask questions, so Evie tossed a pebble at Maeve's window and prayed she was home. The curtain twitched back and a minute later, Maeve came out the back door, pulling her coat over her dress.

"Hey. How did it–" Maeve stopped when she saw Evie's tears. "What in the world happened?"

"Jack Thompson is a bluenose and a… a… oh, I don't know, but something horrid." Evie pulled a handkerchief from her purse and wiped her eyes.

"Come on inside and talk to me. Mama has a headache. She took some powders and went to lie down before supper. We can sit in the kitchen." Maeve led the still sniffling Evie into the bright warmth of the Clement's kitchen.

Evie sat down at the table. "Jack might be airtight, but he is as old-fashioned as Daddy. He had the nerve to tell me he didn't "stop me" from investigating, but he didn't want me to meet Felix Croucher tonight for dinner. I'm not his gal, and I can meet who I want."

"Golly. He sounded like such a swell fella before. Are you sure he isn't just worried that Felix is bad news?" Maeve said.

"Possibly, but it's my choice to make." Evie sighed. "I'm sorry. Between Daddy being angry over my hair, and Jack treating me like I'm on the job one minute and a piece of fragile china the next, I'm frustrated. How am I to crack this case and find Flora if the good guys are as difficult to deal with as the bad guys?"

Maeve stood up and stirred whatever was bubbling in the large pot on the stove. "Aside from Jack being a wet blanket, tell me about today. Did you discover anything? Are you making progress?"

"No, which is why I need your help for tonight."

Maeve sat back down. "What do you need?"

"Felix and I are going to dinner this evening. Strictly professional and it will help the investigation. But I don't feel like I want to be on my own with him. Does that sound silly?"

"No, it doesn't. You don't know this Felix character well enough to go out at night with him. Plus, he's the most likely person to have done something to that Flora gal. He's the one who had her go into the disappearing cabinet." Maeve leaned back in her chair and gave a quick nod of her head.

"I know he is, which is why I have to go tonight. Listen, you said yourself for me not to be such a Milquetoast. Well, I'm tired of sitting at home waiting for the worst to happen, scared to take a chance. If you won't help me, I'll figure something out." Evie got up to leave.

"Hold on. I'm your best friend. I'll help. I just don't like it." Maeve scrunched up her nose, a habit whenever she was thinking hard. Usually, Evie would tell her that her face might stay frozen if she didn't stop thinking so much, but it was no time for jokes. "I've got it. Harold and I will follow you at a discreet distance. We'll get a table nearby. When it's the end of the evening, I'll accidentally bump into you at the restaurant. Harold will insist on driving us both home."

"I'm always amazed at how devious your mind can be. I'm glad you're on my side," Evie joked. "He's picking me up at Aunt Dorcas's at seven. Can you meet me there at six so we can get ready?"

"Sure. Give me an hour to feed the pack of hounds I call my siblings first. Daddy's gone to New York for the week for business, so I'll take a tray up to Mama and let her know I'll be out later. I'll call Harold now."

"You're the best." Evie hugged Maeve.

She walked through the backyard to her own house. The clothes she had taken with her would not do for a dinner date. Mrs. Fortune did her shopping on Wednesdays, so the kitchen was empty. When she peeked into her father's study, she saw he had fallen asleep on the divan in the corner. His snores rattled the picture above his head. Evie pulled a small, knitted blanket out and placed it over him. She crept out and went upstairs.

She hated deceiving her father, but he stuck firmly to his nineteenth century morals and ideas. She hadn't protested his old-fashioned rules in the past because they were both still reeling from losing her brother and mother. The two of them were just trying to survive the grief that weighed so heavily on their lives. Evie hadn't wanted to date or spend a night out with her friends because so many of them had brothers or beaus who had come home from the war. Their joy at a homecoming exacerbated her own grief. She had spent the past four years holed up in the house with nothing but her entertainment and adventure magazines for company. For the past few months, though, Evie had begun to venture out with Maeve and Harold. Occasionally, she would even sing away some of her grief on the stage at The Black Cat. Now, she was ready to move forward with her life, but she feared doing so would cause her father additional heartache. *It's for the best I keep it a secret.*

She looked in her room for something to wear. Her limited wardrobe was out of date. For the past few years, she hadn't paid too much attention to her clothes. She had a few fancier dresses for church, but otherwise she wore plain everyday dresses. She walked up the stairs to the attic. A large trunk sat in the corner. When she opened it, the smell of lemon verbena wafted upward. Evie picked up a blouse and buried her nose in it, inhaling the scent that was her mother. A rush of memories filled her mind. Her mother dotting a drop of perfume on her wrists and collarbone as she dressed for dinner with her father, a gentle smile on her lips when she dotted some on Evie's ten-year-old wrist. She closed the trunk. She couldn't do this. Not yet.

In her room, she pulled out the robin's egg blue dress Maeve had given her. It would have to do. If she were going to continue with her charade as Evie Shaw, she would have to purchase a dress or two that would convince them she was the type of girl willing to go into show business. Careful not to wake her father, she clutched her dress and a pair of black heels and left her home.

Aunt Dorcas was propped up in front of the fireplace when Evie arrived. Her cheeks were pink, and she had a glass of her elixir next to her. She was examining a small statue under a magnifying glass.

"Ah, Evie. How goes the investigation?"

Evie sat down next to the fire. "I'm going to dinner with Felix tonight. He's picking me up at seven."

"Should I play a doddering aunt who doesn't quite have all her faculties or an overbearing distant cousin who controls your purse strings? Wait! I'm a kindly spinster who took you in when an overturned apple cart killed your parents and orphaned you."

"Just be my colorful and wonderful aunt with whom I live," Evie said, laughing. "Maeve and Harold are going to be shadowing me to make sure I'm safe. If you're okay on your own tonight, I'll stay with Maeve afterward."

"Good idea. I want to get the measure of this Felix. If you're in danger, I'll tap the side of my nose. If he seems safe, I'll invite him to play cards on Sunday."

An hour later, Maeve had arrived and the two of them had dressed and were ready to go. Maeve had fixed Evie's hair and added face framing spit curls. She had lined her eyes heavily with kohl. After powdering her face, Evie looked like she could be on the cover of *The Ladies' World*. She and Maeve hurried downstairs to meet Harold, who was patiently waiting with Aunt Dorcas. Evie prayed he hadn't partaken of any elixir. She needed him to have his wits about him this evening.

He whistled when the two of them entered. "You two look swell."

Maeve giggled like a schoolgirl. "Ah. Listen to you, big timer. You're not so bad yourself."

Evie thought if her friend picked any guy to settle down with, she had a winner with Harold. He was fun and not too hard on the eyes.

"Maeve's told me the plan, but if it goes south... well, I'd feel real bad if something happened to you," Harold said.

"Me too." Evie said. "I promise I'll be careful. I appreciate your helping me out. I've got to find out what happened to this woman,

Flora. It's important."

"I don't understand since you didn't know her. But if Maeve supports you, then I guess I do, too." Harold pulled Maeve closer to him and she kissed him on the cheek. "You give the signal, and I will rap that Croucher fellow on his noggin if he gets fresh with you." Harold pulled a blackjack from his overcoat and slapped it against his hand.

"Thanks, Harold. You'll stay close by?"

"I'll park a few cars down from wherever he takes you. Once you're in the restaurant, we'll come in and find a table nearby."

A glance at the mantel clock made Evie realize it was almost seven o'clock. "Felix will be here any minute."

"We'll be in the kitchen until he arrives. Once he's here, we'll go out the back door and be waiting in Harold's car," Maeve said.

A few minutes later, Maeve and Harold ensconced themselves in the kitchen. There was a sharp rap on the front door. Evie shivered even though the front parlor was warm.

"Are you sure you want to go?" Aunt Dorcas asked.

Evie nodded and hurried to open the front door.

Felix stepped out from the dim recess of the doorway and into the front hall. Evie had never seen him in anything but shirt sleeves during their rehearsals. She realized he was quite handsome. He wore a cashmere coat over a brown suit cut in the latest fashion.

"Evie. You look fetching. I've got a taxicab waiting." He motioned towards a waiting car.

"Please come in and meet my aunt. She hurt herself, otherwise, she would come out and greet you."

Felix followed Evie into the front parlor. Aunt Dorcas had been pretending to read a book, but when they entered the room, she put it on her lap. Evie hoped Felix wouldn't notice that her aunt had held the novel upside down.

"Felix Croucher, this is my aunt, Dorcas Harris. Aunt Dorcas, Felix Croucher." Evie realized too late that she had given her aunt's real last name. "She's my mother's sister."

Aunt Dorcas didn't miss a beat. Instead, she turned her most beatific smile on Felix. "It's a pleasure to meet you. My niece speaks quite highly of you."

Felix came over and took Aunt Dorcas's hand and kissed it. "A pleasure to meet you as well. Are you the Dorcas Harris who hiked into the Amazon?"

Her aunt blushed. "I am."

"I read your monograph on butterflies of the Amazon, Miss Harris. You are an amazing woman. I can see where your niece gets her adventurous spirit."

For a moment, Evie thought her aunt tittered. "Please call me Dorcas. Would you like to come and play cards one Sunday?"

"I would be delighted to, but only if you call me Felix." Felix turned back to Evie. "We should get going."

Felix held Evie's coat for her. Once outside, he opened the taxi door for her and placed a rug over her lap. Felix instructed the driver to take them to the corner of Cary and 18th.

Evie had assumed that they would walk to a restaurant near theater row. "Where are we going?"

"There's an out of the way place that you'll enjoy. I–well, I have to admit that I have a surprise for you later this evening, if you're interested."

Evie glanced behind her and spotted Maeve and Harold down the street. Relieved she wouldn't be alone wherever they dined, she relaxed. Evie realized that they were heading towards the river and the docks. For a moment, she wondered if she was going to be kidnapped and stuffed onto an outbound freighter. It was a foolish thought. She had spent too many nights traveling in her head while reading adventure magazines. No one kidnapped women and put them on ships bound for wild and unknown places. That was the stuff of fiction.

"You must come to Richmond fairly often if you've discovered some restaurants more familiar to the locals," Evie said. She wanted to crane her neck out the window and see if Harold and Maeve were behind her. Instead, she allowed herself a quick glance over her shoulder and was relieved to see Harold's old junker hot on the taxi's bumper.

"Yes," Felix said. "You'll discover that when you are on the road, the cities blend into nameless streets and faces. I try to discover something unique and memorable each time I visit a place. It helps me stay connected to the actual world. This place is particularly special. It is owned by an old friend."

Evie thought about what he said. Was he thinking about his spirit world and the hold he believed it had on him? "When was the last time you were here?"

Felix thought for a moment. "About two or three months ago. We play theaters in Pennsylvania, Maryland and Virginia mostly. Ohio is the farthest west the tour goes."

Evie shifted in the seat and turned to Felix. "Someone told me that Flora was from Pennsylvania. She's the gal who was your assistant before, right? The one you said got homesick."

An emotion flitted briefly across Felix's face but was so quick that Evie couldn't determine if it was sadness or anger. "Yes, I suppose that's what happened. Flora and I worked well together. I thought she wanted to be a permanent part of the show, but–never mind, that's old business and we're at our destination. Flora's departure opened the door for you. It was fate."

The taxicab pulled in front of a small building that could have passed for someone's home. She heard music playing from inside, and the sound of people talking. Relieved, she accepted Felix's arm as they walked inside.

Small tables were scattered around the room with red-checked cloths and flickering candles centered on each one. Several couples dined in the close room. It was a very intimate setting. Different from what she had expected when Felix asked her to dinner. It felt like a date.

"This is cozy." She handed her coat to a gentleman who had appeared by their side.

"Ah, Felix, you grace us with your presence again. How are you?" A short, bald man with brown bushy brows that threatened to meet in the middle if he frowned clasped Felix's hand. "And who is this lovely lady?"

"I'm fine, Vano. This is my new assistant, Evie Shaw."

Vano stepped forward and grasped Evie's hands in his. "You will love working with Felix. He has excellent sleight of hand. I remember one time when we were boys and–"

"Oh no, Vano. No stories of my misspent youth. Evie and I need a quiet table where we can discuss the act. She started this week and opening night is only a few days away."

"Yes, yes. The past is the past. I know." Vano gave an exaggerated sigh. He directed them to a table in the corner near the entrance to what must be the kitchen. "Tonight, we are serving *janija* with fresh rolls. You love Tildy's rolls."

"Sounds good. We'll have two bowls."

Vano excused himself, and Felix focused his attention on her.

Evie had never heard of *janija*. Although not a picky eater, she was used to simple southern fare. "What is *janija*?"

"It's a traditional stew with beef, tomatoes, and vegetables. I promise you it is excellent. Tildy is an amazing cook. She and Vano opened this place five years ago, and I stop and eat here every time I'm in the city."

"It sounds like you two knew each other as children?"

"Yes, I immigrated with my parents from Slovenia when I was a child. Vano's family came a few years after we did. We all traveled around the country together. Enough about me. I want to learn all about Evie Shaw. Why vaudeville? Why not make your way to the studios and star in the movies? You're beautiful and should grace the silver screen."

"I'm not brave enough to leave Aunt Dorcas and live so far away. California seems like another planet. The east coast circuit suits me. I'm only a train ride away if I need to return home. She's family and needs me," Evie said with a shrug. "I came to the Bijou on a whim, never imagining you would give me a chance."

"You can thank my brother for that. He doesn't always have the best eye for talent and doesn't think with his head, but this time he chose well."

Evie flushed at the compliment. Before she could reply, Vano appeared at her elbow and placed wine glasses on the table and with a flourish poured a generous portion of a deep red wine into her glass.

"Your dinner will be out shortly, but in the meantime, I thought you might enjoy a glass of wine," Vano said.

"Isn't wine illegal?" Evie asked. She wasn't opposed to alcohol. It flowed freely at The Black Cat where she would occasionally sing on Friday nights. It was an underground gin joint that the law chose to ignore as long as there were no complaints, and the owner passed some dollars to the cops to look the other way. Evie, however, had tasted nothing other than Aunt Dorcas's homemade vintage and whiskey mixed with honey when she had a sore throat as a child. Her occasional sips of gin at The Black Cat had left her gasping.

"If you have the right friends," Vano said with a wink at Felix, "anything is available."

A look Evie couldn't interpret passed between the two men. Felix coughed and looked around the restaurant before returning his attention to Evie. "If it makes you uncomfortable, you don't have to drink it."

She picked up her glass and gave it a tentative sip. The wine's astringency tingled in her mouth. For a moment, she wanted to spit it out. Instead, she allowed it to linger on her tongue. She tasted a hint of leather mixed with something she couldn't discern. She swallowed. "I like it."

"Perhaps you have more bravery in you than you realize," Felix said. "A magician's assistant. Now, a wine connoisseur. What next for you, Evie Shaw?"

"Perhaps I am brave," Evie said. *If he only knew how brave.* "Please tell me about the show. I should know more since I'm part of it now, but I'm ashamed to say, I've never seen you perform."

"So, I'm only famous in my own mind? It's okay. Our show is on the Mid-Atlantic circuit. We travel up and down the coast. Once the new show launches this weekend, we can perform four to five times a day depending on the venue. The only reason we haven't had to perform daily this week is because Mr. Wells did upgrades to the seating and lighting. The workmen made quite a mess. Sawdust everywhere. It took forever to clean. No matter. Mr. Wells wants the big reveal to take place on Friday."

"Mr. Wells?" Evie remembered Mary mentioning he was the owner, but she wanted to hear more from Felix.

"Jake Wells. He owns the Bijou and a string of theaters where we'll perform. I doubt you'll meet him. He's too busy trying to come up with the next big thing in show business. I'm afraid the movies will make our show a thing of the past soon. For now, Marco has kept us in bookings."

"Do we go on stage first?"

Felix laughed. "No. Only the bad acts start or finish a show. We're the headliner, so we are the fourth act right before the closing door chaser. We have twin hoofers who open with their tap-dancing gig, followed by a gal with a dog doing tricks. Occasionally, Betsy will perform with flaming batons to open the show and build excitement."

"Julia. I met her today. She seems nice."

"She's a doll. We're careful since she's only fifteen. The Gerry Society will shut us down in a heartbeat. Her mom's Annie, the woman who spins plates while she sings."

"I've heard about the Gerry Society. Can they really shut down the show?"

"They've arrested Annie quite a few times. Marco bails her out and pays the fine. Will keeps an eye out for them sitting in the audience and gives us a signal. Worse comes to worst, we either skip Julia's act or Annie's if she's sitting in jail. Betsy's baton act comes in handy to fill out the lineup if necessary."

"Gosh. Is it worth it?"

"Sure thing," Felix said. He took a sip of wine. "Annie and Julia are unique acts. They draw in the family crowds which make us the bigger money. The fines are small potatoes compared to what we rake in with the two of them in the show."

Vano appeared at that moment bearing two bowls and a plate with rolls. "Here you go. Miss Shaw, I hope you'll like our traditional Romany food. Enjoy."

Evie looked down at the stew in her bowl, and the scent made her stomach growl. She hadn't realized that Felix and Marco were gypsies. She'd never met one, but she knew a lot of folks considered them on the same level as the coloreds and Italians. Her father said they were all pickpockets and sneak thieves. Evie didn't believe it. Folks were just folks. No different except for their hair or skin. Now, Evie had so many questions she wanted to ask him about his background, but she knew she needed to focus on the missing Flora. Her curiosity would have to wait.

"Will I be ready to perform? How long did it take the previous gal to learn the act? Was she as inexperienced as me?" Evie took a bite of her stew. It was delicious. She followed Felix's lead and dunked a piece of a bread roll into the broth.

Felix didn't respond right away, and for a moment, Evie believed she had pushed too much. He must think her the greenest girl in the history of theater.

"Flora was bright and beautiful, but she was like a moth, flitting from flame to flame," he said finally.

"She wasn't really in it for the long haul then?"

"Flora was a girl who shined on stage, but she wanted the next big thrill of excitement. She wasn't content with the small time like us. She thrived on the rush of danger. I think it's why she first asked to join the show. Magic and the danger of leaving her family."

"She sounds like she wanted a bit of fun, but what do you mean she liked danger?"

"Flora wanted me to take risks with the magic show. She suggested I do a locked water tank like Houdini. I tried to explain that my act is not Houdini's and to imitate him would not bring in the crowds, but she disagreed. She would sneak out after the shows and go to gin joints in the city and come back in the early hours of the morning reeking of gaspers and booze. Mary would have to knock on her door more than once to get her up for rehearsal."

Evie tried to reconcile Felix's description of Flora with the one Jack had given. Perhaps Jack didn't know his sister as well as he thought. Or maybe Felix was lying about Flora to hide something.

"I've never been to a speakeasy. My aunt would lock me in the attic if I did." The lie rolled easily off her tongue. She and Maeve had not gone often, but The Black Cat catered to university students. On Friday nights, they allowed amateurs to sing which brought in the crowds. The owner, Mabel Carter, believed the entertainment helped the booze flow more freely. The Black Cat held petting parties with couples kissing and hugging, but Mabel tried to run a "clean" establishment.

"How does Aunt Dorcas feel about your performing on stage? The money's good, but we aren't considered respectable folks."

Evie scrambled to remember if she had said anything about her family to Felix or Marco. Being a different person was exhausting. She decided she was safe, only giving a partial truth. "She's not ecstatic with me going on stage, but she's an adventuress, too."

"From what I've read, your aunt traveled extensively. It was so exciting to meet her." Felix looked at her bowl. "I see you liked the *janija*. If you're finished, we have someplace to be at nine o'clock."

Evie saw that her bowl was empty. She took another sip of wine. Her head was a little fuzzy. It made her emotionally lighter than she had been in quite some time. She looked around the restaurant to see if Maeve and Harold had arrived while Felix had engrossed her in conversation. She didn't see them. There were only two other couples at tables now, but no sign of her friends. She guessed they had waited outside in Harold's automobile and enjoyed a few stolen kisses in the empty street. Lulled by the wine, she was ready to go with Felix anywhere. She pushed her bowl away and finished the last sip of her wine.

"I'm ready. May I ask where we're going?"

"You can ask, but I prefer to leave it as a surprise. I promise it will be something different from what you've experienced." He threw a few bills on the table and motioned Vano to bring their coats.

"Are you leaving already? Tildy hasn't left the kitchen to visit you," Vano said in protest.

"I'll come see her later this week. Promise."

Felix helped Evie with her coat. He shook hands with Vano, but the man pulled Felix into a hug. "Don't be a *neznanec*."

"I won't. Tell Tildy thank you for the wonderful dinner."

Felix led Evie from the lights of the small restaurant to the unlit street. There were no sidewalks in this area of Richmond, and she stumbled slightly. Felix caught her. She breathed in the scent of him. The antiseptic scent of Brilliantine mixed with tobacco and something leathery. She glanced up at him.

He turned away from her quickly and cleared his throat. "Watch your step. It's only a few blocks."

Evie took his arm and gave herself a mental shake. No more wine. It made her forget what she was here to do. Felix was an attractive man, but he was a suspect, not a man she needed a crush on. First, Jack, now Felix. Evie realized it had been too long since she had enjoyed a man's company.

She looked around for Harold's old heap. It dismayed her to see the street was empty of parked cars nearby. *Where could they be?*

"I can't be out too late. Don't want to be a Flora and miss rehearsal. My Aunt Dorcas will worry, too."

"This won't take long. I want you to experience this with me. I have the strongest feeling that you will understand."

The effect of the wine was wearing off and was replaced with fear. She was down near the docks with a man she had only known for two days. Her father was right. Police work was too dangerous for a skirt like her. She prayed Harold and Maeve were nearby and just being discrete.

Five minutes later, they stood in front of a small one-story home with peeling paint and a front step that was losing its hold on being level. Felix walked up to the door and gave a gentle knock. A woman with white hair pulled into a bun that did not match her youthful face opened it. She wore a long skirt and high-collared blouse that had been fashionable and well-made at one point but was now faded and tired.

"Felix. I worried you wouldn't make it." The woman glanced at Evie. "I'm Clara Morris. Please come in."

Evie followed Felix into the small house. She looked around. The living area was small, but tidy. There was a worn leather chair which at one time had been expensive. Evie noticed a delicate Grecian statue gracing the mantel over the fireplace. A bit of beauty in this tired home. Clara led them through to the kitchen where a scarred wooden table sat with a square board in the middle covered with letters and numbers.

"Clara, this is my new assistant, Evie Shaw. She might be sympathetic to what we're going to do this evening."

Clara nodded. "Good to meet you, Miss Shaw. You've come here to speak to the dead?"

Her words confused Evie. Why were they here and what did this woman expect from her? What did Felix want to show her? The small kitchen was hot and constraining. The wine muddled her mind. She had made a huge mistake coming out with him tonight.

"I–uh, I- "

"It's alright, Miss Shaw. No need to tell us. I can sense that you have someone you need to speak to. If you're not ready to talk about it, I understand," Clara said, her blue eyes kind.

"You can call me Evie. I'm sorry, but what are we doing here?" Evie motioned to the table. "That's a spirit board, isn't it?"

"It is. Have you ever used one before?" Clara asked.

"Certainly not. I mean, no. I don't mean to be rude, but we can't talk to the dead. When a person dies, they go to heaven or hell. There is no spirit world," Evie said. "Anyone who believes otherwise..." She stopped. Felix believed in the afterlife. Despite her misgivings about this woman and Felix, she couldn't risk upsetting him. "I need proof before I can believe."

Felix laid a tentative hand on her shoulder. "Just give it a chance. I promise you that once you see what I've seen, you'll change your mind. Please." He motioned her to sit down at the table.

Clara took a seat next to her. She grabbed Evie's hands, and Evie stiffened at the familiarity of the woman. "Please relax, Evie. This won't hurt and the spirits are more likely to talk to us if you will open your mind to the possibility they exist."

Felix had taken a seat on the opposite side of Clara. His gaze was earnest. "I've spoken to men I last saw dead on the battlefield. They are here with me. They guide me. I know it sounds insane, but if you'll just please try this one time with me…"

Evie looked at Felix, and she saw in his expression that he truly believed that the dead spoke to him. She resigned herself. She needed to discover what happened to Flora, and if gaining Felix's trust by playing along with his interest in spiritualism was what it took, then she would do it.

"What do I need to do?" she asked.

"Place your hand on the planchette." Clara pointed to the heart-shaped wooden object resting atop the spirit board.

Evie rested her fingers lightly on the planchette.

Felix placed his hand near hers. "It will be fine. I promise," he whispered. "Clara has helped me so much since I came home. She brings me peace. Marco tries to help, but he doesn't understand. Please."

Evie nodded. She would hold her tongue.

"I need you to focus your mind and relax. The spirits will not speak to us if the mind and heart are closed to them," Clara said, her voice stern. "Spirits. Hear me. I have loved ones that need reassurance. Need the comfort of your words. Is there anyone who wishes to cross over and speak to us this evening?"

A slight breeze ripple through the room. Evie shivered and swallowed hard. She looked down at the spirit board. Nothing.

"Please set aside your doubts, Evie. You need to allow the spirits to speak to you. I promise it will bring you peace and put their spirits to rest," Clara said. "Spirits. Are you with us?"

Evie closed her eyes and tried to relax. Suddenly, the planchette moved across the board and stopped. It pointed to the word "Yes." She gasped.

"Don't be afraid. Spirits can't harm you." Felix reassured her.

Evie wasn't worried that the ghosts might harm her because ghosts were just something people made up to make themselves believe that their loved ones were still with them. Evie knew ghosts weren't real. She hadn't felt her mother or brother once since they had died. If her mother could come back to earth as a spirit, she would have. Holding firm to that belief, she rested her hands back on the planchette.

"Spirits of those who have left us, are you here?" Clara said in a low voice. "I have a woman with me who has lost someone close to them. She is searching for answers."

Evie suppressed a gasp of surprise. How did Clara know she had lost her family? A tickle of uneasiness tripped across her neck and head. The table shifted slightly, and an icy chill touched her. The planchette slid beneath her fingers towards a letter.

"H." Felix said.

Slowly, it moved its way across the board, stopping briefly on one letter after another until it finally came to rest in the middle of the board.

"This isn't funny," Evie said.

"Spirits aren't tricksters, Evie." Clara's pale blue eyes bore into her. She placed her hand over Evie's. "A spirit is asking you for help."

Evie jerked her hand away. "Felix, I'd like to leave now."

Clara's eyes rolled backward, and she reached blindly across the table and grabbed Evie's hand and held it tightly. "You need to listen to me. A spirit is asking you for help but doing so will place you in grave danger. You must be careful–"

Evie stood up and knocked the chair over behind her. "I'm leaving."

She grabbed her coat and hat from the empty chair next to her and without waiting for Felix, dashed out of the house. She was out the front door and down the sidewalk before she looked to see if Felix was behind her. He wasn't. She glanced up and down the street, looking for a taxi or a trolley stop to take her home. It was empty. She ran, clutching her coat tightly around her. Her heels slipped on the icy streets, and she slowed. She turned her head back and forth. Where was she? She hoped she could find her way to someplace familiar.

Two shadowy figures emerged from a nearby side street. Evie stopped. She was alone in the night near the docks. She realized perhaps she had been hasty in her departure from Clara's without Felix. She wondered why Felix hadn't followed. Was this the grave danger the spirit spoke of? She turned to walk back to Clara's.

"Evie, wait!"

The tightness and fear that had gripped her since arriving at Clara's suddenly left her. She should have known Maeve wouldn't let her down. She walked as quickly as she could in her black heels down the street. When she saw Maeve, she ran the last ten feet and hugged her. "Thank goodness you're here," Evie gasped. She looked over her shoulder.

"Did that fellow Croucher get fresh with you? If he did, I'll wallop him good," Harold said.

"No, Harold, it wasn't him. It was something else. But I don't want to talk about it." Evie gave Maeve a look that hinted she would tell her everything later. "I just want to go home."

Harold guided Evie and Maeve down the block to his automobile. "We stopped down here so no one could spot us."

"You don't understand how scared I was when I ran out of that woman's house. I thought we had lost you before the restaurant. Oh! You two have been sitting out here all night in the cold with no supper. I'm so sorry."

Maeve grinned and reached into the Model T. She pulled out a small hamper. "He thought of everything. Roast beef sandwiches and a little nip of gin, and we were as warm as two puppies in a basket."

Harold helped Maeve and Evie into the seat and tucked a rug around them. "I'll have you ladies back home in two shakes of a lamb's tail."

After two false starts, the motor roared to life and soon had them back into familiar neighborhoods. Ten minutes later, they stopped in front of Maeve's house. Harold walked them to the front door. "It's been a pleasure, ladies, but I've got a dog's life. The old man expects me to be at the desk first thing tomorrow morning. No rest for the wicked and all."

He planted a chaste kiss on Maeve's cheek and turning on his heel, bid them both a good night.

"He sure is swell," Maeve said with a sigh. She hung her coat and hat up on the hall tree by the front door.

"You're lucky."

"He has this friend–"

Evie put up her hand. "Let me stop you before you begin. I love you, Maeve, but I'm just not interested in anymore dates with Harold's friends or Mrs. Galloway's nephews visiting from Baltimore or any other fellow right now."

"Not every man is looking to get married, Evie. Sometimes they just want to have a date with a pretty girl. You have to give a fellow a chance. Harold's friend, Paul, is working doing the accounts for one of the tobacco companies. He's not too hard on the eyes, either. I'm just saying that you need a little fun in your life."

Evie knew Maeve was right, but she knew that if she fell in love with someone, they would want her to stay at home and have babies and keep house. She wasn't interested in that life. To appease Maeve, she said, "I'll consider it."

Apparently satisfied, Maeve said, "I need to go make sure Mama is okay. I'll be back in a minute, then I want to hear all about what got you so spooked in that house."

"I'm going to call Aunt Dorcas and tell her I'm safe."

Evie rang Aunt Dorcas. "I'm at Maeve's."

"Thank goodness. Felix arrived on my doorstep a minute ago looking like he had run the gauntlet. He yelled about spirits and disappearances. I didn't know what to think. I slammed the door in his face and prepared to call your father to go search for you. I'm sure he's still out there waiting for your arrival. I'll tell him you hailed a taxi to a friend's house, and he should go home. I'll expect a full recounting tomorrow."

Evie wished her a good night punctuated with yawns. The evening had exhausted her. She climbed the stairs, pulled the blue dress off, and put on one of Maeve's nightgowns. She sat down at the dressing table and rubbed cold cream all over her face to remove the kohl and red lipstick. As the flannel cloth wiped the day away, Evie watched her face transform from sophisticated woman to a pale-faced girl with a random smattering of freckles across her nose.

Illusion complete, she thought.

Chapter Seven

When Maeve returned from checking on her mother, Evie was already under the covers of the small trundle bed. As children, she and Maeve had spent many evenings telling scary stories to each other by lamplight. Now, Evie felt she had a true story to add to their collection of tales.

"Mother's sleeping and so are the little ones. Now, tell me everything that happened and why you ended up running down the street like hell hounds were chasing you," Maeve said. She slipped out of her dress and put on an old flannel nightgown that had seen better days.

Evie waited until Maeve had cleaned her face and settled under her own quilt before she spoke. She related the dinner at Vano's small family restaurant. She told Maeve what she had gleaned from Felix about some acts in the show. "I may be wrong, but I got the impression there was more to Felix and Flora's relationship than magician and assistant."

"If so, it moves him up to number one on the list of why she may have run off," Maeve said.

"Why?"

"If this gal Flora and Felix had a fight, or she got in a bad way, she would want to disappear. From what you've said, her family is not the kind who would welcome a fellow like Felix Croucher into the family. Sounds like she came from money."

"True, but I didn't ask him if there was something more to their relationship."

"So how did you end up at some shotgun shack in a dangerous neighborhood?"

"The woman who lived there is a spiritualist."

"No!" Maeve sat up in bed. "I thought spiritualism was dying off. No pun intended. Your friend Harry Houdini has helped put quite a number of them out of business."

"Apparently not this gal. Felix asked me to keep an open mind. When Clara used the spirit board, she told me I was in danger. Maeve, I might not be the bravest person in the world, and I've never considered myself scared of the supernatural. I swear I felt something cold dance across my shoulders and the spirit board spelled out *help me, Evie*. Clara told me I was in danger if I helped this spirit. That's why you saw me hightailing it down the street in the cold."

"At least now you don't have to lie to your father anymore," Maeve said. "Tell Mr. Thompson about your suspicions regarding Felix and Flora and wash your hands of the complete mess."

"No. I'm not giving up, yet. If I let some penny theater charlatan like Clara and her spirit board scare me off the case, then I may as well get married and stay home wrapped in cotton taken care of by a husband. What would Nellie Bly have done?" Evie knew using the name of Maeve's heroine would insure Maeve's continued support of her investigations.

"She would have plucked up her courage and dove right back into the case." Maeve sighed. "You're right. You can't let something make-believe like a spirit board scare you off from finding Flora. You might be the best chance of her finding her way home."

"Thanks." Evie stifled a yawn.

"For what?"

"For always believing that I can do anything with a little spit and courage."

Maeve laughed. "That's what best friends are for. I'm glad you're finally believing in yourself." She reached up and turned off her bedside lamp. "Now get some sleep. You have a busy day tomorrow. You need to find Flora Thompson."

The next morning, Evie awoke early. Maeve was still sound asleep, so she dressed and quietly left the house. She would catch up with Maeve later in the day, but for now, she needed to get back on the case. First, she would check in on her father to see how he was without her.

She found him sitting at the dining room table with his head buried in the paper.

"Good morning, Daddy. I was over at Maeve's last night and wanted to drink coffee with you before going back to Aunt Dorcas."

"How is my sister?" Her father peered over the top of his paper.

"She's not letting a broken ankle slow her down. She has plans to go to Paris as soon as she's able." Evie poured herself a cup and sat down at the table.

Normally, Evie didn't get a chance to read the newspaper in the morning. Her father read it every morning without fail as he drank his second cup of coffee. Their routine comprised of breakfast together with brief conversations as he read the articles. Occasionally, a snort of derision or a bark of laughter would break their comfortable silence. Sometimes, he would read her an excerpt of interest. This morning, as her father flipped open the paper to read the inside news, Evie's eyes glanced at the headline and stopped. *Woman's Body Recovered from James River*. It didn't mean that it was Flora Thompson's body they discovered. It could be anyone. Someone could have slipped and fallen. But after last night, Evie had a bad feeling it was Flora who had been found in the river.

She waited impatiently for her father to finish his breakfast and leave the newspaper behind so she could read it. The minute her father left the dining room, she grabbed it before hurrying up to her bedroom.

She skimmed the article before reading it through a second time to absorb all the details. *Police pulled an unidentified woman in her late teens or early twenties from the James River last night. An officer on routine patrol at the docks discovered the body. The victim is approximately five feet in height and of slight build. The victim has dark brown hair and brown eyes and was missing her clothes, which leaves authorities little to assist in identification. Anyone with any information to contact the Richmond Police Office.*

Evie tossed the paper onto her bed. She grabbed her purse and rushed downstairs and out the front door without her hat or coat. At the corner, the trolley was still minutes away from arrival. She considered returning home and asking Maeve to accompany her, but the harsh clang of the trolley bell warned her she had no time to wait. Evie hopped into the car and settled down behind the driver. Her foot tapped a harsh staccato waiting for the ride to end downtown near the Jefferson Hotel.

Fifteen minutes later, Evie stood before the trolley had fully stopped and ran down the steps. She entered the lobby and went to the registration desk. A middle-aged man with wire-rimmed glasses perched precariously on a needle-sharp nose scribbled away with a pencil in a leather-bound book. Evie cleared her throat to get his attention.

"May I help you?"

"Yes, sir. In which room is Mr. Jack Thompson staying?" Evie asked, leaning forward with her hands gripping the edge of the counter.

The clerk looked askance at Evie's request for a man's hotel room number. She felt herself blush, but she lifted her chin and looked him directly in the eye.

"I cannot divulge guests' private information. If you have a seat, I will send a bellhop to see if Mr. Thompson is available to meet with you." He waved at the bank of emerald green and gold velvet wing chairs lining the lobby wall.

Evie sat down on the edge of one chair. After what seemed an interminable amount of time, she saw Jack step out of the elevator. When he spotted her, Jack walked forward, a confused smile on his face. "Miss Harris, what brings you here on this frosty morning? And without a coat?" He led Evie away from the curious eyes of the clerk watching them. "Let me buy you a cup of coffee, and you can tell me why you're here."

Unable to find the words, Evie thrust the newspaper at him and pointed to the headlines. Jack took it and read. His lips tightened and when he finished reading, he crumpled the paper and dropped it on the floor. "It might be Flora. I need to go to the Richmond Police and see if it's her."

Evie grabbed his arm. "Wait. I'm going with you."

"You don't need to."

"I know, but–" Evie stopped. She wanted to say that she could be there for him because death left you empty and cold and sometimes you just wanted another person next to you. She knew what it was like to see the person you knew your entire life without a spark left in their body. To know that they would never walk into the room and smile at you. She didn't say these things out loud. Instead, she just stood silently beside him while the doorman hailed a taxi. They sat together in silence. Jack stared straight ahead, and Evie could see a hardness in his eyes she had not imagined possible. She wondered if she would have had enough strength to look at her brother Peter's body in a morgue.

When they arrived at the police headquarters, Jack went straight to the desk sergeant. Evie recognized the balding man as Sergeant Humphries. As a child, she had called him Humphrey Dumpty because his head had an odd resemblance to a chicken's egg.

"I'm here to see the body of the girl pulled from the river last night. My sister Flora is missing, and I need to see if it's her."

Sergeant Humphries yawned and picked up a pencil. "Name?"

Jack's hands crumpled the hat in his hand, and the muscle in his jaw twitched. Evie stepped forward. "Sergeant Humphries, I don't know if you remember me. I'm Chief Harris's daughter, Evie."

A smile split his greasy face, and he stood up. "Little Evie Harris. I remember you. I used to keep a bag of penny candy in my desk for when you came to visit." His face sobered, and he continued, "How's your daddy doing? I was sorry to hear about your troubles. Your mama was a wonderful woman."

"He's doing okay. Mr. Thompson here has been looking for his missing sister. Based on the newspaper's description, we fear it might be Flora they found last night. Who can we speak to?"

"You must go to the hospital, Miss Evie. They've taken the body to the morgue. If it is her, Mr. Thompson, you come back here to the station to talk to Detective Mann."

"Thank you, Sergeant. I appreciate your time," Jack said through stiff lips. He turned and strode out of the police station.

Evie dashed after him. "It might not be her, Jack."

"I've got a gut feeling that it is. That no-good son of a–" Jack stopped. "Sorry. I know that Felix Croucher did something to my sister. I'm going to prove it and when I do, God himself won't be able to stop me from killing him."

Evie didn't know how to respond to Jack's anger and grief. When her brother had died in the war, it had devastated her. She had been angry with everyone, but many families had lost their sons and brothers. Their collective grief as a nation had provided some measure of comfort. The flu had taken her mother a few months later. It was senseless, but the deaths weren't because of a single person or action. There was no focus to her grief and anger. It had just seemed unfair. This felt different.

When they arrived at the hospital, the woman at the entrance directed them to go to the basement where they would find an orderly who could take them to identify the body. They took the steps down, their shoes echoing on the cold, white tiles. The sign over the swinging doors showed they had arrived at their destination. Jack hesitated a moment before pushing through them, Evie close on his heels.

An older man sat behind a battered gray metal desk. His grizzled hair was cropped close and his mahogany skin was wrinkled and furrowed. His low, deep voice resonated in the quiet space. "May I help you?"

Jack opened his mouth to speak, but words didn't come out. Evie sensed that the man beside her was losing strength. He feared what was behind these doors. She stepped forward. "We're here to identify the girl pulled from the river last night. The desk sergeant told us to come here."

The man stood up slowly, his large bones creaking as he towered above them. He lumbered forward and motioned to follow him. He guided them to a large, cold room lined with metal tables covered with sheets and what Evie knew were dead bodies underneath. The sickly-sweet smell of decay permeated the air, and Evie fought back the bile that rose in her throat.

"Miss, go back and wait in the other room. It ain't pretty when a body come up out of the water." The orderly stopped in front of a table and touched the edge of the sheet, waiting for Evie to leave before revealing what lay beneath.

Evie closed her eyes for a moment to steel her resolve. She opened them and moved close to Jack. "I'm okay."

The orderly pulled back the sheet to reveal the girl. Despite herself, Evie let out a loud gasp of horror. This was not the dead body of a girl who had died quietly in her sleep or suffered the ravages of illness like her mother. The water had not been a kind grave. Her skin was bloated and blackened, and bits of twigs and grass knotted themselves into her brown hair. Blackened bruises circled her arms.

Jack lurched forward and reached out his hand to touch the girl's face but stopped short. He closed his eyes and swallowed hard. "It's my sister. It's Flora. I recognize the small birthmark on her neck. She always joked she would never get lost because she had a small map of Europe etched on her-" He reached out to touch his sister again. "Aw, Flora. Look what that bastard did to you."

Evie reached for his hand and squeezed it. "I am so sorry, Jack."

Jack's jaw tightened, and he gripped her hand. "I need to make arrangements to take her home."

The orderly covered Flora with the sheet and motioned for them to follow him back to the desk. "Have a seat. You got to fill out papers identifying the body as your sister, and then you got to fill out a form for us to release the body to you."

Jack and Evie sat in the chairs by his desk as he pulled out the required forms and slowly filled them out. After what seemed like days, he pushed the papers forward toward Jack and indicated where he needed to add information. Jack's hand tightened around the pen so tightly the veins popped, Evie feared it would break in his hand. Flora's name and her date and place of birth.

He signed his name and pushed the papers back at the orderly. "Do the police know how she died?"

The orderly's eyes slid around the room. He leaned forward and whispered, "I ain't supposed to say nothin', but someone hit your sister in the side of the head and dumped her in the river. They say someone murdered her."

Evie thought he was stating the obvious. A girl like Flora Thompson wasn't like the loose women who exchanged money for favors. Unsavory characters sometimes beat those women, and the cops would find them dead by the docks. It was Richmond's dirty little secret that the cops and politicians didn't like known. Evie had overheard her father talking to one of his fellow cops when she was younger. Someone had done this terrible thing to Flora, and Evie knew in her gut there was a link to Felix's vaudeville show.

She and Jack left the morgue. She wanted to say something to him, but any words that came to her mind seemed inadequate. She knew all the platitudes. Evie had heard them all when friends and family had come to the wake for her mother. They were snake oil on a gaping wound, and all it did was sting and make you scream.

"The pain will lessen with time," a lady from the church had said. "Time heals all wounds."

Evie had been tempted to say, "Unless the wound gets infected and rots, then time is the enemy of a wound." She hadn't though. Instead, she had nodded politely and allowed them to pat her head like she was a small child. Her father hadn't offered any words as a balm to her pain. She couldn't blame him. He was still reeling, as she was, from the news of Peter's death when his wife had contracted the Spanish flu. They dealt with their grief and pain by withdrawing from the world and each other.

Evie hesitated, then took Jack's hand and held it. They walked together out of the silent sterile halls of the hospital and out to the noise and dirt of the city.

"You need to stay away from Croucher and the rest of his bunch. I'm going down to the theater and beat the truth out of every one of them." Jack's face was white with anger. His hand tightened on Evie's, and she winced from his grip. "Let me get a taxi to take you home."

"No. I'm going back to the theater today. Jack, you can't go down there and start a ruckus. Go home to Pennsylvania. You need to be with your parents when you break this to them. This isn't the news you want to give someone through a telegram or telephone call."

At the mention of his parents, Jack shrank further into himself. "This will kill my mother."

"Go home," Evie repeated. "I'll be in touch if I learn anything new. I'll speak to my father and see if he has learned anything from his pals on the force."

Jack gave her a resolute nod. "I don't like it, but I can see you're determined. I can't stop you. All right, but you need to check in with Harry or someone every day until I come back. Promise?"

"Promise."

Jack hailed a nearby taxi. He waited until she was seated and paid the driver before he spoke again. He leaned through the open door and looked in her eyes. "You are either the bravest woman I know or the dumbest, but either way, you need to stay safe for me."

To her surprise, he gave her a fierce kiss then shut the door. He tapped the roof of the taxi and stepped back on to the curb. The taxi pulled away before Evie could respond. She reached up and touched her lips, unsure of what to think.

Chapter Eight

Evie walked to the side entrance and tried to quell her nervousness about seeing Felix after the previous evening's fiasco. She closed her eyes and took a few deep breaths. Flora's death had left her reeling. Now, here she was, an hour later, walking into the den of a possible killer. She closed her eyes and thought about what she could say to smooth over her sudden flight from last night's seance session with Clara.

"Late night?"

Evie's eyes focused. Betsy had pulled a cigarette from a silver filigree case. She silently offered one to Evie. She took one and placed it between her lips like she was a gal who lit up a gasper with her morning coffee. Truth was, she and Maeve had tried one they had snatched from Peter's dresser, but it had caused them to collapse in a paroxysm of coughing. She looked around to make sure there was no one nearby. She didn't want a passing patrolman to catch her smoking. He might not arrest her, but he would make sure word got back to her father. If she were a man, she could smoke like a chimney with impunity, but it was still against the law for a woman to smoke in public. Defiantly, she leaned in to allow Betsy to light the tip of her cigarette.

"I went to dinner with Felix last night," Evie said. She gave a small inhale, enough to give the semblance that she knew what she was doing.

Betsy arched her brow. "Really? I would have thought Felix had learned his lesson about stepping out with the hired help."

Evie's body grew hot. "It wasn't a date. It was a business dinner. What do you mean by stepping out with the hired help? Did he date his previous assistant?"

Betsy took a deep draw from her cigarette and blew out a ring of smoke. "Felix has a tendency to fall in love with the newest bit of fluff that floats into the theater. He won't ever commit to any gal. He still holds a candle for his first love."

"You didn't answer my question. Was he seeing the gal who worked with him before me? Flora, wasn't it?" Evie held the cigarette to her lips and took a small puff. She stifled a cough. "I want to be prepared in case he gets fresh with me. You can never be too careful with fellas these days."

"Flora was always giggling and carrying on with Felix. She wasn't a floozy. Flora just liked to have a good time. He took her to a few gin joints and tried to get her to join him when he went to spiritualists. Then when he showed more than a passing interest in her, she changed her tune and chased after a man who wasn't available." Betsy stubbed her cigarette out on the wall behind her before pushing herself away from where she leaned. "Come on. It's freezing out here and you've got no coat. Let's get to rehearsal."

Betsy pulled the alley door open. Evie dropped the cigarette on the sidewalk and crushed it under her shoe. The orchestra was tuning their instruments, and the cacophony of violins and cellos practicing their scales echoed from the orchestra pit. Evie hurried to the dressing area. She pulled the sheet and changed into her costume before she could rethink her plan to stick with the investigation. When she was ready, she hustled to the wings of the stage to wait for Annie to finish her song.

Will sidled up next to her, rolling the disappearing cabinet in front of him. He gave her a nod. "Annie can really belt out a tune, can't she?"

"She has an impressive set of pipes on her," Evie agreed. "I wish I could sing like her."

"I'm sure you have a great singing voice. A beautiful voice for a beautiful girl." Will didn't make eye contact with Evie.

Evie cut her eyes sideways, not sure if he was being nice or being fresh. She went with the former to see if she could glean any information about Flora from him. Felix might show her the door after last night, so her chance to investigate would be gone. "Thank you. How are you? I haven't spoken to you since I started rehearsing."

"I'm fine. Keeping busy repairing props and running errands for Ma and Marco. You think you're gonna stick with the show once we finish here in Richmond?" Will shuffled his feet and still wouldn't meet her eyes.

"If I don't make a total sow's ear of my first appearance, I am. Why? Gals don't stay with the show very long?"

"Some do. Some don't. Seems like the pretty ones don't last. I figure as pretty a gal as you are, you've got your heart set on Hollywood and the picture shows."

"Oh, I don't think I have the looks for the movies. I heard that gal, Flora, didn't go back home. Guess she caught some director's eye, and he whisked her away from the stage and onto the silver screen. Wouldn't that be a hoot if something like that happened to me?"

Will scowled. "Flora—"

"Flora what?" Marco asked.

Will started at the sudden appearance of Marco from behind a stack of instrument cases. "Nothing, Mr. Croucher. I was telling Evie here that some gals head off to Hollywood rather than sticking with the show, which is a mistake. This show is destined for big things. I'd best be getting back to my work. Miss Shaw." Will nodded and limped away quickly.

Marco's hooded eyes swept over Evie in her skimpy costume. She had the urge to run screaming back to the dressing room and wrap herself with a blanket to get away from his penetrating gaze. He smirked at her as if he knew what she was thinking.

"You seem to fit in just fine with the crew, Evie. How are things going with my brother? Is he behaving himself?" Marco asked.

"Behaving himself? He's been a perfect gentleman." Evie wondered how many assistants Felix had been romantically entangled with.

"That's not what I'm asking." Marco lowered his voice. "My brother has been a little, how shall I say this, odd since his return from the war. He has a tendency to see things... I want to make sure he's done nothing to scare you away from the show. I'm depending on Felix to keep his act together until we leave to go to the next venue. He's the big draw for the audience and without him the show would have to close."

For a moment, Evie considered telling Marco about Felix taking her to see Clara last night and his insistence the spirits influenced his magic. She thought about how sincerely Felix believed that he could see the dead, but he still seemed so lucid. She looked at Marco with his cold, calculating manner and the way he made her skin crawl. "No sir. He's been fine. If you'll excuse me, I see Annie's finishing, and Felix hates for me to be late to the stage."

Slipping on stage, Evie hurried over and picked up several of the props Annie used during her comedy singing act. "Let me help you carry these backstage."

Annie eyed her suspiciously. "Well, aren't you the helpful little one? I can carry it myself. Don't need some young fluff crowding in and treating me like I'm ready for the rocking chair."

"I didn't mean—"

Annie didn't wait for Evie to finish but snatched the hats and scarves from her and stalked offstage. Flustered by the woman's open hostility, Evie stood with her mouth open until Felix walked on stage.

"Don't mind Annie. She's prickly, but her heart is pure gold. She's just feeling her age." Felix looked down at his feet. "I want to apologize for my behavior. You could have been hurt out on the streets late at night. I behaved badly."

Evie put up her hand to stop him. "Only if you'll forgive me. Dealing with death unsettles me. It was foolish to dart out of Clara's house. Fortunately, I happened upon a taxi and decided to go to a girlfriend's house to calm down. I didn't want to upset my aunt. I'm sure you understand."

I really should go into show business. I just gave a world class performance.

Felix looked relieved. He looked around the stage. "Where's my top hat? I must have forgotten it backstage."

"I'll get it. I want to say hello to Mary. Her rheumatism has her out of sorts."

"I'm sure she has plenty of medicinal whiskey to make it feel better," Felix said with a sardonic twist of his lip. "Go on then. Be quick."

Evie hustled off the stage and into the back area. Mary wasn't amongst the costumes, but she heard muffled voices coming from down the hallway. She hadn't ventured into this area, so she was eager to see what lay farther down in the theater offices. She arrived at a door with a frosted glass window with the word *Private* painted in gold lettering.

"I can't take it anymore!"

Evie stepped back and looked around. That was Betsy's voice. When she saw no one in the hallway, she leaned back and pressed her ear to the door.

"Shut your mouth! You'll do what I tell you, or I swear I'll kick you out on the street to starve. When I'm through with you, no one will ever want to look at your pretty face ever again."

"He's your brother, Marco. I can't do it."

Evie could barely hear Marco's reply. "It's because he's my brother. He's got to keep it together until we make it back to Youngstown or the show is through."

"Are you sure it's safe?" Betsy's voice quivered.

"Yes, and it'll calm him. Listen, baby, I'm sorry I raised my voice. You know I love you, right, doll? My man swears it's safe. They give it to women after childbirth all the time." Marco's voice slithered through the door. His tone had turned from angry to crooning.

"I suppose it will be all right. I'll put it in his water."

"That's my girl," Marco said.

There was silence for a minute, then Betsy said, "I'd best get out there. The new girl might decide to make eyes at Felix if I'm not there to stop her. We don't need any more trouble."

Evie stumbled away from the door and hurried down the corridor to the rack of costumes. She spotted Felix's hat and snatched it before rushing back to the stage. What in the world was Marco giving Felix?

"Ah, there you are Evie. I hope Mary's feeling better. Let's start with my ring toss trick then we'll move on to some others. I want to run down the entire act this afternoon. We open in a day and a half, so you need to have this down cold." Felix took his top hat from her in exchange for the silver rings.

Evie wanted to warn him that Betsy planned to drug his water, but she didn't know how. Instead, she grabbed the three large rings and stepped over to the side. The orchestra was rehearsing for the magic show, and the upbeat music they played galvanized her spirits. She tossed the first two rings to Felix, which he easily caught. At his nod, she tossed the final one at him and he juggled them into the air at a faster speed until finally he caught them all and when he pulled his hands apart, the three rings were connected. Felix then rotated the rings, and they were free and flying up in the air once again. When he caught them, Evie grabbed them away from him and prepared for the next trick. Will had wheeled the wooden box for the sawed lady trick onto the stage. Without missing a beat, Felix began his patter.

"Ladies and gentlemen, I will now saw my lovely assistant in half." Felix held out his hand to assist her into the box. Evie spotted Betsy squeezed into the lower half, a bored expression on her face.

"Excuse me," a voice from the seating area shouted over the lively strings of the orchestra.

Felix squinted against the canned lights and made a shushing movement at the musicians. "The theater's closed. We open up on Friday. You can come see the show then."

A shadowy figure walked down past the orchestra and stood next to the stage. It was a uniformed police officer. Evie gulped and prayed it wasn't someone who might recognize her despite her new look.

"Officer Samuels. I need to speak to you."

Felix helped Evie out of the box. She eased out of the stage lights and into the shadows. She watched Felix. He wiped his hands on his trousers. Evie saw perspiration dotted his upper lip and forehead. "Sure. I'll meet you backstage. If you walk over to those curtains, you'll find the entrance."

Felix waited until the officer had stepped away, then he hustled over to help Betsy out of the box. "Go get Marco," he whispered to her. "Evie, I'll be back in a minute. Why don't you take a break? Go see Mary. We'll take it from the top when I return."

After Felix left, Evie waited a moment before going to the side stage and peeping around to see where the officer was. She spied him talking to Felix near the ladies dressing room. Fortunately, the disappearing cabinet was between them, so she crouched behind it and pretended to be fixing her shoe. She leaned forward to listen.

"Flora's dead?" Felix asked.

"Yes, sir. It's my understanding she worked for the show." Officer Samuels peered down at the notebook in his hand. "Her brother, Jack Thompson, reported her missing and claimed you folks said she had run off home. Seems to me, she didn't make it very far."

Flushing an angry red, Felix stuttered, "Now hold on a minute—"

Officer Samuels held up his hand to stop him. "I'm not accusing you of anything. Just stating the facts as I see them. When was the last time you had any contact with Flora Thompson, Mister...?"

"Croucher. Felix Croucher. Flora was my assistant. We had a performance on Saturday night at seven o'clock two weeks ago. We performed our final illusion, and that was the last time I saw Flora."

Officer Samuels licked his pencil, then jotted some notes. "You didn't find it strange she finished a performance, then up and disappeared?"

Felix shook his head. "To be honest, Flora had been acting a little strange. I put it down to homesickness. Not everyone is cut out for the vaudeville circuit. I assumed she packed her things and returned home."

"Assistants come and go." Marco strode out from the wings. He held his hand out to the policeman, who hesitated before shaking it. "Marco Croucher. I manage this show and the people. My wife said you needed to speak with us."

"Yes, sir. One of your gals, a Miss Flora Thompson, has turned up dead. We're trying to locate who might have seen her last."

Marco was silent for a moment before answering. "I guess that would be my brother, Felix. Last time I saw or spoke to her was when she was getting ready to go on stage to perform that Saturday night. I'll be honest. It surprised me she walked out without at least picking up her last pay packet." He leaned forward and lowered his voice, and Evie strained to hear him. "Officer, she was a bit fast and loose if you get my meaning. Personally, I thought she ran off with one of these boys who hang around at the back entrance hoping to make time with some gals from the show. You know how some of these modern women are."

Officer Samuels snapped his notebook shut. He nodded his head. "You are right. Young ladies wearing short skirts and putting on war paint when they should be home. I said as much to my missus when she put on some lip color. Miss Thompson must have run afoul of one of these longshoremen or other vagabonds who come in from the docks. Hard to track down a murderer when he's probably on the next ship to Shanghai."

"It's a shame. Flora was a beautiful girl. I'll send my condolences to her family," Marco said. "Thank you, Officer. I appreciate you coming down here and letting us know what happened to poor Flora. Is there anything else I can do for you?"

"No, sir. You've been most helpful, Mr. Croucher. Sorry to have disturbed your rehearsal. May have to come check out the show. I practice a few sleights of hand card tricks myself every now."

Marco put a friendly hand on the policeman's shoulder and guided him off the stage towards the front of the house. "Come with me and I'll get you tickets for the Saturday show. You can bring your wife and children. We're a family friendly show."

Evie eased back. She couldn't believe Marco's assertion that Flora was a floozy. She hadn't met the girl, but surely Jack couldn't be that unaware of his sister's character. So, she liked to drink a little illegal hooch and have a good time? From what Evie heard from Maeve, many young people and some not so young were out enjoying life. After the war, people wanted to have fun.

Something was going on, and the police were more interested in closing the case than learning who killed poor Flora and dumped her in the river. Despite her earlier misgivings about Felix and continuing with the show, Evie knew there was no way she could leave now. She stepped out from her eavesdropping spot. "Felix? What was all that about?"

Felix failed to meet her eye. Instead, he stared after Marco and the officer, his face a taut mask.

"Felix?"

He shook his head as if awakening from a bad dream. Evie saw a glint of tears in the corner of his eyes. "What? Oh, sorry. I was thinking about poor Flora. She was a special gal. Full of life and fun. It's hard to imagine someone snuffing out a bright light like her."

"Gosh. How horrible! Are you okay?" Before she could stop herself, she put a hand out and touched his arm. Felix gripped her hand. She gasped from the strength in his fingers.

He released her hand and pulled away from her touch. "It seems like everyone who comes close to me ends up dead. Perhaps you should flee as far away from me as possible before you meet the same fate as Flora," Felix whispered.

Not sure what to say to his warning, Evie decided now was her chance to find out more information. "I overheard you telling the policeman that Flora had been acting strange."

"She was such a vibrant slip of a girl who laughed at everything. The last couple of days before she..." Felix stopped and looked up towards the roof. "The days before she disappeared, she was different. I asked her what was wrong, but she would shrug it off and say it was nothing. She would hurry out of the theater after rehearsals finished. I thought maybe she had met someone. The day she disappeared, she seemed down. It's why I thought she returned home."

Evie weighed what he said against the little Jack had told him about his sister's last communication with the family. "Do you think someone was bothering her? Will said there were fellas that hang out in the alley trying to pass the time with some girls after the show."

Felix snorted. "The only fella I saw trying to pass the time with Flora was Will himself. He has a tendency to make himself a pest with the ladies. I can't blame him. His mother keeps him on such a tight leash that the only girls he might meet are the ones who are part of the show. Flora would never leave the theater by herself. She was careful."

"Will hasn't gotten fresh with me, but I'll definitely watch out." Evie decided she had learned all she could for the moment. If she probed any more into Flora's time at the theater, Felix might get suspicious. "I know that the show has to open on Friday night, and I definitely need more rehearsal time. Should we take it from the top?" She reached down and picked up the silver rings and walked over to her place on the stage.

Felix stepped center stage and bowed. "Ladies and gentlemen, the spirits warned me we have nonbelievers here tonight. By the time the curtain falls, you will all believe in magic."

Chapter Nine

Three hours later, Evie was sitting at the dinner table with Aunt Dorcas. She had made them a light supper of cheese on toast and soup. Lacking domestic skills herself, Aunt Dorcas was content with Evie's cooking. Evie told her aunt about the previous evening with Felix and the mysterious Clara, then the discovery that Flora was dead.

"You need to be careful, Evie. Felix isn't the only person who could have killed Flora. This Marco character sounds dangerous." She stood up and used her cane to hobble to the china cabinet at the side of the room. Dorcas returned to the table with a small wooden box. "Here. This is for you. It's small enough to conceal in your handbag."

Evie opened the box and gasped. A small gun with a pearl handle nestled in the red velvet lining. "I can't carry a gun."

"Why not? I taught you how to shoot when you were twelve. This has gone from a missing girl to a murder. You're no quitter, so I won't suggest you stop investigating, but you need to be safe. Take the gun."

Evie reluctantly nodded her head. She picked it up, surprised how slight it was. "I suppose I would feel safer with it."

"It holds two shots. Make sure you shoot them where it counts." Aunt Dorcas gave her a grim stare. "Don't hesitate because it could cost you your life if you do."

Supper was subdued after that, and they talked about Aunt Dorcas's upcoming trip to Paris. Evie cleared away their dishes and washed up before excusing herself to go to bed. Tired, but too stimulated from the day's events, Evie stared up at the ceiling and thought about everything she had learned. Leaning over, she opened the drawer of her nightstand and pulled out a piece of stationery and a pencil. Across the top, in capital letters, Evie wrote "suspects" and underlined it. Underneath, she jotted down Felix, Marco, and Betsy's names. She stared at her list, contemplating each one.

Flora had been a beautiful girl who, according to Betsy, had flirted with Felix but nothing more. She had also said Flora became interested in someone else. Who? Evie didn't think this was true. She had heard a note of jealousy in Betsy's words, and there was something between Felix and his sister-in-law Betsy. Mentally, she moved Betsy's name higher on her list of suspects. Felix had worked closely with Flora, and Evie suspected something more to their relationship after her conversation with Betsy.

Marco seemed to have a roving eye and had bribed a policeman, but did that make him a killer? Evie doodled leering eyes next to his name as she considered. What did he have Betsy put in Felix's drink? A nerve tonic or something much more sinister?

Will was a possibility, but he seemed genuinely upset by Flora's death. To be fair, she added him to the list. Underneath Will's name, she wrote "unknown." The killer could be someone she hadn't met yet. Will had hinted that men liked to wait at the alley door to waylay girls from the show as they left. Had Flora run afoul of one? Sighing, she slipped the piece of paper back into the nightstand and closed her eyes. Tomorrow was her last rehearsal before opening night. She needed all her wits about her.

***

The next morning, fog shrouded the city. Evie decided to walk the fifteen blocks to the theater, but she soon regretted her decision. The sidewalks were icy, and she slid as much as walked. She stopped and waited for a trolley to finish her journey. Clutching her jacket closer to her, she was glad she had worn her woolen stockings underneath her dress. Evie envied the men in their warm suit coats and pants and wondered if anyone had frozen to death from fashion. The trolley finally pulled up and minutes later deposited her at the block by the theater.

No one was smoking by the alley door today, and Evie hurried inside. Annie was backstage with Julia and her dog, Sammy.

"If it ain't the greenhorn. Thought for sure you'd leave after the first few days," Annie said. She stacked a box labeled "china plates" onto another one marked the same. They looked heavy, so Evie hurried over to help. She struggled to lift one while Annie made it look easy.

"Thanks for helping. I was running low on plates for my act, and I was worried they wouldn't get here before opening."

"Mama bet the Topper twins a nickel you wouldn't last a day. I knew you had backbone the minute I met you." Julia gave Evie an approving grin. "Are you ready for opening night?"

"I hope so. Felix wants me to run through the act today without stopping so we can get our timing down," Evie replied. She heard a sharp whistle and saw Will motioning to her. "I'm late. I'll talk to you later."

Evie hurried over to Will. "Sorry I'm late. The sidewalks were a mess."

"You need to get changed. Felix is in a tither over something and has been shouting for you to get onstage."

Evie grimaced. "I'll be right there."

She grabbed her costume off the rack near the changing area and donned it as quickly as she could. Shivering from the cold that had permeated the theater from the outside, she trotted to the stage. Felix was pacing and seemed deep in thought.

"I'm so sorry I'm late." Evie began but stopped when Felix looked up at her. His eyes were red and sweat dotted his forehead. "Are you okay?"

Felix stared at her a minute in shock. He wiped his hand over his brow and seemed to recover. He walked to the side of the stage where his water pitcher sat. He poured a glass and gulped it down before returning to stand next to her. "I'm fine. I thought you were someone else for a moment. Ready?"

Evie wondered if Betsy had doctored Felix's water. Should she say something? Stepping closer to him, she said, "Who did you think I was, Felix? Flora? Did you think I was Flora? Do I look like her?"

Felix backed away and failed to meet her eyes. "I don't want to talk about her. We need to get started. Tomorrow is your debut. You need to make sure you know the act."

Evie ignored him. "Please answer me, Felix. I need to know what is going on. What happened to Flora? Do you know?"

Felix threw up his hands and turned on her. "I don't know. The spirits aren't talking to me. She was here one minute and gone the next. It was as if they took her."

"Who? Who took her?"

"The spirits!" Felix grabbed her arms, and Evie winced at their iron grip. His eyes were feverish. "They didn't approve of her."

"You're hurting me." Evie struggled, but his hands clamped down even harder.

He leaned in close and whispered, "They took her, and now they've gone quiet."

"Let me go, Felix. Please. You're hurting me." Evie let out a small sob.

The sound seemed to break the trance he was in. Felix released her and stepped back. "I'm sorry. Take a break." He turned and stumbled towards backstage.

Evie stood there. Was this the reason why Marco wanted to drug his brother? To make him act like this. Or was it to stop him from hearing the spirits? Evie wished she knew. With a shaking hand, she wiped the tears off her cheek. She closed her eyes and took a deep breath. She needed to compose herself before he came back. Opening them, she saw Mary watching her from the far corner by the front curtain ropes.

Realizing someone had spotted her, Mary stepped out. "Chin up, Evie. Felix gets like that sometimes. He ain't been right since the war. Mr. Croucher tries to help him, but sometimes he can't be helped. Come get a cuppa and calm your nerves. When he comes back, he'll be acting like nothing happened."

Clutching her arms around her, Evie followed Mary to her work area. Mary poured a cup of tea and reached into her sewing basket and pulled out a flask. She dumped a liberal amount of amber liquid into the tea, then handed it to Evie.

"Drink up. It will warm you up. It's a cold as a witch's teet in here." Mary eased her large bottom onto her stool. "Mr. Felix has spells every now and again. It makes him hear and see things that aren't there. He didn't mean you no harm."

Evie didn't answer. Instead, she took a deep sip of the tea and shuddered. Her eyes smarted as the liquid burned its way down her throat. She didn't know what Mary had poured in there, but it packed quite a wallop.

"What's in the tea?" Evie gasped after a moment.

Mary gave a wheezy laugh that turned into a cough. "It's the best

Irish whiskey on the east coast. That will put hair on your chest and pep in your step if you drink enough."

"How did you get whiskey? I thought only bathtub gin was available around here."

Mary shushed her. "Not so loud. I have my sources. I take a nip now and then to help my rheumatism. You wouldn't turn me into the revenuers for something used for medicinal purposes now, would you?"

Evie shook her head. The whiskey did seem to be calming her nerves. She felt a warmth in her stomach that was spreading slowly to her fingers and toes. She took a smaller sip. "I might have a touch of rheumatism myself."

Giving her an approving nod, Mary said, "Felix is a good man. He wouldn't hurt a fly. He just gets confused."

Evie looked down at the red handprints on her arms. They would be bruises by tomorrow. *How would that play out on stage with the audience?*

Aloud, Evie asked, "Do you think I look like Flora?"

Mary squinted at her. "A little. Your outside might be similar, but I suspect your insides are different."

Evie started to ask her what she meant but stopped when she saw Marco coming in the back door. She took a big gulp of tea and ignored the fire it ignited in her gut. What did they say? Liquid courage indeed. Standing up, she straightened her costume and headed to the stage. She was careful to keep her head down and act as if she hadn't noticed Marco's entry.

"Evie, a word." Marco called after her.

Her steps faltered, and she steeled her nerves before turning around. "Yes?"

Marco quickly covered the space between them. He was uncomfortably close to her, and Evie took an involuntary step back. "I wanted to speak to you before you went onstage with Felix. He had a difficult night."

Evie stifled the urge to ask if it was because of what Marco had Betsy put in his drink. "I'm not sure I understand."

Marco considered her before speaking. "He saw things in France that I can't even imagine. It's changed him. Let's just say his eyes may have been closed, but his sleep was not restful. If he acts out of sorts, please keep this in mind."

She remained silent and allowed his words to settle into her mind. Would Peter have been like Felix if he had come home from the war? She couldn't even imagine the horrors her brother and Felix had experienced.

Marco must have taken her silence as acceptance because he placed a hand on her bare arm. "Thank you for understanding." He hesitated then said, "Felix is a good man. He's everything I'm not. Anyway, you'd better hurry along now. You don't want to keep my brother waiting."

With that, Marco walked away, and he left Evie standing there with her mind in turmoil. She wanted nothing more than to put her street clothes back on and put Felix and Flora behind her. She could apply for a job in the typing pool at the newspaper. She could ask Ruby to book her at The Black Cat as a paying gig. She was always complaining that the girls wouldn't stick around as soon as a good-looking guy came flashing a few bills at them. She was so deep in her own planning that she didn't hear Will until he cleared his throat.

She gave a small start and whirled to face him. "Oh! Will, it's just you."

He gave her a wry look that twisted his harelip into a caricature of a smile. "Sorry I wasn't the man you wanted to see."

"I didn't mean it like that. You startled me. I guess my nerves are jumpy since that policeman was here yesterday."

Will's brows lowered, and he tilted his head. "Why? You didn't know Flora. It's nothing to do with you."

"I didn't know her, but someone killed a girl who worked this show. What if they come back? Maybe coming here was a bad idea. Felix was..." she hesitated, not sure if she should say anything more.

"He has his moments, but you would, too, after all he's seen and done. Can't say as I wouldn't be a little touched myself if I went to war. This bum foot of mine kept me home," Will said, a touch of defensiveness creeping into his voice. "You can't quit. I'll make sure no one bothers you. I promise you'll be safe."

Will seemed so sincere in his promise that Evie felt some of her earlier fear from the encounter on the stage fade. She was not a quitter. "I'd best get onstage. I don't want to keep Felix waiting. I have a show tomorrow."

She didn't see Felix anywhere, but it didn't matter. She would work on climbing down through the trapdoor without making a sound. She still had a little difficulty, so it wouldn't hurt to practice. She opened the curtains of the disappearing cabinet then closed them behind her. It was dark with only a hint of light creeping through a small gap between the edge of the curtain and the rest of the box. She used her fingers to explore the floor beneath her. The hole to pull up the trapdoor was inches in front of her. Hooking her finger through, she pulled the door up and clambered quietly down the rungs of the ladder. Today, there was only one lantern lighting the space. Evie glanced towards the area where she had found the button and dried blood. It was nothing but shadows everywhere else. Anyone could hide down here, and she would never see them. Frightened by the thought, Evie raced quickly to the other end and climbed up and into the light of the backstage area. She needed to come back and look closer at the stain on the basement floor, but she would have to do it tonight. And she would not be alone.

Chapter Ten

"How are we supposed to get in there?" Maeve whispered. She held a small flashlight in her hand. Her words came out in puffs of steam in the frigid night air.

"I put a piece of chewing gum on the lock as I left this evening. It's just enough to make it easier to jimmy the lock," Evie said. She slipped a screwdriver out of her pocket. She moved to the door and shoved the metal tip between the jamb and the lock.

"Here. Let me do it." Harold took the screwdriver from her and with a pry and a pop, the door was open. The three of them slipped inside the theater.

"I don't even want to know how you knew to stick gum in a lock," Maeve said. She shone the light around the hallway leading to the backstage area. "This place is spooky at night."

"Daddy telling tales about sneak thieves over dinner taught me bad habits," Evie said. "Follow me."

Evie turned on her own flashlight and led Harold and Maeve through to the ladies dressing room. She shone the light around the space. Shadows danced under its beam giving the ominous appearance of devils in firelight. "I'll search here. You two see if you can find anything in Marco's office down the corridor."

"What are we looking for?" Harold asked.

"Anything related to Flora. Personal belongings. Papers." Evie said.

Now that she knew Flora was dead, Evie needed to find out if she left the theater under her own volition, ready to return to Pennsylvania or not. If she did, someone killed her outside of the theater. If that were the case. it would make it harder for Evie to discover what happened to her.

Evie went into the costume area. There were several enormous trunks in one corner. Evie assumed they held props and costumes for the various acts, but she wasn't sure. She opened the first one to find it full of plates and canes for Annie's spinning plate act. Closing the lid, she moved to the next one. Inside were several costumes for men. An old battered top hat and several old coats. Nothing that would belong to a petite woman like Flora. The third one was locked. Evie reached to pull a bobby pin out of her hair and cursed when her hand found her short bob. She hurried over to the dressing table and found a large bobby pin. Kneeling in front of the trunk, she eased the pin around until she heard a click. *Ha! Harry Houdini would be proud of my lock picking skills!*

Opening the trunk, she realized at once that this was what she was looking for. Several women's outfits were folded neatly and stacked on the right side. On the left was a coat with a mink collar. It was the same coat Evie had seen Flora in that night only weeks ago at The Black Cat. She pulled it out of the trunk and quickly searched the pockets. She pulled out an envelope and a slip of paper. She picked up the flashlight to read the envelope when she heard a noise at the alley door.

She shut the trunk and tiptoed across the floor. She had no way to warn Harold and Maeve, but knowing her intrepid friends, Evie was sure one of them was lookout while the other searched. The voices were louder now.

"I'm going to fire that worthless Will. He's supposed to make sure the theater is locked up tight every evening."

"Marco, calm down. I'm sure it was a simple oversight. The police have everyone flustered coming here yesterday about Flora. Come on and let's get what you need and go. I'm ready to have some fun."

Evie had made her way toward the stage. She peered around the corner to see Marco and Annie coming down the hallway. She closed her eyes and prayed they wouldn't go to his office. As they came closer, Evie realized they were coming to the stage. She moved swiftly to the disappearing cabinet and stepped inside.

"I must have dropped them when I was watching Felix's rehearsal earlier this week. That new assistant of his is quite the looker."

"Marco, you wouldn't dare do that to me. She's not your type. A little too wet behind the ears for your taste," Annie said. "If I thought you were interested in her, I would scratch her eyes out."

Evie couldn't believe it. Marco and Annie. What about Betsy? She could hear them walking down the rows of seats. "No need to be jealous, doll face. She's more Felix's type. Soft and gullible. Ah! There they are. If I missed getting the shipment because I lost the keys, it would piss off Frankie."

"Want to have a little fun on the stage?" Annie's voice was husky.

Evie heard the low rumble of Marco's laugh. They were coming back on the stage. She was breathing so loud she was sure they could hear her. She needed to get out of the cabinet. Closing her eyes, she reached down and eased the trapdoor open. Moving swift as a mouse, she stepped down through the door and into the gloomy space under the stage. Once her feet found the brick floor of the cellar, she eased across to the corner where she crouched down behind one of the wooden crates. She didn't dare turn the flashlight on for fear of the light being seen through the floorboards. Instead, she closed her eyes and prayed that Harold and Maeve had made their way outside without being caught.

The sound of footsteps tapped across the stage above her. Muffled laughs made their way through the darkness to her ears. She couldn't make out the words, and she wasn't sure she wanted to know what they said. Betsy was a beautiful woman, and Annie was several years older than Marco. She dared not move when the footsteps were directly over her head. Something scurried over her hand, and she bit back a squeal of fright. Could she make it to the other side and get backstage without them hearing her? Evie waited. Surely, they wouldn't stay at the theater all night.

Evie shivered as the damp and cold of the unheated space worked its way through her layers of clothing. Trying to distract herself, she ran through the lyrics of her favorite songs by Marion Harris. As the words from *I Ain't Got Nobody* danced in her mind, a whisper of breeze lifted her hair.

Where did that come from? She moved closer to the wall. *Had someone opened the trapdoor?*

Not daring to breathe, Evie waited to see if someone came down the steps. For a moment, she wondered if Felix's ghosts were keeping her company, but dismissed it as nonsense. She was frightened enough without thinking about spirits. The noises above her head had stopped, and she heard Marco and Annie walk across the stage towards the wings. She uncurled from her hiding spot, and her tense muscles protested the move. Standing up, Evie stepped slowly across the floor, feeling her way along the wall until her hands found the ladder leading to the backstage area. Not wanting to risk being spotted, she waited five minutes longer to make sure they had left.

Once she felt safe, Evie clicked on her light to find the stain on the floor. She found it and knelt down to inspect the edge of the box and the bricks below it. Her hand traced along the outer edges of the spot. It was dry, but Evie could clearly see it was a reddish-brown stain and larger than she first believed. It must be blood. It had flowed through the cracks of mortar between the bricks and between the crates. If it was Flora's blood, Evie knew this is where she must have died.

"Evie!"

She jumped as her whispered name echoed around her. Was that Maeve calling her name?

"Evie, where are you?" Maeve's whisper was louder and more strident.

Her shoulders slumped, and she breathed a sigh of relief. "I'm underneath the stage. Are they gone?"

"Yes," Maeve whispered. "How do you get back up to us?"

"Give me a minute. I need to check something," Evie called. She turned on her flashlight and clambered over the crates. Where had that breeze come from? Evie didn't really think it was spirits. When she spotted it, she knew her theory had been correct. Behind the wooden crates was a set of metal wooden doors secured with a heavy lock. Evie licked her finger and held it up. She felt a small wisp of cold air across her finger. She had found her ghost.

Evie climbed down then tucked her flashlight under her chin to hold as she climbed up to the backstage area and pushed open the small hatch. Her head popped through the opening, and she grabbed her light to shine around the space. Harold put up a hand to shield his eyes from the beam.

"Sorry," Evie said.

Harold hurried over to help her. When she was standing next to them, Maeve pulled her into a hug. "You scared the gee willikers out of me. We didn't know what had happened to you."

"I'm fine. I heard them coming, so I stepped into the cabinet and made my way through the trapdoor."

"Who were they?" Harold asked.

"Marco Croucher and Annie McAlrony. Marco is the show manager and Annie is one of the acts. Funny thing is that Marco is married, and it isn't to Annie. He's two-timing his wife, Betsy."

"You said he gave you the heebie jeebies," Maeve said. "Now you know why. I wonder why they were here so late at night."

"Marco was looking for some keys he had dropped. I heard him say Frankie would be upset if he missed a shipment because of missing keys. I wonder what kind of shipment. Maybe props for the show?"

"I doubt you would be here close to midnight to look for some keys for a delivery of magic props," Harold said. "Besides, Maeve and I found some interesting things in Marco Croucher's office."

He pulled a small black notebook from his jacket pocket and handed it to her. Evie shined her light over it. She flipped through several of the pages.

"It looks like some kind of code with dates," Maeve said.

Evie scanned through the list of abbreviations written on the left-hand side of the page. "It's locations. I recognize some letters. Look. Here's P-I-T next to 1/05/22. The show was in Pittsburgh in January. Right after it is YOU which is short for Youngstown. Jack said the show left and went there next."

Harold pointed to the next column. "20g BW. I don't know what that could mean. Do you think it's related to tricks they use?"

"It doesn't seem like a code for any of the tricks I've learned," Evie said. "This next column has to be money. $100 for Pittsburgh and then $250 for Youngstown. Is Marco keeping track of ticket sales at each location?"

"I don't think so," Maeve said. "We found a book of accounts in his desk. It has ticket sales, payroll, expenses, and everything listed out."

"We'd better put this back where you found it and get out of here," Evie said. She walked to the back room Marco used as his office. The desk was meticulous. No stray papers scattered along the top, unlike her father's desk. Evie felt like this was the desk of a man who liked to have control. She did a quick search and found a small cobalt blue bottle shoved in the back of the top drawer. She read the label— *Nerve*

Tincture. This must be the bottle Marco had given to Betsy to dose Felix. She returned it to its hiding spot. Taking a sheet of paper from a small box in the bottom drawer, Evie scribbled down a page of the codes and the corresponding dates and locations. Placing the pen back exactly where she'd found it, she closed the desk drawer and motioned they should leave.

The three of them walked down the block to where Harold had parked his old Model T. He helped them into the car and tucked heavy blankets around them. It took several attempts to get his old hay burner started, but soon they were on their way to Aunt Dorcas's house.

It surprised Evie to see the lights still on. Maeve had decided to stay the night and accompany Evie to the theater before continuing on to the newspaper to work her Friday shift in the typing pool. After walking them to the front door, Harold gave Maeve a kiss and bade them both goodnight.

When Evie opened the front door, she saw Aunt Dorcas leaning on her cane and waiting for them. "Aunt Dorcas, why are you still awake? You should rest that ankle."

"How can a body rest when they know their favorite niece is out and about town in the middle of the night? You were on the case, weren't you?" Aunt Dorcas leaned forward, eager to hear the details.

"I told you she would know we were up to something," Evie said to Maeve. She hurried over to help her aunt into the front room. "We had quite an adventure this evening. Let me get you settled and help you prop that ankle, and then we'll tell you all about it."

"If it weren't for this blasted ankle, I'd have gone with you," Aunt Dorcas said.

Evie guided her to a large chair in front of the fire while Maeve grabbed a pillow and a footstool to prop the injured leg. Once everyone settled into a comfortable spot, Evie told Aunt Dorcas the events of the evening.

"Let me see the code you copied," Aunt Dorcas said. "I can't gallivant around the city at midnight because of this ankle, but my brain is sharp as ever."

Evie hurried back to the front hall where she had hung her coat and pulled the folded piece of paper with the code out of the pocket. The envelope and slip of paper she had found in Flora's pocket fell to the floor. In the fear of discovery at the theater, Flora's belongings had completely slipped her mind.

"In all the excitement from earlier, I forgot I had found this in a coat I recognized as Flora's." Evie held up the envelope and slip of paper. "It's a letter addressed to Jack. Do you think I should read it or wait and give it to Jack?"

"Read it," Maeve said.

"Read it," Dorcas echoed.

"I think he would understand if it helped find out what happened to Flora," Maeve said. "If it were me, I would want every lead followed."

Evie lifted the flap of the unsealed envelope and pulled out two pieces of paper. She read the letter and as she came to the second page, she realized why Flora had considered coming home. "Listen to this. 'Something odd is going on at some of our circuit stops. Will Mason, the props man I wrote you about, will disappear as soon as the troupe arrives in town with the truck full of wooden crates and comes back later if at al. I asked him about it, and he said he was running errands for Marco and to mind my business. You know me, Jack. I'm not one to let that sleeping dog lie. I've got a show in an hour, so I'll close here. Give my love to Mother and Father. Love, Flora.' The letter is dated a few days before she disappeared."

"Tell me about this props man Will," Aunt Dorcas said.

"He's quiet and mild-mannered. He offered to walk me to the trolley at night, and he seems like a gentleman," Evie said. She sat down on the settee. "I don't think he likes Felix. I caught a look he gave him the other day, and it gave me the chills. Will's mother, Mary, is the costume mistress. She is a hard worker and likes a little elixir just like you, Aunt Dorcas."

"What's the other piece of paper you found?" Maeve asked.

Evie unfolded the slip of paper. "It's a receipt for one week's rent at Mrs. Brompton's Boarding House. It's dated the day Flora disappeared."

"She wouldn't have paid for a week's rent if she was planning on leaving town," Aunt Dorcas said. "Let me see the code you copied. I've used a cipher or two in my earlier days during the Spanish-American War. I might be able to crack it."

Evie handed Aunt Dorcas the paper with the codes. Her aunt peered down at the paper. Her forehead crinkled in concentration. Maeve and

Evie stayed silent so she could think.

Aunt Dorcas pursed her lips, then set the piece of paper down. "I think I might know what this means, but I need to talk to a friend who may shed more light on this. He lives in Norfolk. I can't drive with this broken ankle, so I'll need you to drive me, Evie."

"I can't drive," Evie said.

Aunt Dorcas's snorted and shook her head. "Still? It's about time you learned. I'll call my friend tomorrow and see if we can drive down on Sunday."

Evie stood up. "I'd best get some sleep. Tomorrow, or should I say today, is my first performance in front of an audience."

"Harold and I plan to go tomorrow," Maeve said. "I'm sure you'll be the star of the show."

Evie felt relief she would have a friendly face in the audience during her big performance. Suddenly, she knew for sure Flora had died in the theater. "I'm positive Flora never left the theater. In fact, I think she was killed during the final trick which rules Felix out if I'm right."

"Why do say that?" Maeve asked.

"Because Flora's clothes, shoes, and her expensive coat with the mink collar were still in the theater. Someone put them in the trunk, and I guarantee it wasn't Flora."

Chapter Eleven

The next morning arrived much too early for Evie. She'd failed to close the silver drapes in her room the night before, so the morning sun shone through the windows and eventually forced her to open her eyes. Sitting up, she raised her arms to stretch then stopped. Tonight, she would be on stage before hundreds of people.

Evie wrapped herself in her favorite dressing gown, then peeked in on Maeve. She was still asleep. Evie let her rest. It was even eight o'clock and Maeve didn't have to be at the newspaper until ten for her Friday shift. Maeve's father was the editor of the newspaper. What Maeve wanted was to write stories, but her father insisted she learn the newspaper business from the ground up. Mr. Clement was proud his oldest daughter had taken such a keen interest in journalism.

Downstairs, Evie found Aunt Dorcas already at the kitchen table with a cup of coffee. Her aunt looked none the worse for the late evening. In fact, her cheeks were rosy, and her eyes sparkled when she saw Evie.

"I've been awake for hours, but I let you sleep. I've been thinking about the receipt at the boarding house. She paid rent through until last week. Do you know if Jack picked up Flora's belongings already?"

"I don't know," Evie said.

Jack had mentioned he didn't know where Flora had been lodging while she was in Richmond. Evie couldn't believe she hadn't thought of finding out where she and the rest of the troupe boarded. Surely it would have been one of the first places the police would have checked when Jack reported his sister was missing.

"I have an idea," Aunt Dorcas said. She took a sip of her coffee and motioned for Evie to have a seat. "I think you should talk to Mrs. Brompton to see if she has Flora's belongings. You're a cousin sent by the family to retrieve her things."

"What if the police picked up her belongings?" Evie asked.

"You could say that communication must have been lost amid funeral preparations," Aunt Dorcas replied.

Evie agreed it would be an excellent cover. "I have to be at the theater by ten, so it will have to wait until tomorrow. I have something else I need to take care of first, and I hope you'll help."

Her aunt arched an eyebrow and peered over her cup of coffee. She waited for Evie to continue.

"I need to tell Daddy what I'm doing. I hate lying to him even more than I hate how he treats me like a child. I need to come clean and let him know I'll be performing tonight before someone sees me and tells him."

Aunt Dorcas pondered Evie's words before she spoke. "I have never known my brother to be levelheaded outside of the police force. I think he used up all his common sense dealing with criminals every day. Let's hope now that he's retired, he will listen to reason. I'll telephone him now and invite him to breakfast. I'm sure I have something in the pantry that can pass for food."

"I'll call. You need to rest your ankle. Then I'll whip us up some eggs and toast. I think I saw a jar of Mrs. Fortune's pickled watermelon rinds, too. It will do in a pinch for jam."

Evie picked up the handset in the front hallway and asked the operator to connect her to ST7299. After a series of clicks, Mrs. Fortune answered the other end.

"Harris residence. Who may I say is calling at this ungodly early hour?"

"Mrs. Fortune, it's me, Evie. Is Daddy awake?"

"He is." Mrs. Fortune lowered her voice. "Are you in trouble? Do I need to come to the county lockup and rescue you?"

Evie laughed. "No. Nothing so serious."

"Hold on, and I'll get your father."

Evie heard the handset being laid on the table, and the heavy footsteps of Mrs. Fortune walking away to find Evie's father. A minute later, her father's deep voice boomed across the line, causing Evie to pull the telephone from her ear. Her father believed the louder he spoke on the telephone, the easier it was for the person on the other end of the wire to understand.

"Evie, why are you calling so early in the morning? Is something wrong with Dorcas?"

"No, Daddy. She's fine. In fact, she and I would like to invite you to breakfast." Evie sucked in her breath, waiting for his answer.

"Evie, you know I eat breakfast promptly at seven-thirty every day. What's my sister up to? Has she talked you into any hare-brained schemes?" Evie imagined her father's eyes narrowing and his teeth clenching his pipe tighter.

"No. Can you please come by this morning for coffee? I wouldn't ask if it wasn't important."

Her father's voice softened, and Evie could hear a note of concern. "Is everything alright with you? I know we parted on harsh words, but I didn't mean to upset you. I—"

"I need to talk to you face-to-face," Evie said.

"I'll be there in fifteen minutes. Let me see if I can convince the old Buick to start this morning."

Evie disconnected the line and returned to the kitchen. "He'll be here in fifteen minutes. Should I wake Maeve?"

"Definitely. My brother won't dare bluster and bully with three women as his foes. I suppose I should get presentable." Aunt Dorcas stood up and rested a hand on Evie's shoulder. "Do not let my brother intimidate you. You're a grown woman, and it's time he treated you as such."

Evie knocked on Maeve's door as she opened it. Maeve gave a small snort as she awoke then sat up, giving Evie a sullen look. "Please tell me there's coffee." She glanced at her bedside clock. "It's not even nine o'clock. I could sleep for at least another half hour."

Maeve flopped dramatically back down onto the feather pillow and pulled the burgundy cover over her eyes. Evie shook her head. She walked over to the bed and pulled the covers off of her best friend and said, "Daddy's on his way over so I can tell him I'm performing at the Bijou Theatre."

Maeve's eyes flew open. She sat up and grasped Evie's hands. "You've gone cuckoo, haven't you?"

Laughing, Evie pulled Maeve from the bed and handed her a

dressing gown. "No. I need to tell him before someone else does." She glanced at her watch. "You have less than ten minutes now to get dressed and downstairs before he arrives. You and Aunt Dorcas are my reinforcements."

Evie left Maeve muttering small curses involving fleas and camels under her breath and went to her own room to dress and brush her hair. She splashed some cold water on her face and pressed her fingertips to the puffy circles under her eyes. She wished she had some miracle cream to make the dark circles disappear but settled on a touch of powder. She exited her room just as there was a knock on the front door. Maeve popped out of her room, dressed if not ready, and the two of them walked together to greet her father.

He stood stamping his feet on the stone steps at the door. He took his hat off as he stepped inside and handed it to Evie. "It's cold as a frog's tail this morning. I hope you put the coffeepot on the stove, Evie. Hello, Maeve. You're looking lovely this morning." George leaned over and pecked Evie, then Maeve, on the cheek. "Where's your aunt?"

"In the kitchen," Evie said. "It's warmer in there than in the front parlor."

George walked through to the back of the house where the kitchen had been added in 1913. Prior to that, there had been a small building that had served as an outdoor kitchen. When Dorcas bought the house, she'd insisted on knocking it down and modernizing. She loved foods from various countries and would often try to concoct a new exotic dish. Unfortunately, her cooking skills were usually not up to the challenge.

Pushing open the swinging kitchen door, George greeted his sister. "Good morning, Dovie. I see you've banged yourself up again. You'll never learn."

Aunt Dorcas gave her brother a sour look. "Listen, Georgie boy, I will never stop living and exploring the world. Something an old goat like you will never understand."

George leaned down and gave his sister an affectionate kiss. "I suppose you're right, Dovie. It's what keeps you interesting. Otherwise, you'd be an old spinster."

She batted her brother on his arm and laughed. "You're a horrible brother. Evie, get your father some coffee, please."

Evie hurried to the cupboard and pulled out an enamel mug. She filled it full of coffee and set it in front of her father before pouring two more cups for herself and Maeve. She sat down at the table next to Maeve.

"I've always wondered why you call her Dovie, Mr. Harris," Maeve said.

He took a sip of coffee before answering. "She tried raising doves when she was a young girl. Other little girls her age wanted a kitten or a puppy, but not Dorcas. She had to have something different. She convinced our father to get her a pair of doves. She spent every morning with them trying to train them to jump on her finger and take food from her hand. Eventually, they did. It was around that time that I started calling her Dovie."

"What happened to the birds?" Evie asked.

Aunt Dorcas gave a sad shake of her head. "I accidentally left the cage open one day, and they flew away. No loyalties in the dove world. I should have asked Father for a parrot."

"As much as I enjoy reminiscing, you asked me over for a reason." Her father turned his gray eyes toward Evie. "What is going on?"

Evie's fingers pleated and unpleated her skirt while she thought about how to start. "It's like this, Daddy. When Jack Thompson came and talked about his sister… and when Houdini said he knew Mama, I felt like… I wanted to…"

Holding up his hand, George stopped her. "You're not making sense. Stop dithering and get to the point, Evelyn Jane."

"I'm investigating Flora Thompson's disappearance by working at the Bijou Theatre." The words shot out of her mouth and tumbled over each other in her rush to confess.

Her father sat back and stared at her. He opened his mouth to speak, then closed it. He picked up his cup of coffee and stared at it like he was waiting for an oracle to tell him how to respond. He took a sip and when he set it down, he finally looked at Evie. "Did my sister put you up to this?"

"What? No!" Evie looked at her aunt, then her father. "This was my decision. Aunt Dorcas had nothing to do with this. I saw Flora before she disappeared when I was… out one evening. She was so vibrant and full of life. She was everything I'm not."

George's brow furrowed. "What are you talking about? You're a wonderful girl. You make some foolhardy decisions, but—"

Evie stood up and slapped her hand on the table. "I am not a girl! I'm a grown woman, Daddy, and it's time you realized it. The show hired me as the new magician's assistant, and I'll be performing on stage tonight."

Her father's lips thinned as she spoke. He scowled at Dorcas and jabbed his finger at her. "This is your doing. I will not have my daughter performing on a stage like a common strumpet. Evie, get your coat. You're coming home with me!"

Maeve gripped Evie's hand under the table. Aunt Dorcas grabbed her cane and struggled to her feet. Her jaw pushed forward, and she narrowed her eyes. "Now you listen to me, George Harris. You and Evie have been walking around like ghosts in that house for the past four years. She's finally shown a bit of gumption and did something with herself, and I'll be damned if she's going to stop."

George's face whitened at his sister's profanity. He stood up and knocked the chair over. Without a word, he strode out of the kitchen. A moment later, they heard the front door slam.

The women sat frozen in silence. The only sound was the ticking of the hall clock. Maeve cleared her throat and stood. She gave Evie's shoulder a quick squeeze. "I think I'll get my things and head to the newspaper. I'll see you at the theater tonight, Evie. Dorcas, thank you for your hospitality."

After Maeve left, Evie got up and righted her father's chair. She sat down in it and looked at her aunt. "I'm sorry I dragged you into this, Aunt Dorcas. I knew it would upset Daddy, but I didn't realize he would be so quick to blame you."

Aunt Dorcas snorted. "George has been blaming me since the day I was born. I let it roll off my back like water on a duck. He's so full of hot air, he could have helped me fly that hot air balloon." Her face turned serious. "I love my brother, but he has to loosen your reins before you do something foolish."

"More foolish than investigating a murder?" Evie asked, her lips twisting into a grimace. She sighed. "I'd best be getting ready. We have one last rehearsal before our opening performance this evening. Here's hoping I don't make as big of a mess of my performance as I did talking to Daddy."

Forty-five minutes later, Evie arrived at the theater with only moments to spare. Out of breath, she yanked open the back exit to find a man sporting a dark mustache dominating his florid face. She stumbled backwards, slipping before the man reached out and caught her.

"Pardon me, miss," the gentleman said once he let go of her arm.

"It's my fault, sir. I was in a hurry and didn't look where I was going."

He held the door open for her, and Evie walked inside. He followed behind her and closed the door. "I'm Jake Wells. A pleasure to meet you, Miss...?"

"Harris... I mean, Shaw. Evie Shaw. You own the theater, don't you?" Evie mentally shook herself for the slip of the tongue.

Mr. Wells nodded. "I do. You're the new assistant Marco was telling me about this morning. How do you like working for the Crouchers?" He indicated that Evie should walk with him. She had to take two steps for each of his long strides.

"I like it very much," Evie said. "It's such a wonderful opportunity."

"Hmm... I suppose. To be honest, I considered canceling their contract when I decided to modernize the theater seating this month. It seems all anyone wants is more films and less live shows." He stopped and turned to her. "I'm surprised a beautiful young woman like you hasn't already hoofed it to California to try her fate with the silver screen."

Evie could feel the heat rising from her neck into her face from his attention and compliment. She hated that she could never hide her embarrassment. Her cheeks always betrayed her. "I don't know that I have the presence for movies. To be honest, this is my first professional job in show business."

Jake Wells stroked his mustache. "Marco has a tendency to hire untested assistants. Let's hope you turn out better than his last one. If you'll excuse me, I have a meeting to attend."

He turned and left her standing open-mouthed.

"Are you going to stand there or are you going to get ready for rehearsal, dearie?" Mary asked, touching Evie on her shoulder. "You look like you were a million miles away."

"Oh, I'm sorry, Mary. I just met Mr. Wells." Evie followed Mary to the backstage dressing area. She grabbed her costume from the wooden rack and went to change. Before she stepped into the alcove, she turned back to Mary. "Mary, did Mr. Wells meet Flora?"

Mary studied her for a moment. Her large, gapped teeth worried her bottom lip as she picked up a pair of black men's trousers. "I suppose he did. He always stops by his theaters if he's in town."

Evie pulled the curtain shut and changed. She continued to talk to Mary as she unrolled her stockings. "How many theaters does Mr. Wells own?"

"Several." Mary was silent for a moment. "Last I heard, he had over forty. Mind you, we don't go to all of them. Marco likes to stay along the coast more often than not. Will told me Marco changed the schedule and now we are off to Norfolk next. My rheumatism can't take much more of the cold and damp. What I wouldn't give for a show in Arizona."

Evie buttoned up the bodice of her costume. She combed her fingers through her bob and pulled the curtain open. "Forty theaters? Goodness. Mr. Wells must be a successful businessman."

Mary narrowed her eyes. "Don't be getting any fanciful ideas in your head now, girl. If you came here to hook yourself onto Mr. Wells, you can leave now. Felix doesn't need any gals flitting off after a man again."

Evie's eyes widened, and she held up her hands. "I'm not interested in Mr. Wells."

Pursing her lips, Mary sat down on a stool and threaded a needle with black thread. "Best be getting on stage. You'll need all the practice you can before tonight's performance."

"I suppose your right," Evie said, hurt by Mary's snub. "I wouldn't want to do anything to embarrass myself or the show."

Mary mended the tear in the trousers without looking up. Evie turned away and walked to the stage area. She could hear Annie finishing her singing act. The orchestra would remain in the pit for Felix's rehearsal. Felix had explained the day before that the right music would add suspense to each trick. It was all part of the show.

Evie stood in the side stage shadows and watched Annie spin her plates while singing. The fierce concentration the woman exhibited all the while belting out *How Ya Gonna Keep 'Em Down on the Farm* amazed her. Evie loved to sing, but she couldn't perform like Annie in front of a huge crowd. When Annie caught her last plate and curtsied, Evie couldn't help but applaud.

Out of breath, Annie sauntered off the stage. "Let's hope the crowd tonight likes my act as much as you did. How ya' doing, Evie? Ready for your first actual performance?"

Evie blew out a breath. "I hope so. I've never been so nervous in my life. At The Black Cat—"

Annie snapped her fingers. "The Black Cat? Aha! I thought I recognized your face. You were the gal up on stage belting out *Jazz Baby*. You told me you had never really performed on stage."

Swallowing hard at being caught in her own lie, Evie said, "I've sung tunes on their amateur nights. It wasn't anything professional."

Annie scowled. "You're just like all the other young gals. Coming in here with your fresh looks and bobbed hair, trying to push out us old-timers." She poked her finger in Evie's face. "Let me tell you something, girlie, the likes of you won't outshine me. The singing act is mine."

Annie stomped off the stage, passing her daughter, Julia, without so much as a pause. Julia came and stood next to Evie. "What's the matter with Mama? She looked madder than a wet hen in a summer storm."

"I'm afraid that's my fault. She found out I like to sing a few songs occasionally. She thinks I came here to steal her act." Evie shook her head. "I could never perform as good as she does. I can warble notes, but nothing like your mother."

Julia put a hand on Evie's shoulder. "Don't let her bark bother you. She's worried that Marco won't keep her on until next season. Mama thinks he'll replace her with someone younger and prettier. I tell her not to worry."

"I don't want to sing on stage!" Evie protested. "I enjoy working with Felix. It's exciting and—"

"Do tell," Marco said. He sauntered over to Evie and Julia. He snaked his arm over Evie's shoulder. "Tell me how much you love working with my brother. Is it the thrill of the stage or something else? My brother is like catnip to certain types."

Evie's stomach clenched at his touch. She felt like a snake in the thrall of a charmer. "I like the work. It's fun to learn how the tricks work."

"Leave her alone, Marco." Felix appeared from behind the curtain and yanked his brother's arm off of Evie's shoulder. "Don't you have a meeting or a wife to attend to?"

Marco's hands clenched and unclenched at his side. His jaw

tightened, but he didn't say a word. Instead, he turned on his heel and left.

Julia's eyes were wide. "It doesn't pay to make Mr. Marco angry, Evie. I'd be careful if I were you."

Julia scurried off stage, leaving Evie alone with Felix. Evie looked down at the floor, embarrassed that Felix may have heard her gushing about how much she enjoyed working on stage with him. Her feelings were also tinged with fear at Julia's warning about Marco.

"I'm glad you like working with me," Felix said. His dark eyes flashed. "Good chemistry on the stage between performers makes a better performance for the audience. And don't worry about my brother. More often than not, he is all talk and no action."

And the other times? Evie wondered. Instead, she said, "I'm ready to rehearse. I want to make sure I'll not make a fool of myself this evening."

"We'll start with our entrance. We've done it without music, but today, we'll work with the orchestra."

Their rehearsal with the orchestra passed in a whirlwind of color, movement, and sound. Betsy joined them onstage for a number of the illusions, including the sawed lady trick. Quieter than usual, Betsy wore her street clothes— an out-of-fashion long-sleeved dress— rather than her costume. Felix lifted an eyebrow at her appearance.

"Mary's repairing a small tear to the lace on the bodice of my costume," Betsy said.

She finished her portion of the rehearsal then scurried from the stage without another word to Felix or Evie. Felix's eyes followed her departure and a hint of sadness passed over his face before he returned his focus to Evie and their next trick. By the end of their time on stage, Evie felt she could perform every illusion with her eyes closed. At one o'clock, their scheduled time on stage finished, and Conrad the Human Pretzel waited impatiently in the wings for his chance to rehearse.

"We don't have a long break before we need to be back here for the show," Felix said. "Would you care to join me for a late lunch?"

Evie hesitated. Their dinner together had not gone as she had thought, but it had been nighttime. A lunch date would be quicker and not involve a spiritualist. "I'd be delighted. If you'll give me fifteen minutes to change, I'll meet you near the entrance."

Evie hurried to the ladies' dressing area and pulled the makeshift curtain shut so she could change. As she buttoned her blouse, Evie heard a woman trying to stifle a sob. She tucked her blouse into her midnight blue skirt, then stood waiting to see if she had misheard. A sniffle and muffled crying met Evie's ears. She gathered up her pocketbook and pulled open the curtain. The sobs came from the space the women used for makeup and hair. Evie tiptoed across the wide-planked floors and grimaced when her foot found a board that emitted a loud creak.

"Who's there?" Betsy's voice called out.

Evie found Betsy in front of the vanity mirror wiping her eyes with a handkerchief. The heavy pancake makeup on Betsy's face had been partially removed, and Evie gasped at what she saw.

"Where did you get a blackened eye?" Evie asked. She leaned down and peered at Betsy's reflection in the mirror. "Are those bruises?"

Betsy picked up a compact and using a large pouf tried to cover the marks on her face and neck. "It's nothing. I fell."

The bruises circled her neck in an ugly blue-black necklace that her high-necked blouse had failed to hide. "Those bruises aren't from a fall. Betsy, what happened? Did Marco do this? Are you okay?"

Betsy whirled around on the small chair, her face dark. She pointed at Evie with her varnished red nails. "Do not tell anyone about this, you understand? This is not your business." The words were spat at Evie with such venom that she reeled back.

Evie's face flushed. "I—I'm worried about you. You can't let him hit you."

Betsy snorted. "What do you think I can do to stop him?"

"Was Marco drunk when he did this?" Evie had heard some men were brawlers when they drank.

"No. It would have been easier to get away from him if he had been." Betsy applied some liquid blush to the apples of her cheek. Looking at her reflection, she added a small touch more to her left cheek. "He thought I'd been snooping in his office. I tried to tell him I hadn't, but he wouldn't listen. Like there's anything that would interest me. It's not like he keeps the theater receipts in the open."

Evie's stomach dropped. She thought she'd placed everything back as it was last night, but something had caused Marco's ire. "I'm sorry."

Betsy applied a vibrant red lipstick to her lips and turned to look at

Evie. "Don't be stupid. You've nothing to be sorry for. It's not your fault my husband is a brute."

If only I could fix this, Evie thought. "Why would he get so upset if you went into his office? It's just theater business, correct?"

Betsy put the lipstick lid back on the tube. "Marco has other business interests. He doesn't allow anyone in his office, not even his latest *paramour*."

"Paramour?" Evie raised her eyebrows. Did Betsy know about Marco and Annie?

Betsy stood up and turned toward Evie. "Listen, doll, don't be naïve. No man stays faithful to one woman for long. Marco has a wandering eye. He always has and he always will." She shrugged her shoulders. "He keeps me fed and clothed, which is more than my father did. A girl's got to eat."

"I'm sorry," Evie said again. It seemed a limp apology for everything Betsy had endured, but she didn't know what else she could say.

Betsy waved away her apology. "Stay away from the Croucher brothers, Evie. Find yourself a nice guy who'll treat you right. Have a couple of kids and a happy life."

She picked up her fur wrap and walked away, leaving Evie standing there wondering if Betsy was right. She also wondered if Marco's fists had been used on anyone else recently— like Flora Thompson.

Chapter Twelve

There was a knock, and Evie turned to see Felix at the entrance to the ladies dressing area. "Are you ready?" he asked.

She allowed him to help her into her winter coat. Offering his arm, they walked out of the theater and down Broad towards Grace Street. Evie pointed out the site where workers were busy constructing a new department store, which would compete with Thalhimers for people's business.

"Have you always lived in Richmond?" Felix asked. He guided her around an icy patch.

"Always. My mother's family arrived in Virginia in the late 1700s. My father was originally from Maryland. Family story is that he was taking a train to North Carolina to find work. The train got stuck in Richmond because of an overturned coal car on the tracks, so he had to spend the night. He was walking from the station to find something to eat when he spotted my mother. He introduced himself and decided that the city streets of Richmond and my mother were much more appealing than the jack pines of North Carolina."

Felix was silent for several minutes before speaking. "My parents were performers. I don't think Marco and I lived in one place for more than a few months before my parents were off to join the next show. It must be nice to know who you are and to have ties to a place."

Evie considered this. She had often felt stifled by her family, but now she could see that having a home and a family weren't always a negative. "I miss my mother."

Felix had stopped in front of a small diner. He opened the door for

Evie. The place was deserted except for a laborer sitting at a corner table focusing on his bowl of stew. They slid into a booth and a waiter handed them a menu. It was a simple menu with familiar dishes like lamb stew and hash with a choice of rice or beans. Evie decided on round steak with mashed potatoes and blackberry cobbler. Felix chose a dish of pig knuckles with red beans. Once the waiter had left them with a promise to return in a moment with two glasses of tea, Felix focused his attention back on Evie.

"If it's not too painful, may I ask what happened to your parents?"

Evie almost protested that it was her mother who had died before she recalled Felix believed both her parents had passed. "The Spanish flu took them both back in 1918. I was by my mother's side when she left this world."

"You could see her again," Felix said, his eyes intense.

She didn't want a lecture on her mother being in a better place. She had heard all of that from the preacher when he came to the house after the funeral. "I don't mean to be rude, but I would rather have my parents here with me than in heaven."

Felix shook his head. "I'm not talking about heaven and hell. To me, those are elusive ideas that hold no interest. I'm talking about summoning your mother's spirit back here to earth so you can speak to her. Clara can make it happen."

The waiter had returned with their tea, giving Evie a small reprieve as she planned a response. "I don't believe in ghosts, Felix. I believe once you die, you're gone. Back to the stars or to the ashes and dust from whence we all came. I used to believe in God, but…"

His hand covered hers, and Evie found a slight comfort in his touch which surprised her. "You lost your faith when God took your parents."

It wasn't a question, but an affirmation of her belief. She nodded her head. "I can't believe in a higher power who would take good and kind people from the world."

"It's a conundrum many people struggle with after the events of the last several years. It's why I've taken an interest in spiritualism. I'd like to talk about the other night at Clara's house. I think I surprised you, and I apologize. It was unfair of me."

Returning to that night in her mind, she saw the table with the spirit board and how someone or something tried to communicate with her.

She knew the parlor tricks that clairvoyants used, but at that moment in Clara's dimly lit kitchen, she had felt a presence. It hadn't been her mother or brother. She would have recognized them. The warmth of her mother's smile or Peter's infectious laughter and pranks were as much a part of her existence as her own heart beating. She would have known. Instead, she had felt something dark and unsettling. Could it have been Flora's spirit trying to communicate with her?

"It frightened me a little," Evie admitted. "I know you are a believer, but I don't know that I'm willing to suspend my disbelief. Too many years hearing Reverend Willett preaching from the pulpit."

He sipped his tea. Grimacing, he dipped his spoon into the glass sugar bowl on the table. He stirred several spoonfuls into the glass and seemed mesmerized by the swirling brown liquid. "I joined the Army trying to convince others I was more American than Slovenian. I was trying to prove something to myself and all the men who looked askance at me when they heard my accent."

"I barely hear it when you speak."

Felix smiled. "Hours of talking in front of a mirror. Marco thinks I'm ridiculous to turn my back on our heritage, but I'm not. I love America. So many opportunities. No long bread lines. No hungry children begging in the streets."

"Not that you see. We have our own poor. They're simply better hidden than they are in other countries. Maybe it's not as noticeable, but years ago, it was horrible. Fortunately, we're seeing more businesses open. R. J. Reynolds is hiring more men. Things in Richmond are improving."

The waiter brought their lunch, and the two of them concentrated on their food rather than spirits and the poor. Felix took a slice of bread and dipped it into the pig's knuckle broth. "Rich men get richer. Poor men break under the burden of their greed. It's the way of the capitalist world. It's why my parents came to this country. We wanted our chance to get rich, too."

Evie didn't know what to say. She was aware of the claims of the Bolsheviks regarding the tobacco companies. Her father often railed about the "blasted anarchists and their fool ideas," but she didn't know enough to comment. Now, she wondered if she should pay attention to politics and what was going on in the outside world. For so long she'd been treading water, trying to survive day-to-day tasks and overcome the loss of her mother and brother. She had no idea what had gone on in the world outside of her small circle. It had only been the past couple of months that the crushing weight had been lifted from her chest. She felt as if she resurfaced and found life had moved forward without her. Maeve had helped by dragging her out to some gin joints. They discovered The Black Cat. It had been music and performing which had lit a small spark in her heart again.

Felix continued, "When I was in France, I saw my friends die. The smell of burning and the cries... it's seared into my memory. I go to sleep with their cries in my head. The smell permeates my waking hours. The only time it's quiet is when I am on stage or when I intentionally invite them into my world. Clara helps. She's created a doorway for them to come and speak to me. My long-lost friends are my spirit guides."

She had no response for Felix. What would he say if he knew Marco dosed him with nerve tonic? Evie knew many of them contained opium. Was it the drug that made him see hallucinations of his fallen comrades? Evie had only experienced war from the home front. While disillusioned with much of life, she was still grateful for her warm, safe home and the stability it gave her. She couldn't imagine the horrors Felix had seen. She put her hand on his. "I'm so sorry you had to see the things you did. To be honest, I don't know if I was a man who had fought in battle that I wouldn't believe in the afterlife, too. I've lost my parents, but I have to believe that they have moved on and aren't lingering here on earth."

Felix grasped her hand. He threaded his fingers through hers. The intimate gesture felt familiar and oddly comforting to Evie. "I'm not asking you to believe. I'm asking you to keep an open mind. Wasn't it Shakespeare who said 'There are more things in heaven and earth, Horatio'?"

Evie rolled her eyes heavenward, searching her memory and coming up empty. "I was more interested in music in school than Shakespeare, I'm afraid."

"Really? Do you sing or play an instrument?" Felix asked.

Evie hesitated to reveal this part of her life. "I like to sing. When I was younger, I always thought I would end up on stage. Not that my family would have allowed it, but a girl could dream."

"Have you ever performed on stage?"

Evie thought about lying, but decided it was easier to tell the truth. "You might think it's silly, but I've sung a couple times at a place called The Black Cat. It's a little hole-in-the-wall gin joint behind a pawnshop."

Felix snapped his fingers. "I knew you looked familiar, but I couldn't place your face. I saw you perform when I took Flora after we arrived in Richmond. A friend of mine plays in a band that performs there."

Evie tried to hide the surprise in her face. "You took Flora to The Black Cat?"

Felix released her hand. He picked up his fork and ate, avoiding her gaze and her question. After a moment, he swallowed and looked across the table at her. "A group of us went one night. Annie, Marco, Flora and me. I liked Flora. She enjoyed a good time and brought joy into my performance. I thought she liked working with me, but perhaps she liked the thrill of being onstage and the center of attention more. We went to dinner a few times, and I took her to hear music at the gin joints. It wasn't a big romance. We were strictly friends."

Evie didn't know how to respond. "Did Flora have a boyfriend?"

Felix considered her question. He took another bite of his food and chewed slowly. He put down his fork and sighed. "I am a cad to say this, but I think she may have been more interested in my brother than me."

Evie's eyes widened. "Marco? He's married to Betsy. What makes you say that?"

Felix's lips thinned. "My brother isn't famous for his fidelity. I could be wrong, but Flora was asking me a lot of questions about Marco before she... before she disappeared. I assume it was because she found him as fascinating as other women have."

Marco had claimed women were enamored of Felix, but perhaps it was the opposite. Marco exuded power and confidence. The combination had made fools of more than one woman. Evie saw resignation in Felix's face. She remembered her first day at the theater and the scene between Felix and Betsy she'd witnessed. Felix had begged Betsy to let him help her. Now, after seeing Betsy's bruises, Evie understood his pleas. "I hope you don't find this too forward, but may I ask about you and Betsy?"

Felix's sharp bitter laughter rang out in the empty restaurant.

"Betsy? What can I say? I left to go to war, leaving my fiancée in my brother's caring hands. I come back to no fiancée and a new sister-in-law."

She cringed. "I am so sorry," Evie said, and she was. "I can't imagine how you feel. You and Marco seem so close. Isn't it difficult working with her then?"

"Yes, and no. Marco is an opportunist. He always has been and always will be. I think Betsy is, too, but I didn't see it. Love being blind and all."

Felix dipped his bread back into the broth and took a bite. After he swallowed, he continued, "Marco will always be my brother. When I came back from France, my head was all scrambled. He took care of me until I was back on my feet. I owe him my loyalty."

Evie picked at her food and considered Felix's words. She couldn't fathom a brother betraying a brother. She knew it had happened during the War between the States. Brothers fighting brothers. Father against son. She supposed she was lucky. Peter had been Evie's biggest advocate when he had been alive— from fighting off boys who had tugged her pigtails when they were young to supporting her when she talked to her parents about attending university. Would Peter have encouraged her involvement in this latest adventure? She had to believe he would.

"I got the sense that Betsy didn't care for Flora. Is it because of Marco?" Evie asked.

"Possibly. Or it could have been because Flora and I went out a few evenings. Betsy might not want me with all my damage, but she doesn't want any other woman to want me either," Felix looked at his watch. "We'd best finish and return to the theater or Marco will box both our ears for lateness."

Evie scooped up a bite of blackberry cobbler. She savored the tang of the berries while she thought about everything she had learned about her new theater family.

Chapter Thirteen

The alley door swung open just as Felix reached out to open it for Evie. Will stepped out and frowned when he saw Felix and Evie together before quickly schooling his face into a bland mask. "Marco is looking for you both."

If he could have snarled like a dog guarding a bone, Evie believed Will would have. *Why does he hate Felix? Could it be because of Flora, or was it something else entirely?*

Evie didn't have time to linger, however, because she could hear Marco shouting Felix's name. The two of them trotted to the backstage where Marco paced the floor.

"Where the hell have you been, Felix?" Marco snapped. He saw Evie behind Felix and scowled. "And you. What do you think you're doing catting around my brother? I hired you to do a job, not make doe eyes at Felix. Get changed and get ready. We're going through the show one more time before the doors open."

"But—" Felix said.

Marco grabbed Felix by his shirt collar and pulled him close. "Do as I say, little brother."

"Or what?" Felix knocked Marco's hands away. He pushed his jaw out and poked Marco's chest with his finger. "I'm not the same man I was two years ago, so don't threaten me. And don't threaten Evie."

Felix stepped back and without another word, grabbed Evie's hand and pulled her after him to the dressing area. She wanted to look behind her to see Marco's reaction, but she knew to keep quiet and get ready for the show without getting in between the brothers. She thought back to Marco's comment about Felix and how he claimed he kept his brother focused. Perhaps Felix didn't need his brother's assistance after all. She had just watched the mouse attack the tom cat and win.

Felix didn't stop until they were at the ladies dressing area. Mary glanced up from where she sat with a needle and thread between her fingers and one of Julia's costumes in her other hand.

Felix dropped Evie's hand. "I'm sorry he spoke to you like that. My brother can be crass and overbearing. He means well, but sometimes, it's too much. A man can only abide so much, even from his kin."

For the first time, Evie noted an accent tinging Felix's words. The accent he had tried so hard to shake. The stress of the situation, Flora's death, Marco's anger, and whatever else the spirits were placing on his soul, were clearly affecting him. Evie downplayed her reaction to Marco's vulgarity. "Marco is probably nervous about the show tonight. I'm sure he didn't mean what he said."

Mary watched their exchange with curious eyes. "He has been pacing around here like a badger worrying after a worm."

Realizing they had an interested audience, Felix turned from Evie to Mary. "I'm going to change. Mary, do you have my new top hat?"

"Right here. It's tip top fancy and ready to grace your handsome head." Mary handed him a coal black top hat with a red satin band circling the brim.

"Evie, I'll see you on stage. Again, I'm sorry about Marco." Felix gave her one last lingering gaze before turning on his heel and walking away from her.

"I noticed that you and Felix came in together," Mary said, her lips pursed as she focused on Julia's costume. Her fingers poked the needle through the velvet bodice and pulled up a stitch. "I hope you're not getting yourself starry-eyed over him. It won't amount to anything."

"He just took me for a bite to eat to calm my nerves. I have no interest in Felix. I plan to focus on my career. Not a man." Evie lifted her nose in the air.

"Harrumph. It's girls chasing after a career that's made it so hard for my Will to find a good girl to settle down and give me grandchildren. I don't understand you young things thinking work is something glamorous. I've spent forty years stitching and cleaning after other folks. There's no glory in it." She finished her repairs, then bit the thread in two with her teeth.

"Will's a nice man. I'm sure he'll find himself a gal," Evie said.

Mary cut her eyes sideways. "He *is* a nice man. A hard worker, too. When he's done here at the theater, he goes to work running errands for Mr. Croucher. One day, he'll be running a theater. You mark my words."

Evie didn't know what to say, so she nodded her head in agreement. She found her costume for the magic act hanging on a rack outside the dressing stalls. She changed and moved to the makeup area to apply thick kohl around her eyes. Betsy had advised her that with the lights and distance from the audience, it was better to wear heavier makeup with exaggerated lines. She spent a minute lining her lips into a distinct Cupid's bow before filling it with a deep red lipstick. Satisfied with her results, she fluffed her bob and adjusted the feather fascinator that was part of her costume.

When she arrived at the side stage, she watched Annie finish her act. Felix leaned against the wall, eyes closed. His lips moved silently, and Evie wondered if he was praying or talking to himself. Rather than disturb him, she sank back into the shadows to wait for her turn on stage.

Two minutes later, Annie dashed offstage, laughing, her plates and wands clutched in her hand. She glanced over at Felix as she passed. "Another perfect rehearsal, Felix. Let's hope the luck holds for you and your newest assistant. You seem to run through them rather quickly, don't you?" Annie gave a malicious grin and continued on her way.

Felix didn't respond. Instead, he brushed off his hat and placed it on his head. From Evie's viewpoint, his black hair and eyes gleamed despite the dark, giving him a devilish air. She stayed put. A loud rumble broke the silence as Will pushed the disappearing cabinet past her. Felix followed behind Will. Evie watched as Felix instructed Will on placement.

"It's imperative tonight goes off without a hitch. Make sure you put all the props on the stage correctly. I want the audience astounded by my performance. Plus, it's Evie's debut as my new assistant."

Evie peeked around the curtain and listened.

"I know what to do, Felix," Will said. "Your brother already gave me my orders for the night. Evie will do a wonderful job, I'm sure. The two of you seem to work well together."

"She's a hard worker. Bright, funny, and a looker to boot. I'm glad Marco hired her on to the show," Felix said. He opened and closed the cabinet curtains, checking for anything that might distract the audience.

"Do you know if she has a boyfriend?" Will asked.

Felix stopped and gave Will a sharp look. "Don't start sniffing around her, Will. You made a fool of yourself over Flora. Don't make the same mistake with Evie."

Will walked off the stage without replying. As he passed by, Evie heard him mumble, "I'm not the one who's sniffing around her."

She waited a minute before she stepped from the shadows onto the brightly lit stage. Her shoes clicked across the floor, alerting Felix to her presence.

Felix looked up. "You look fetching, Evie. I'm sure you will knock the suspenders off the crowd with your good looks and your performance. Nervous?"

"A little. I'm worried I'll trip over my own two feet. I'm happy I don't have to talk."

"You'll do a wonderful job. Just follow my lead. You ready?"

She nodded, and their rehearsal began. The act started with the magic rings, and Evie managed to not drop one while tossing them to Felix. After that, Felix did his card tricks and Evie's participation wasn't necessary. She saw Betsy stepping into the sawed lady contraption backstage while Marco helped her. Will stood watching, his expression inscrutable, waiting for his cue to wheel it onstage.

Although the disappearing cabinet trick usually ended the show, Felix had her run through it one additional time. She still had difficulty opening the hatch, and he thought it would benefit her to do it twice. Felix whipped the curtains back to demonstrate the box was empty. All the while, he kept up a steady patter. "Ladies and gentlemen, my next trick will astound and amaze you. My lovely and vivacious assistant, Evie, will disappear right before your eyes."

He held his hand out to Evie to guide her into the cabinet. As she stepped towards him, there was a sudden whirring sound above her. When she stumbled back, a large sandbag crashed to the floor. It split open and spilled sand across the floor.

Evie's hand covered her mouth. "Oh my goodness!" She felt the color drain from her face and for a second, she thought she might faint.

"It almost hit me."

Felix ran across the stage to her. He clasped her to him before pushing her back and looking at her face. "Are you okay?"

Evie nodded, unable to speak. Will and Marco dashed onto the stage. Betsy followed behind them. Marco looked up at the rafters and frowned. "Will, I told you to check those ropes. They looked worn out last time I was up there. They could have killed someone. We can't afford another week's delay."

Heaven forbid you should lose money because a sandbag killed me. Aloud, Evie said, "I need to take a moment to collect myself. I'll be right back."

As she fled past the dressing rooms, she stopped. Evie felt like someone was watching her. She glanced around and saw Annie smirk and saunter back into the makeup area.

A moment later, Evie leaned against the ice cold bricks by the alley door. She didn't care that she wasn't dressed for the weather. She had practically run from the building in her dash to get away from the stage, Annie's nasty looks, and Felix. He was the one who knew where she stood on stage. Was the sandbag falling truly an accident or something much more sinister? The bite of the wind whipped down the alley and the pale sun emitted no warmth. She was chilled to her core from the weather and from fear. The door opened, and Betsy stepped out. She had Evie's coat in her hand.

"Thanks," Evie said, tugging it on over her costume. She shivered and her hands shook as she buttoned the top button. "Don't suppose you have a cigarette to share."

Wordlessly, Betsy pulled a silver cigarette case from her coat pocket and opened it for Evie. Putting one between her own lips, Betsy flicked a match against the brick wall and lit both their cigarettes. "You okay?"

"Not really, but I will be. I won't let a silly accident ruin tonight's performance."

Betsy inhaled and blew out several small circles of smoke. "Good for you." Without looking at Evie, she asked, "Do you believe in curses?"

"No. I don't believe in goblins, ghosts, or things that go bump in the night either. Why?" Evie took a tentative inhale. She gave a small cough, but her nerves seemed to steady.

Betsy leaned against the wall and eyed Evie. "Felix seems to have bad luck wherever he goes. I'm sure you know that he and I were engaged at one time."

"He told me a little. I didn't think it was any of my business," Evie said. "I'm only his assistant. I'm not interested in his personal life."

A low chuckle came from Betsy. "You really are naïve, aren't you? Felix has taken a shine to you. Just like he took an interest in Flora and the girl... what was her name? Audrey. Each one had a bad ending."

"Audrey? I didn't know about her. What happened?" Evie inhaled again, deeper this time. Her hand shook as she lowered the cigarette.

"She broke her leg when a board on the stage in Pittsburgh snapped under her. I think someone tampered with it. She had to go home. In stepped Flora to fill the void. And we know what happened to her. Now a sandbag almost kills you. Felix and his magic act are cursed."

Betsy's statement left Evie speechless. Instead of responding, she inhaled deeply, causing a paroxysm of coughing. By the time she had recovered, Betsy had ground out her own cigarette and opened the door to go back into the theater. Evie waited a moment before following her.

When she walked back to the stage, she found everyone in chaos. Marco was shouting at Will. Felix stepped between the two of them and held both at arm's length.

"I told you I checked those ropes, and they were good. Better than good. I tugged on each one myself. I'm not taking the blame for this one. Someone must have gone up there and tampered with them." Will stepped back from Felix and crossed his arms.

Marco raised his fist. "If I find out it was you trying to sabotage my show, I'll see that you never work again."

"Why would he sabotage the show, Marco?" Felix turned to his brother. "You're not making sense."

"Someone was in the theater last night and went into my office. The only people who have keys right now are me, Jake Wells, and Will. So you tell me who else could have come in here and tampered with my office and with the ropes. Jake Wells?" The scorn in Marco's voice told Evie what he thought of that idea.

"No one has been here. No one tampered with the ropes. It was an accident. We have a show to put on, so now is not the time to point fingers at each other," Betsy said, laying a hand on her husband's arm.

Marco jerked away from her touch, but his posture relaxed. "You're right. We have to put on a successful show this weekend. We need the income. Finish your rehearsal. We've got a little over an hour before we open the doors." He stalked away, leaving everyone silent in his wake.

Will stirred first. He checked the placement of the cabinet before turning to Felix. "It's ready to go. And Felix, I really made sure those ropes were safe. I don't know what happened."

Felix placed a hand on Will's shoulder. "I believe you."

Betsy followed Will off the stage. Evie watched him assist her into the box for the sawed lady trick. Evie's hands were shaking and sweaty. She wiped her palms on the skirt of her costume, then pasted a false smile on her face before turning to Felix. "Ready?" Evie asked.

Closing the space between them, Felix gently grasped her arms. "Are you sure you want to do this? Annie could fill in."

"Nonsense. It was an accident. Accidents happen all the time, and what kind of assistant would I be to run at the first sign of trouble? Now, I believe you were getting ready to place me in the disappearing cabinet."

Felix leaned down and gave her a light kiss on her cheek before releasing her. He turned to the imaginary audience and announced, "I shall now make my beautiful and brave assistant, Evie, disappear."

He held out his hand to her, and without hesitation, Evie grasped it. His fingers tightened briefly before twirling her into the cabinet. When the door closed and darkness surrounded her, Evie took a deep shuddering breath. She could do this. Quick as a cat, she squatted down and found the small finger hole in the floor and lifted it. She scrambled down and found herself in the dimly lit space under the stage. Suppressing her fear, she jogged across the brick floors and climbed up into the light. As she hoisted herself up, a hand reached down and grasped her wrist.

A gasp escaped her lips. Will pulled her up. "Sorry, Evie. I didn't mean to startle you. I wanted to make sure you were okay."

"I'm fine. Thank you." She smoothed her skirt with her hands. "I'd best get back to the wings. Our next trick is in a moment. We can't leave the audience waiting."

A wry smile twisted Will's cleft lip. "That's the spirit. I need to roll it on stage. Betsy's probably getting a cramp tucked into the box."

As she trailed after Will, she heard Felix talking. His fingers tapped a rhythm on his top hat that rested on a small table. A moment later, he reached into the hat and pulled out a white handkerchief. With the incantation of magical words, the handkerchief transformed into a white dove which he released. It flew up to the rafters where it nestled amongst the lights.

"Ah! Good timing, Evie. Let's do the next trick, then the disappearing cabinet once more, then we can relax before we open the doors."

Felix and Evie performed the sawed lady illusion, then the disappearing cabinet once more. Conrad the Human Pretzel waited in the wings to finish up the show as Felix left the stage. Conrad nodded to Evie. She wondered what it would be like to bend yourself into a tiny ball and roll across a stage. Would it hurt? She couldn't imagine doing some of the contortions she had seen him practice backstage.

"Hi, Conrad. Are you ready for tonight's show?" Evie asked. She had been introduced to him and the twins who opened the show, but as yet, had not taken time to know him.

"I've been doing this for years. The question is, are you ready?" Conrad gave her a smile. His blue eyes were kind, and his white bushy brows and beard gave him the appearance of a skinny Saint Nicholas.

"I think so. How long have you been with the show?"

Conrad tapped his bottom lip. "With this show, only a year. Before this gig, I was with a traveling circus based out of Georgia."

"You must have known Flora. Even though I hadn't met her, it saddened me to hear that someone had murdered her. It's made me a little nervous." Evie shuddered, which was only a slight affectation.

"Stay away from the men who flock to the back alley entrance after the show, and you'll be fine," Conrad said, patting her on the arm. "It was probably one of those cocksure young men who always chase after any young lady on her own. Now, I'd best get on stage. You can never get enough rehearsal time."

Conrad left Evie pondering his words. She had seen no men hanging out behind the theater, but the theater had been closed for the new seating until this week. Both Felix and Will insisted Flora wouldn't have walked out of the theater on her own. She would have to pay attention after the show. She hurried back to the dressing area where she found Mary by the kettle.

"Join me for a cup of tea, Evie. It will calm your nerves." Mary invited her to sit on a chair near her work table.

Mary put a cup that Evie hoped was clean in front of her and poured tea into it. After making her own cup, she returned the kettle to the hotplate and settled her bulky frame onto a chair. It creaked under her weight. "I hope you're not still distressed about Marco and his tussle with Felix. You know how brothers are. Best friends one minute and brawling the next."

Evie hesitated before she said, "My brother, Peter, and I used to bicker constantly when we were young, but as we grew older, he became one of my closest confidantes."

"Will your brother be coming tonight to watch you perform?" Mary took a sip of tea and grimaced. She spooned sugar into the cup and stirred it before taking another drink.

"My brother was killed in the war. I never realized how close we really were until he was no longer there for me to talk to." Tears welled in Evie's eyes.

Mary clucked. "Poor child. You know what it's like to lose somebody then. My Will wanted to serve, but with his foot... well, people called him a coward, but the Army wouldn't take him. Girls would turn their back on him in the street. It wasn't right. He's a good man, my boy is."

"He's been very kind to me," Evie said, trying to ease Mary's distress. "He even offered to walk me to the trolley."

Nodding her head, Mary said, "That's my Will. Always looking out for the girls. I raised him right. I'm glad to see you appreciate him. Not like others."

"What others?" Evie asked.

Mary waved her question away and stood up. "You finish your tea, love. I need to visit the facilities and get things in order for Julia. I had to mend a tear on the dog's costume. Silly creature gnawed a hole in his cloth collar."

Evie took a sip of her tea, which had cooled. She grimaced at the bitterness and added a bit of sugar. She walked the cup to the hotplate and poured in more hot tea. As she did, she spotted something under the table leg. She bent down and picked up a crumpled bit of paper. Looking around to see if anyone was near, she laid it on the table and smoothed the wrinkles from the paper.

Will, please don't wait to walk me to the trolley. A friend is taking me out for a late supper after the show. F.

A sound from the alleyway startled her, so she tucked the note into her bodice. She would bet a slice of Mrs. Fortune's sweet potato pie that the note to Will was from Flora. Will liked to offer his gentlemanly service of an escort to the trolley to more than just her. He used to offer to escort Flora, too, but clearly, Flora made other plans. Did those plans include Felix? Or someone else? Evie needed to find out, but for now, there was no time to investigate. She had a show, or as Felix would say, an extravaganza, to prepare for.

Chapter Fourteen

It was show time and Evie's nerves were tauter than the orchestra's violins. She stood in the wings with Felix and Betsy watching Annie's final number. It was amazing to watch the woman spin the plates on a stick while wailing a tune and dancing at the same time. It was definitely a talent that Evie didn't have, nor did she think she wanted to cultivate. She would stick to plain old singing in front of a microphone at The Black Cat without the use of props. If the audience wanted more, they could look elsewhere.

Annie held the last note of *How Ya Gonna Keep 'Em Down on the Farm?* When the orchestra finished playing, she gracefully caught the spinning plates and curtsied to the audience. She took a moment to bask in the cheers before giving one last curtsy and a cheeky grin, then she pirouetted off the stage. Annie was shiny with sweat and her mascara and kohl had smudged under her eyes from the hot house lights, but Evie saw the triumph of a performance done well. Evie hoped she could share in that same elation after she and Felix left the stage.

The orchestra played the opening chords for the magic act. Felix leaned over and whispered in her ear, "You will be fantastic, Evie. See you onstage." He winked and strutted out with a flourish of his cape.

Twenty-five minutes later, Evie had disappeared from the cabinet and was waiting to take her bows with Felix. She hadn't missed a beat or a cue. Although her ears had thrummed with the beat of her heart when she had stepped on stage, the lights had kept her from seeing the audience as more than just blurs in the seats. She had taken a deep breath and pretended there was no one else there but Felix and her. By the time she stepped into the cabinet for the last trick, her cheeks ached from smiling. It was fantastic, and she couldn't wait to do it again.

Betsy sidled up next to her and gave her a friendly shoulder-to-shoulder bump. "You did great. You really did."

Heat suffused her cheeks, and her grin grew wider. "Thanks. Maybe Marco will keep me on since I didn't trip over my own two feet."

At the sound of her husband's name, Betsy's face changed. Her eyebrows furrowed, and she grimaced. "For now." She turned to Evie. "Listen, there are some things you need to know if you're going to stick around. You want to get a drink with me when we're done?"

Evie didn't hesitate. This was just the opportunity she needed to find out more information about the show and Flora. "Yes. I'm dying for one after tonight."

Betsy laughed. "I've got the place for us to go. I'll meet you by the back door after we take our curtain call. Come on. We need to get out there."

Betsy grabbed Evie's hand. With Felix standing between the two of them, they took a bow. Felix stepped forward. "My assistants, Evie and Betsy. Didn't they do a fine job, ladies and gentlemen?"

Evie and Betsy dropped into a quick curtsy, then sprinted from the stage, the applause thundering behind them. Felix joined them a moment later. "Evie, you did as well as I predicted. You're a natural on stage. I am so proud of you."

A side glance at Betsy told Evie that she wasn't thrilled with Felix's praise, but she hid it and said, "I told Evie she was great. Maybe we can keep an assistant for more than a month this time."

With a quick spin on her heels, Betsy left. Felix's eyes followed her retreating form for a moment before turning back to Evie. "Do you want to go somewhere this evening to celebrate? Perhaps a drink at The Black Cat?"

The thought that she might run into someone at The Black Cat who knew her as Evie Harris and not Evie Shaw sent a shiver of dread down her spine. "I'd love to, but I already promised Betsy I would go with her. Perhaps another time."

Felix inclined his head. "It would be good if Betsy and you got to know each other better. She's had a tough time and could use a friend." He hesitated before he continued. "I worry about her. My brother isn't always the kindest person."

Evie didn't respond. What could she say? She didn't know Marco, but from what she had observed, he was quick with his temper and his fists. He wasn't the type of person Evie had experienced. Her father might be gruff, but he had never even raised his voice to Evie's mother. In her world, a man who struck his wife was not a man, but a coward.

Instead of saying what she thought, Evie said, "I'm sure Betsy and I shall be grand friends. Do I need to do anything else tonight?"

"Will and Mary lock up the theater when we're done. The front of the house takes care of closing up the ticket booth and making sure the audience is clear. The cleaners come in early in the morning to get everything spiffy for tomorrow night's performance. We're done for the night."

"Well, thank you again for giving me a chance," Evie said. "Have a good evening."

"You, too, Evie."

As she walked away, she heard him whisper, "And be careful."

Twenty minutes later, she had changed out of her costume and back into her street clothes. She had removed her stage makeup, and she had applied a thin line of kohl to accent her large eyes and used a light hand to apply her lip color. She was as presentable as expected after a late night and a long day. She slipped her coat on and tucked her short hair under her blue cloche.

Betsy was leaning against the door frame waiting for her. She had removed her stage makeup, too, but had reapplied it with a heavier hand than Evie. The powder wasn't enough to conceal the blackened eye from a close inspection. The heavy eyeliner only emphasized her exhaustion and the bruises. "Ready?"

"Yes. Where are we going?" Evie asked.

"Just wait. It's a little hole-in-the-wall joint some family of mine run. They serve the best gin rickeys, and their music is always hopping."

They walked out the door. A shadowed figure separated himself from the brick wall and stepped in front of them. Evie assumed it was one of the reputed fans that waited at the alley door.

"Ladies, can I escort you to a taxicab or trolley," the man said. The voice sounded familiar, but a heavy handlebar mustache and an old-fashioned bowler obscured the face.

"Scram," Betsy said as she reached into her pocketbook. She pulled out a small knife with a dangerously sharp tip. "We're not interested."

The man backed away, holding his hands in the air. "No need to get feisty. I thought I recognized Evie when I was in the audience. I knew her when she was young. I felt it my duty to come and escort her back to her home."

The cloud that had blocked the moonlight scudded away, and Evie peered closer. She stifled a gasp. It was Harry Houdini in disguise.

"Oh, my goodness. I didn't recognize you." Evie put a hand on Betsy's wrist so she would lower the knife. "I haven't seen you in a month of Sundays, Mister…"

"Houlihan," Harry said, stretching his hand out to Betsy. "Erick Houlihan. I'm an old family friend of Evie's. Nice to meet you."

Betsy hesitated before dropping the knife back into her pocketbook and extending her hand. "Betsy Croucher. Sorry about the knife, but we get all sorts of characters hanging out by the theater trying to get fresh with some girls."

"No harm done," Harry said. "You did a wonderful job this evening, Evie. I would love to visit with you. I'm only in town for one more day. I'm taking the Sunday evening train to head to New York. Are you free tomorrow evening after the show?"

Evie wasn't sure how to navigate this subterfuge, but she saw the subtle nod of his head and said, "I am. It would be nice to talk to someone who knew my parents before they passed. Shall we meet here? Say nine-thirty?"

"Excellent. Let me get you ladies a cab. You shouldn't be out unescorted if there are young Lotharios on the prowl."

Harry walked them to the street and raised his fingers to his lips and whistled. A black cab idled at the end of the street and pulled forward. Harry opened the door for Betsy and Evie, then he handed a dollar to the driver. "Make sure they get safely to their destination. Mrs. Croucher, a pleasure to meet you. Evie, I'll see you tomorrow. Have a good evening."

He closed the door after they were safely inside and tapped the top of the cab's roof before stepping back. Evie felt the tightness in her shoulders leave when the car pulled away from the curb.

Betsy eyed her. "Your friend is more than a friend, isn't he?"

Puzzled, Evie said, "I don't know what you mean. He's old enough to be my father."

"He acted like he hadn't seen you in a while, but he called me Mrs. Croucher. How did he know I was married?"

Evie thought quickly. She glanced at the pocketbook with the evil-looking blade that Betsy had clutched in her hand. "He must have seen your wedding band and realized you were a married woman. Mr. Houlihan is very observant. I could never escape his watchful eyes when I was a child up to shenanigans."

Betsy leaned back and chuckled. "For a moment I thought you were trying to pull a fast one on me. I guess I'm a little on edge with everything that's been happening at the theater."

Evie wanted to talk, but the cab had pulled up to the address Betsy had provided. In front of them was a drugstore with advertisements for liniment hanging in the window.

"Are you gals sure you're in the right place?" the driver asked.

"Yes," Betsy replied. "My friend lives down the block. We'll walk from here."

"If you're sure," the driver said, tipping his hat before driving off and leaving the two of them standing on a dimly lit street corner.

With a small shiver, Evie looked around. The street was deserted, but despite the lack of people, she heard a faint sound of thumping. Betsy grabbed her hand and pulled her along behind her. "Come on. The party's already hopping."

The two of them went down the alley until they reached a beat up red door with the words *employees only* scrawled in white paint. Betsy rapped twice, then four times, followed by a final rap. There was the sound of a hasp being moved and near the top of the door, a small window appeared.

"What do you want? Don't you know what time it is?" a deep voice boomed.

"I'm so sorry, sir. I must have forgotten to wind my watch," Betsy said.

There was the sound of another lock being turned, then the red door swung open and light spilled out into the gloom of the alleyway. A giant of a man with tight black curls and a boxer's broken nose stood before them. "Bets! Woman, you've been in town but you haven't stopped by to say hello. Get in here and give your favorite cousin a hug."

Betsy stepped into the giant's embrace and allowed his bear-sized paws to hold her. He pushed her back to look her over and scowled when he spotted the bruises that makeup didn't quite hide. "You need to leave him, Bets. If not, I won't be responsible for the damage I do."

Betsy gave him a playful tap. "I'm fine, Sam. You can't afford to get in trouble with the law. Just leave it alone. This is my friend, Evie. Be a doll and pour us a drink."

Sam nodded to Evie. "Sam. Nice to meet you."

Sam led the two of them down a short flight of stairs to a cellar that had been transformed. Instead of the gloom of dank bricks and dirt floors, pine boards stretched across the room to a cherry bar with a brass rail. They had scattered several small tables around the room. Every chair held a man or woman with a glass in their hand. A small band with a piano man, a sax player and a singer were playing a familiar tune. Giddy couples danced and laughed on a makeshift dance floor. Cigarette smoke and sound filled the air. Evie loved it.

Sam went up to the bartender and said, "Gino, fix my cousin, Betsy, and her friend a drink." He slid coins onto the bar. "Bets, I've got to get back to my post. Friday night's our busiest night. Come visit with me before you leave."

The bartender slid two drinks across the bar to Betsy and Evie before pocketing the coins. "I gave that an extra kick just for you since you're related to Sam," he said with a wink.

Evie picked up her glass and took a tentative sip. "Whew. That packs a wallop."

Betsy took a big gulp and smacked her lips. "Just how I like it. Come on. Let's see if we can find someplace to sit and talk."

Chapter Fifteen

Evie followed Betsy to two chairs near the stage. They had to squeeze their way past several cheek-to-cheek couples while holding their drinks high to keep from spilling them. Betsy pulled her cigarette case out of her purse and offered one to Evie.

"Thanks." She looked around at the mix of people occupying every available space. "This place is really crowded."

"It usually is. My uncle owns the pharmacy upstairs and lets my cousins run the joint." Betsy smiled and waved at a couple sitting across the room. "That's my cousin Freddie and his wife, Polly."

"I didn't realize you were from the area," Evie said, taking a sip of her drink. It was stronger than Aunt Dorcas's elixir, but the bartender had added some Coca-Cola to smooth the taste. She knew it would keep her awake for hours. Coca-Cola always made her jittery.

Betsy sat back in her chair. "I'm not. My family's from New York, but three uncles moved down to DC and Richmond for better business opportunities. This is my mom's family. Italian through and through. My uncles never forgave my mother for marrying a mutt and a Protestant to boot."

The music changed from a slow waltz to a fast-moving tune. Evie's foot tapped in time with the music, and she hummed the familiar song under her breath. She took a drag of her cigarette. This time, she didn't embarrass herself by coughing. She watched the dancers trot by and sipped her drink.

"Can I ask you a question about Felix and Marco?" Evie asked.

At first, Betsy didn't answer her, and Evie wondered if perhaps the music had drowned out her words. But then, Betsy gave a long sigh and tapped the ash from her cigarette into a metal ashtray. "Go ahead and ask. Our show is like an incestuous, gossipy family. I'd rather you find out things from me than listen to that cow, Annie."

Surprised by the bald frankness of Betsy's words, Evie plunged forward with her interrogation. "Felix told me that the two of you were engaged before the war, but you ended up marrying Marco while he was overseas. Why?"

Betsy watched the band as she spoke, not meeting Evie's gaze. "You have to understand what life was like for me growing up. We lived hand to mouth because my father was a shiftless man who liked to drink every penny he earned. My mother worked seven days a week in a shirt factory. If not for her, we would have all starved."

"But your uncles—"

"Ah, my uncles. They would help occasionally, but when Uncle Anthony found out that the money he'd given Mama went to the bar, he and my uncles refused to help anymore. I left and went on the road with a burlesque show when I was fifteen. One less mouth for them to feed is what I figured."

"Are your parents still in New York?" Evie asked. She couldn't imagine what Betsy's life had been like. Her own father indulged in an occasional glass of whiskey before the Volstead Act, but he was a believer in law and order, even if he didn't agree with it.

"My mom died from tuberculosis about a year after I left. My sister, Teresa, married a man who might as well have been Papa. My father disappeared a week after we buried my mother. His body washed up in the East River a few days later. I can't say I was sorry." Betsy finished her drink and gazed down at the empty glass.

Evie didn't know what to say. Betsy hadn't answered her question about Marco and Felix, but she felt like Betsy needed to get her story out the only way she knew how. She waited to see if she would continue.

Instead, Betsy stood up with her empty glass in her hand. "I'm going for another. I'll bring you one, too."

Evie almost demurred but thought better of it. She needed to gain Betsy's trust, and if drinking liquor in a basement speakeasy was the only way to do it, then by golly, she would do it. She allowed her eyes to drift across the dance floor to where Betsy's cousin sat with his wife.

He was a handsome man with pitch-colored hair and a pencil-thin mustache. His suit coat draped over the back of his chair. A black leather shoulder holster was stark against his white shirt. When he turned and shifted to watch the band, his eyes caught hers. She looked away, embarrassed he had caught her staring.

A glass appeared in front of her. She took it from Betsy and set it down next to her empty one. "Thanks."

Betsy settled back in her seat, then leaned across the table. "Are you keen on Felix?"

Startled, Evie opened her mouth to protest, but found she couldn't. She found him attractive, and she enjoyed his company earlier at lunch. Did that mean she fancied him? She didn't think so, but it had been so long since she had dated anyone that she couldn't properly tell. "I don't think so. To be honest, I have little experience with men. I haven't stepped out with anyone since my… for some time."

Betsy regarded her through half-closed eyes as the smoke from her cigarette filled the air between them. She sat back. "I guess I'll take you at your word. You seem fairly honest. Not that I can stake a claim to both him and Marco. Damn, I'm such a mess." She ran her hand through her hair.

"Are you still in love with Felix?"

"No… yes. I don't know. I should have never married Marco. Felix left, and I didn't think he was coming back. I got scared. I never wanted to be hungry and eating watered down soup with stale bread again." Her eyes grew misty and stared into space, lost in her memories. "I met Felix and Marco when they were a two-bit act in a dive outside of Cleveland. The two of them performed card and mind reading tricks together. What a sad sight that was, let me tell ya.

"I offered to be Felix's assistant, so Marco stepped back and took over as manager. We got gigs in some nicer houses, and eventually, we added new acts. Felix and I grew to love each other. When he enlisted, I fell apart, and Marco stepped in to fill the void."

A man with slicked-back blond hair and a sad attempt at a mustache appeared at their table. "Ladies, my friend and I were wondering if you would do us the honor of a dance." He indicated a whippet-thin man with bulging eyes and an unfortunate overbite which gave him the appearance of a frightened ferret.

"I, uh, no thank you." Evie stammered without giggling. She

decided she shouldn't have another drink, or she would have hell to pay tomorrow.

Giving a half-shrug, the man turned away. Once he left, Evie leaned across the table to Betsy. "Marco didn't have any qualms about dating his brother's girl?"

Betsy lit another cigarette and inhaled. "Marco wants what Marco wants, and I was unattainable because of Felix. Once he had me, he lost interest. I was such a fool," she said, bitterness tinging each word.

Evie couldn't imagine being in Betsy's shoes. In love with one man, but married to his brother through desperation. The very idea stiffened her resolve to never marry. She wouldn't ever be placed in that position if she had any say.

"I don't think Felix will ever forgive me for breaking his heart. Not really," Betsy continued. "And Marco will never forgive me for loving his brother more than him."

The music stopped and the band announced they were taking a quick break. Evie was glad that the noise had lessened. She loved music, but the heavy smoke, the booze, and the noise made her head throb. She needed to get her information, then convince Betsy to call it a night.

"Was Felix interested in Flora?" Evie asked, trying her best to sound nonchalant.

Betsy gave her a sharp look. "Flora? You keep gnawing at that bone. Why are you so interested in them?"

"He's mentioned her a few times, and he seemed to care about her. I was just curious about their relationship. If it was more than business." Evie shrugged, trying to show she couldn't care less if Felix took an interest in her.

"Flora liked a good time. If someone promised her fun, she was the first one at the door with her flame red lipstick and champagne tastes. She liked a night on the town and wasn't choosy who took her."

Betsy said this without rancor. Evie tried to reconcile Betsy's view of Flora with the picture painted by Jack Thompson. "She was a floozy?" Evie asked.

Betsy waved at the smoke in front of her face, then laughed. "Nah. She would slap the face of any fellow that got too fresh with her. Flora liked to have fun. Music, drinking, good food. To be honest, it surprised me she lasted with the show as long as she did. We all knew she came from a good family, and it was just a chance for her to go on the road away from Pittsburgh. Flora wanted adventure."

"And now she's dead," Evie replied. She took another sip of her drink before she continued. The Coca-Cola did little to cut through the harshness of the liquor. It did, however, cut through Evie's reserve and made her nerves jump. "What happened the night she disappeared? Did you see her that evening?"

Shaking her head, Betsy said, "I saw her before the show started, and we performed the sawed lady together. I left before the act finished."

Evie waited for Betsy to continue. She didn't want to seem overly interested lest Betsy get suspicious, however, she wanted to jump across the table and ask Betsy if she had killed Flora out of jealousy. Instead, she leaned back in her chair and took another small sip of her drink and looked casually around the room.

"I should've stayed that night. Flora had asked me if I wanted to go to The Black Cat. I promised her I would, but I didn't. Now, she's dead, and it's my fault."

Evie looked up sharply. "What do you mean? Your fault. Why didn't you stay for the curtain call?"

"I had gotten into a fight with Marco earlier. He hadn't come back to the hotel the night before. Flora had come in that afternoon to get ready for the show and appeared exhausted. I guess I put two and two together and figured they had spent the night together. It hurt me," Betsy said. "Not Marco. I'm used to his indiscretions, but Flora was my friend. Or at least, she was my friend, which is why we had made plans to go out for a drink."

"So you left without asking Flora if she had been with Marco?" Evie prompted.

"Well, I had talked myself into confronting her after the show, but Will came and asked if I could take Julia back to her room. She had eaten some bad fish and needed to go home, and Will couldn't find Annie anywhere. I took her back to the boarding house and stayed with her until she fell asleep. When I went to the theater the next day, I found out nobody had seen Flora and she hadn't shown up for the evening's performance. Annie had to fill in and was steaming mad about it."

"You couldn't have known you wouldn't see her again. And who knows, maybe whoever killed her would have hurt you, too."

Betsy pulled a handkerchief out of her purse and dabbed at the tears that had formed while she had talked about Flora. "I suppose you're right. Stupid little git had to get murdered before we could sort things out."

Betsy's tears seemed real, and her face filled with sorrow at Flora's death. *And I can cross you off my list of suspects who might have murdered Flora.*

Chapter Sixteen

The next morning, Evie's head beat out a tattoo of pain. She had no one to blame but herself. After Betsy's tear-stained confession about Flora, Evie didn't feel like she could leave her. So instead of going home, the two of them had continued to sip the paint varnish liquor in the makeshift bar. It wasn't until the band had called it quits for the night that the two of them had grabbed their coats and stumbled up the stairs to bid Sam goodnight. He had found somebody to cover the door and gave them a ride. He dropped Evie off in front of Aunt Dorcas's before continuing on to Betsy's hotel. Betsy had been softly snoring in the sedan's backseat. Evie whispered her thanks to Sam for the lift and tiptoed into the house so as not to wake her aunt.

Now, she hunched over her coffee while Aunt Dorcas puttered in the kitchen with her cane. "Aunt Dorcas, have a seat. I can fix you breakfast. You shouldn't be putting weight on your ankle." Evie opened one eye and immediately regretted it. "I didn't wake you when I came in, did I?"

Aunt Dorcas thumped a tin of headache powders down on the table in front of Evie, causing her to wince. "I was out like a kitten after nursing. I take it you had an excellent debut. Oh, I wish I could have been there to see you on stage." Aunt Dorcas sighed and sat down, propping her foot up on a kitchen step stool. "Your mother should have gone on stage. She had a beautiful singing voice."

Evie thought about her mother, Rose, and how she had filled the house with music. Always singing when she sewed or cleaned, it brightened the atmosphere of the house on even the cloudiest day.

Now, their home was devoid of song, except for Mrs. Fortune's occasional humming. It was from her mother that Evie gained her love of music. Rose had encouraged Evie's passion and the two of them would sing with the Victrola, much to Peter's chagrin. He had a tin ear and would complain that Evie sounded like a cat squalling, but he had said it with affection.

"Yes, she did," Evie said. "I didn't make a mess of the performance, and Felix seemed pleased. Guess who was waiting for me at the back door?"

"Harry Houdini?"

"Yes," Evie said, narrowing her eyes. "How did you know?"

Aunt Dorcas refilled Evie's coffee cup before replenishing her own. "He stopped by the house to see you. It appears your father had gone on the warpath and shouted down the Jefferson Hotel until Houdini finally calmed him. Harry came by here after he had dropped your father off at your house. He said he convinced George you weren't in any immediate danger, and he would see you home after the performance."

Evie took some headache powders and chased them down with a sip of coffee. "He stopped to see me after the performance, but he didn't see me home. Instead, I went to a hole-in-the-wall gin joint with Betsy Croucher."

Aunt Dorcas arched her brow and leaned forward, resting her face in her hands. "Tell me and don't leave out a thing. I must live vicariously through you because of this confounded ankle."

Evie relayed the events of the previous evening, leaving nothing out. "I believe Betsy, so I'm crossing her off my list of suspects." The powders were helping her head stop thumping, and the coffee had woken her up. "After breakfast, I'm going to head over to the boarding house where Flora stayed and gather her things. Maybe I'll find something there."

"I think you need to take someone with you when you go. That neighborhood is close to the river and there are some interesting characters."

"I'll call Maeve and have her go with me. The two of us together will be fine," Evie said.

She stood up and prepared a quick fry up of scrambled eggs with a slice of ham for the two of them. By the time she finished cleaning up the kitchen, Evie felt more like her old self. She had learned her lesson regarding rot gut alcohol. She would stick to Aunt Dorcas's elixir. It tasted better and didn't leave you feeling like a parade marched on your brain all night.

An hour later, she and Maeve had ridden the trolley to the neighborhood near the river. The street they were looking for was a block and a half from the stop, but the sun was out and finally melting away the last of the winter snow and ice that had held on to the city for so long.

"Harold and I didn't have the best seats, but we both thought you did an outstanding job on stage. I mean, when you disappeared from that cabinet at the end of the act, I gasped. For a moment, I feared you wouldn't return just like Flora. Silly," Maeve said with a self-deprecating giggle. "Ever since we were at the theater, I've been looking over my shoulder like a nervous Nellie. You'd think I was the one undercover."

"I'm glad you were there. What do you think about Betsy? Do you believe her?" Evie asked. She had told Maeve about the drinks and girl-to-girl conversation of the previous night on the trolley ride.

"I do. Marco sounds like a real cad, but Betsy married him for security and broke Felix's heart. That speaks a little to her character. I think Betsy is one of those gals that will always survive regardless of who she might step on. I would still be cautious around her if I were you," Maeve said.

The boarding house was a two-story square structure with white clapboards and black shutters with paint beginning to chip. There was a stoop with an overhang by the front door and a hand-painted sign next to the door said, *Rooms for rent. Inquire inside.*

"Do we knock?" Maeve asked.

Evie tried the handle. It turned easily, and she opened the door and called out. "Hello? Is anyone here."

There was the sound of a chair scraping from a room nearby and heavy footsteps coming toward them. A moment later, a stout woman with graying brown hair pulled back into a severe bun appeared. She waved them inside. "Mind that you shut the door behind you. Don't want the cold to get inside." She wiped her hands on an apron she had tied around her middle. "Are you here to rent a room? I've got one that came vacant this past week. You two would have to share, but it has a trundle, so it shouldn't be a problem."

"Uh, no. I'm Flora Thompson's cousin, Evie. I've come to get her things if you still have them. My aunt and uncle were too upset to do it themselves, so I offered to come collect them," Evie said. She hoped her similar looks to Flora convinced the woman of her good intentions as a relative.

Maeve glanced at her out of the corner of her eye and gave Evie an encouraging nod. "I'm Maeve, a family friend. I came with Evie for moral support. It's been such a trying time for everyone."

Maeve pulled a handkerchief out of her purse and dabbed at some nonexistent tears. She even sniffled a little to add authenticity to her performance. Evie made a mental reminder to go to Maeve for any acting tips because she was pulling all the stops out with this act.

"Oh, you poor thing. Come into the kitchen and have a cup of coffee with me. I've got a chicken stewing on the stove for tonight's dinner. I need to keep an eye on it, so the pot doesn't boil over." The woman turned and headed towards the back of the house. They followed close behind her.

The kitchen was spotless and filled with the smells of cleaner and cooking. They sat in the chairs closer to the stove and thanked her for the cups of coffee she placed in front of them. After pouring her own, she sat down at the table. She pushed a stray hair that had escaped the bun away from her face. "Where are my manners? I'm Mrs. Brompton. I run this boarding house. I couldn't believe it when the police stopped by to let me know someone had murdered Flora. Can you believe it? She was such a sweet young thing, too." Mrs. Brompton's eyes were wide. "Such a shame. She was going back home to Pittsburgh after the show closed, too."

"Really?" Evie asked. "I hadn't realized she wasn't staying with the show."

"Oh, yes. She wasn't like the other women on the circuit. That's mostly who I rent rooms to, you know. Girls in the theater. I have one or two who work in the burlesque." Mrs. Brompton lowered her voice to a whisper on the word burlesque. "I run a strict house. No hotplates. No smoking in the rooms. And no men. Flora didn't give me any reason to watch her when she came in after a show. Unlike some of these girls."

"I'm sure it will comfort the family that Flora had someone who cared about her wellbeing," Maeve murmured.

"Yes," Evie chimed in. "My aunt and uncle need any bit of comfort they can find right now. So, my cousin didn't have a young man she was stepping out with? The only reason I ask is because in a letter I received, she hinted that she was interested in someone."

Mrs. Brompton tapped her bottom lip with her finger and looked up at the ceiling. After a moment, she snapped her fingers. "There was one man who came by here looking for her. It was the day before she disappeared. He was a nice enough. Walked with a bit of a limp. Flora wasn't here, and he left. Otherwise, no, she didn't have any gentleman callers. Not that came here, anyway."

Will. Why would he come looking for Flora?

Evie asked, "Are any of the other women from Flora's troupe staying here?" She hoped the answer was no. If not, she would send Maeve up to gather Flora's items.

"Well, now, Annie McAlrony and her daughter, Julia, stay here, but neither one is home right now. I could take a message and have Annie contact you. Are you local or…"

"No, ma'am. I took the train down from Pittsburgh. Maeve is a friend from school, so I came down to visit her for the day and gather Flora's things. I'm leaving to go back home on tomorrow's train."

Mrs. Brompton stood up. "That's too bad. I'm sure it would please Annie and Julia to meet you. Julia especially seemed fond of Flora. Closer in age and all."

"Did Flora and Annie seem friendly," Maeve asked.

Mrs. Brompton had gone to stir the pot on the stove, but at Maeve's question, she stopped and put the spoon down on a metal rest. "Now that you ask, I got the distinct impression that Annie wasn't as enamored of Flora as Julia seemed to be. Annie's always prickly. Very sensitive about her looks, that one is. Thinks she's getting old, when she's only in her thirties. My aching back and feet know old! You bright young things. You wear me out."

Evie gulped the tepid coffee and stood up. "We don't want to take up more of your time. Are Flora's things still in her room?"

"No, love. I packed them back into her travel case. I waited to put out the sign that a room was available, hoping she would come back, but then the police told me she had died. I can't really afford to leave the room empty." She said the last bit with a touch of defiance.

"Perfectly understandable." Evie reassured her with a smile.

The tension that tightened Mrs. Brompton's face retreated with Evie's words.

"If it's not too much trouble, could I see the room where she stayed? The two of us were so close when we were younger." Evie allowed her voice to trail off and gave a slight hiccup of a sob.

"Of course, dear. Let me get the key." She patted Evie on the shoulder and walked across the room to a small desk. Opening the top drawer, she pulled out a skeleton key, then she handed it to Evie. "First door on the left at the top of the stairs. Take your time."

Evie gave a quick side nod of her head at Maeve towards Mrs. Brompton. Maeve understood Evie's intent because she turned to Mrs. Brompton and asked, "How long have you been running this house?"

Evie moved swiftly up the steps and found the room that had been Flora's. Using the key, she unlocked the door and entered the sparsely furnished room. There was a simple iron bed with a colorful patchwork quilt. Evie sat down on it. The springs creaked beneath her. She gazed around the room to see it as Flora had. There was a narrow chest of drawers that was scratched and worn. A mirror sat above it. In the corner was a small sink with a towel bar. That was it.

Evie got up and walked over to the dresser. She opened each drawer and moved her hand around to feel for any items left behind. Her hand came back empty. She moved back to the bed and got down on her hands and knees. A trundle bed tucked neatly underneath left no room for any item of substance. Still, she patted her hand around on the thread-bare rug. Her finger caught on something small and sharp. Carefully, she used her fingertips and flicked the item out from under the bed.

An earring lay on the floor before her. Evie picked it up. It was a jade drop set in sterling silver. It was lovely and quite delicate. She reached her hand back under the bed, but she couldn't find the matching earring. Perhaps she would find it in Flora's belongings. It was possible that another tenant of the boarding house left it behind. She had spent too much time in here. Mrs. Brompton would grow suspicious if she lingered any longer. Pushing herself off her knees, she tucked the earring into her purse, then straightened her skirt. Evie went to the sink and dampened her fingertips under the spigot. She patted a small bit of water under her eyes so it would appear as if she had been crying. She looked in the tarnished mirror above the dresser and, satisfied with her appearance, headed downstairs.

Mrs. Brompton had refilled Maeve's coffee cup and the two of them chatted amiably over a plate of shortbread cookies. At the sound of Evie's approach, they looked up and stopped talking.

"Oh, you poor dear," Mrs. Brompton said. "This must have been difficult for you, and here I am chewing the fat. Can I get you anything? Another cup of coffee? A cookie? Your friend has been telling me about her job down at the newspaper. You modern girls with your careers. If I got a job outside the home, my Leonard would spin in his grave."

Mrs. Brompton nattered on about her husband, but Evie had stopped listening. She heard footsteps on the front step. She hoped it wasn't Annie coming back to the boarding house. There would be no way she and Maeve could talk their way out of things if it was. She heard the squeak of a hinge, then the sound of something falling on the floor. The footsteps retreated. Evie glanced down the hall and saw a handful of white envelopes on the floor in front of the door.

"Your mail is here." Evie tried to keep the relief from her voice. "You've been most kind, Mrs. Brompton. We'd best be going. You said you had Cousin Flora's things packed?"

"Yes, dear. Right here in the front hall closet."

Evie and Maeve followed Mrs. Brompton to the door underneath the stairs. She opened it with a skeleton key that resembled the one Evie had used to go into Flora's room. Mrs. Brompton pulled out a leather travel case with a matching valise. She set the two bags on the floor in front of Evie.

"That's odd," Mrs. Brompton said, her brows lowering. "I put a small little lock on the bag, and it's gone. I didn't want anyone to think I hadn't secured her belongings. It's mostly nice girls who stay here from the traveling shows, but occasionally you get one with sticky fingers."

"Perhaps you meant to put in on there and forgot. I'll tell my aunt and uncle you kept Flora's belongings secure," Evie said.

Relief washed over Mrs. Brompton's face. "You're probably right. I was so distressed to hear about her murder that I plum forgot, I'm sure. I packed up her things about three days after she went missing. I waited because I heard someone moving around in her room. I thought it was her, but when I knocked, nobody answered. I figured I was hearing things. It's an old house, and the lead pipes like to bang and shimmy sometimes."

Evie grabbed the suitcase and handed the valise to Maeve. "We'd best be going. Thank you again for all of your help. Did Flora owe you anything? I'll make sure my family settles her account."

Waving the offer away, Mrs. Brompton said, "No. She paid in full each week."

Evie and Maeve walked to the door, but before she opened it, Evie turned back to Mrs. Brompton. "I'm sorry, but I have one more question. When was the last time you saw Flora?"

Mrs. Brompton thought about it before answering. "It was Saturday morning on the day she disappeared. She came down and had coffee and toast before getting ready to go to the theater. Around one o'clock, an automobile arrived for her. She dashed out the door with a wave. It was the last time I saw her. Flora never came back."

Chapter Seventeen

They hurried away from the boarding house after bidding Mrs. Brompton a good day. Flora's case was heavier than Evie first expected, and she was grateful when Maeve offered to switch.

"Carrying my little brother has given me muscles," Maeve said. "What's the hurry? The trolley comes on the quarter hour. We've got over ten minutes before the next one arrives."

Evie glanced back over her shoulder. As they left, she could have sworn she spotted a woman of similar build and coloring as Annie walking down the sidewalk. Annie's red hair was hard to miss. It wasn't until they were safely around the corner that Evie slowed.

"I thought I saw someone from the theater. I didn't want to take a chance we'd been spotted," Evie explained. She slowed her pace only slightly. She couldn't relax until they were safely on the trolley heading back home.

"Did you find anything upstairs in Flora's room?" Maeve asked. Her long legs easily keeping pace with Evie.

"Not really. I found an earring under the bed. It might have been Flora's, but it's just an earring."

"I discovered that Mrs. Brompton keeps a closer eye on the tenants than one would think," Maeve said. "She knows the comings and goings of everyone. Guess who has been by the boarding house."

"Will?"

"Yes, but only the once. Marco," Maeve said, crowing his name. "And he didn't just come by to see Annie. He picked Flora up the day she disappeared."

Evie stopped. "Marco? Not Felix? Are you sure?"

Maeve stopped, too. They were at their trolley stop, so she set the bag down on the sidewalk. "Definitely Marco. Mrs. Brompton knows them both since the show always has acts stay at her boarding house. Will and Mary board at a small place down the street that rents to families. She confided in me that Marco had been coming by the boarding house to pick up Annie at least two previous times in the past year. I guess Richmond is a regular stop on the show's circuit."

"Interesting," Evie said. "Marco gave me the willies the first time I met him. It seems his eyes and hands wander more than I suspected the day we met. We already knew he was two-timing Betsy with Annie. It's interesting he picked up Flora and not her. Perhaps Betsy's concern about Flora and Marco wasn't entirely unfounded."

The trolley arrived, and Evie was happy to hop on and get away from the boarding house. When they arrived back at Aunt Dorcas's, Maeve and Evie hurried inside moments before the storm that had moved in while they were at Mrs. Brompton's finally released its promised downpour.

"Whew! That wind picked up since we left this morning. And I was thinking the sunshine was here to stay. I'm glad I don't have to leave for the theater for another two hours. Maybe this will all blow over," Evie said. She set the hat box down and hung her coat up on the tree by the door.

"I'm going to phone my mother to let her know I'm staying here for the time being. Besides, I want to see what's in that suitcase." Maeve picked up the phone that hung on the wall in the front hallway and asked the operator to connect her. After a brief exchange, Maeve joined Evie in the front parlor where she had laid the suitcase and valise on a table.

Aunt Dorcas thumped in. "I thought I heard you two. The wind is whipping outside, isn't it? Are those Flora's things?" Using her cane, she maneuvered herself onto a royal blue winged-back chair with thin black pinstripes and propped her foot on her zebra footstool. "Don't let me stop you. Open it."

"You're very royal with your commands," Maeve joked.

Evie opened the case. Inside were several dresses and undergarments, all jumbled together. A pair of black t-strap shoes similar to Evie's bone-colored ones were underneath the clothes.

Another pair of low-heeled shoes were next to them. There were also two pairs of stockings and a sterling silver brooch in the shape of a peacock. Underneath the stockings were letters tied together with string. Evie untied them and glanced at each envelope. They were all from Flora's parents, and there was one from Jack. She didn't feel right reading them, so she put them down on the table. She found no brushes or makeup packed in the bag, so Evie assumed they were still at the theater. It was a little odd since surely Flora would have wanted to do her hair in the morning before she went out for the day. Evie made a mental note to check with Mary on where Flora's personal items were at the theater. There was no pocketbook either.

"That's everything. Nothing hidden in any seams that screams 'my murderer is…'" Evie felt a wave of disappointment. She had hoped to find something of significance in Flora's belongings. "It is odd the suitcase is such a mess. Mrs. Brompton's house was tidy. I can't imagine she packed Flora's clothes like this. Perhaps someone did search the case."

"Hang on," Maeve said. She had opened the valise and had laid the items neatly in a row. "I've found a bracelet made of jade and silver in a jewelry case. It's quite an expensive piece and looks to be part of a set. It should have earrings and a necklace to match, but they aren't in the case."

Evie moved over to Maeve's side and picked up the necklace. "It matches the earring I found underneath the bed. Flora's clothing is well-kept and expensive. Her shoes are polished and don't have scuffs. She took care of her things, but she was careless with expensive jewelry. Strange."

"There's nothing else in the box beside this cloche. This would look beautiful on you, Evie. You and Flora must have similar coloring," Maeve remarked.

"She could have passed as my sister," Evie said.

"Well, the belongings are a bust," Aunt Dorcas said. "What time are you leaving for the theater?"

"I need to be there no later than three o'clock for the early show at five. On Saturdays, they do two performances."

"Maeve, call Harold and see if he would be good enough to escort an old woman to the theater. I'm tired of being cooped up in this house, and I want to see my favorite niece on the big stage. You can come, too."

Maeve chuckled. "Somebody needs to supervise you around my handsome fellow. I'm sure he'd be delighted to catch the show again."

"Then it's settled." Aunt Dorcas clapped her hands together, then she tried to stand but lost her balance and fell back into her seat.

"Goodness! Let me help you." Evie dashed over to her aunt and put her hands under Aunt Dorcas's elbow. Once she knew her aunt was balanced, Evie handed her the cane. "Let me cook us a light lunch. We can eat and go through everything we've learned."

"Uh… em…" Aunt Dorcas's cough did little to disguise her laugh.

"I can cook," Evie protested. She looked back and forth between her aunt and best friend as they finally stopped trying to disguise their chuckles.

"Thank goodness Mrs. Fortune stopped by and left plenty of food for us," Aunt Dorcas patted Evie on her shoulder. "Don't worry, love. I never learned to cook well either, but I do like to experiment with exotic flavors. A girl can either spend her life toiling over a hot stove or enjoy life and have adventures. My choice will always be adventure."

Twenty minutes later, Maeve and Evie had laid out the slices of ham and thick cheese that Mrs. Fortune had sent over with a fresh loaf of bread. Maeve placed homemade peanut butter cookies on a cabbage rose-patterned china plate. Evie poured three glasses of milk. It was a feast fit for three amateur investigators who needed food to fuel their sleuthing.

They related everything they had learned from Mrs. Brompton. When they finished sharing their facts, Aunt Dorcas didn't speak for a moment. She took a last bite of her sandwich and swallowed before putting a finger up. "First, someone searched Flora's suitcase. That much is obvious. Second, there was something going on between Flora and Marco Croucher. Was it an innocent work relationship or something else?"

"If I ask Jack, he would say it was an innocent relationship on Flora's part, but now, I'm not so sure. Flora was a fun time girl. We need to determine if it included having a relationship with a married man," Evie said.

"Third," Aunt Dorcas continued, putting another finger in the air. "Flora never made it back to the boarding house. Was she murdered in the theater or after she left?"

"My money is on inside the theater. Evie found blood and Flora's mink-collared coat in the Bijou," Maeve said, nibbling at a cookie. "Oh, these are so good. Do you think Mrs. Fortune would make me my own personal stash? If I brought a tin of these to the house, the little monsters would eat them all and not leave a crumb for me."

"Focus, Maeve," Evie said. "You're right. I think someone killed her in the theater. There was blood under the stage and the torn costume. Here's what I can't figure out. They found her nude in the river. How did the murderer get her out of her costume and carry her body from the theater? It's a couple of miles from the Bijou to the river."

Maeve snapped her fingers. "A car. They had to have access to a car. You couldn't hail a taxicab with a body."

"Will has a truck. He uses it to run errands for Marco and haul props," Evie said. "He also had a crush on Flora. Marco has an automobile, too, if he picked up Flora."

"You need to find out where Will was the night Flora disappeared," Aunt Dorcas said. "Speaking of which, you'd best get ready if you want to make it to the theater on time. I'm going to lie down for a bit before the show. Maeve, you're welcome to rest yourself or you can listen to the wireless radio."

Evie helped her aunt settle down on a tufted chaise and covered her with a blanket. Afterward, she and Maeve cleaned up the kitchen, rehashing the day's events. Maeve excused herself to call Harold at his office to ask him to take them to the theater. Evie went upstairs to have a wash and reset her hair before leaving for the Bijou.

Once she was ready, she peeked in on Aunt Dorcas, who snored softly next to the fire. Maeve sat in a chair opposite her and had fallen fast asleep herself. Evie opened the door, praying it wouldn't squeak. The rain had stopped, but the wind continued to shake the trees and windows. Evie pulled her coat tighter and held onto her cloche so it wouldn't tumble off her head with the first gust. She had just started walking down the street to the trolley stop when an automobile pulled up beside her. Evie ignored it and continued to dash so she would be at the stop on time. A loud honk made her jump. She turned and was surprised to see her father sitting behind the wheel of his Buick. He beckoned to her and jumped out of the driver's seat to hustle her into the passenger side.

"Thank you, Daddy. The wind is ferocious," Evie said, once settled under a car rug.

Her father grunted and pulled back into the street. Evie wanted to ask him why he was there, but she knew her father. He did everything in his own good time. At least he turned down the street that would take them to the theater district. She half-expected him to drive her back to their home and lock her in the attic until she "came to her senses."

"Harry came to see me," George said. "He told me you did an excellent job during the magic act. Your mother would have been pleased."

Evie didn't respond. Instead, she waited for her father to continue. After a minute, he said, "Since my retirement, the investigating teams have focused on busting up illegal liquor in cahoots with federal agents rather than stopping crimes such as a young woman's murder. The new chief thinks Flora Thompson ran afoul of a vagrant or someone traveling through the area. They've closed the case."

"But, Daddy—"

He held up his hand to stop her. "I don't agree with their decision. Although I'm vehemently opposed, I would rather know what you're doing rather than pull out my hair wondering if you are okay. If you're determined to be pigheaded—"

"I'm smart, and I'm capable, Daddy. I'm not the young girl you remember from before Mama died. I've grown up, and I'm capable of taking care of myself." If the car hadn't been moving, Evie would have been tempted to get out and walk the rest of the way to the theater.

"I know that, Evie," her father mumbled. "It doesn't mean that I don't want to turn back time. To go back to when we were a happy family. When your mother and Peter were..." He didn't finish because he bit back a sob.

Evie didn't know what to say. Her father had not cried once in the past four years. Not when the telegram arrived telling them of Peter's fate in France, and not the day her mother had passed away in her sleep after valiantly fighting the flu for two weeks. But now, four years later, her father pulled the car to the side of the road and buried his head in his hands. Evie sat frozen in shock. She sat in silence until he pulled a handkerchief out of his pocket and wiped his eyes.

He looked down at the handkerchief and gave Evie a sad smile. "I remember when your mother embroidered my initials on this. I thought it was too fancy for a policeman, but she insisted, saying it added a touch of class. I miss her, Evie. God, how I miss her."

"I miss her, too," Evie whispered. She touched her father's arm, and he clutched her hand.

"Promise me you'll be careful. You'll not take chances, and you'll check in with me every day."

"I will," Evie said. It was an easy promise to make.

"You find anything that points to one of those theater people," he spat the last part out, "you will bring it straight to me to handle."

Nodding, Evie said, "I promise, Daddy. I'm braver than you realize, but I'm not willing to take foolish chances with my life."

"I love you, Evelyn Jane," he said gruffly.

"I love you, too, Daddy."

Her father cleared his throat. "Ahem… well, I… how is the investigation going? What about these Croucher characters?"

"Marco Croucher gives me an uneasy feeling. He has a hot temper, and he mistreats his wife."

George pulled the car back onto the street and focused his attention on the windshield. "Back when I was on foot patrol, I would get a tingling on my neck if I ran into a thug on the street. Nine times out of ten, my feelings were right. It's how I rose through the ranks so quickly. I paid attention to my gut and my tingly neck."

"I don't know if he's the one who killed Flora, though. I need more time. One thing is for sure, there is something going on with the troupe."

They had arrived on theater row. Her father parked the car a block down from the Bijou. He let the motor idle while Evie relayed some things she found. She left out her late night escapade breaking into the theater. It wouldn't do to make her father fret needlessly now that she had done the deed.

"I'll be in the audience watching. If there is anything that makes you fear for your safety, tug on both earlobes and I'll charge the stage."

Evie laughed at the image of her father leaping across the orchestra to tackle someone. "I'll be fine. Aunt Dorcas, Maeve, and her beau will be here tonight, too. Harry is meeting me after the show so we can talk. Please don't worry about me."

At the mention of Harry Houdini's name, her father scowled. "It's his damn fault you're in the mix."

"Daddy, you can't blame him. No one forced me to go down to the theater and stick my nose in. I know you won't understand, but for the first time since Mama died, I feel like I have a purpose."

He sighed. "I understand. I don't agree, but I understand. I've been puttering around like an eighty-year-old man looking for a hobby myself since I retired. It was a mistake to leave the force. Now, I've got nothing but time on my hands to sit and think about Rose and Peter."

Evie glanced at her watch. "I have to go, or I'll be late." She leaned over and kissed her father on his cheek. "Thank you, Daddy."

Her father smiled. "For what?"

"For understanding why I have to do this. And Daddy, as far as everyone with the show is concerned, I'm an orphan living with my invalid aunt."

"I'm surprised Dorcas allowed you to call her an invalid. Damn fool woman with her hot air balloon."

"Bye, Daddy." Evie didn't wait for her father to continue. He could rail about Aunt Dorcas's shortcomings for an hour with barely a breath between each complaint. She hopped out of the car and walked up the street at a fast clip. She didn't want to risk Marco's wrath by being late today.

Chapter Eighteen

Evie arrived in the dressing area to chaos. She could hear the raised voices before she even walked through the alley door.

"I told you I needed it repaired before this evening," Annie yelled.

"And I told you I would get to it when I could. I've been working my fingers to the bone for weeks trying to make new costumes for Felix's act," Mary said, her voice loud and angry. "Last I checked, you don't pay me my weekly wages."

"I'll be talking to Marco about you. It's about time he replaced you with someone younger and with a better attitude," Annie said, her voice rising to a screech.

Evie watched Annie turn on her heel and stalk away down the hallway to Marco's office. She waited a minute before daring to enter the ladies dressing area. Mary muttered under her breath as she picked up the dress Annie had tossed next to the sewing machine.

"Is everything okay?" Evie asked. She pulled her costume from the rack.

"Yes. Some people are too big for their knickers. I don't take orders from that one." Mary slammed a bobbin of thread into the machine. She placed her foot on the treadle and sewed the hem of the dress.

Evie didn't stay to talk. She figured now was not the time to probe Mary for information about her son and Flora. She quickly changed into her costume. She pulled the curtain aside. "Oh!"

Marco stood in front of her. "Hello, chickadee." His insolent eyes looked her up and down.

Evie fought the urge to grab her coat and hold it in front of her. "I made sure I was on time today, Mr. Croucher."

Marco didn't say a word. Instead, he strolled slowly around her. Evie felt something akin to bugs crawling across her skin. When he reached out a fingertip to pluck a stray thread from the sleeve of her costume, she flinched away from his touch.

"Do I make you nervous, Evie? No need. I'm only inspecting my troupe to make sure everything is as it should be."

"Th—thank you, Mr. Croucher. Being the boss of a show must be a great deal of work." Evie fought to control the stammer in her voice.

He leaned against the wall and watched her. His gaze made her feel like a piece of raw meat tossed in front of a starving wolf. "I told you to call me Marco. We're all family here. No need to stand on formality. Traveling on the road like we do, everyone becomes close."

"Marco, then. Sorry, I forgot. Was there anything you needed? I should probably find Felix to let him know I'm here." Evie edged away from him.

Marco straightened and stroked a finger over his mustache. "Yes, go run and find my baby brother. He's always in need of a new sycophant."

Evie turned before he touched her again. As she left the dressing area, she spotted Annie standing by the costumes watching Marco and her. Evie felt jealousy emanating from Annie's glare clear across the room.

She didn't find Felix. Instead, Julia was center stage practicing tricks with her dog. Evie relaxed and watched Sammy's antics. It helped push the moment with Marco from her mind.

"She's good, isn't she?" Betsy said from behind her.

Evie turned. "She really is. How long has she been performing with the show?"

"Ever since Annie joined the act. She used to juggle while her mother sang and spun plates, but Marco got the idea to get her a dog. The two of them spent hours training the hairy beast. Marco has always had a soft spot for animals and children."

"You don't like dogs?" Evie asked.

Betsy shrugged. "I got bit by a mastiff when I was a kid. It took months for the wound to heal." She lifted the edge of her skirt to show Evie an ugly purple scar which ran from her thigh down to her knee. "They had to remove a large piece of my skin and restitch the wound when it became infected, so I prefer cats to dogs."

"Understandable," Evie said. She was a cat person herself. Peter had always wanted a dog, but her mother didn't think the city was a place for one. Rose believed dogs should be able to run free in a field chasing rabbits and squirrels, not cooped up in a small yard. Evie knew the feeling. "Is Felix here?"

"I saw him heading towards the men's area earlier. He'll be along soon, I'm sure. How's your head after last night?"

Evie grimaced. "Let's just say I'm not prepared for a repeat performance. There wasn't enough black coffee in the world to make me feel human this morning."

Julia finished her performance and whistled for Sammy. The two of them trotted off the stage and paused by Evie and Betsy.

"Golly, it's hot on the stage today. I sure hope the Gerry Society ladies don't show up tonight. Mama heard they might." Julia was a fast-chattering magpie.

"I've heard about them," Evie said. "I didn't realize they were so active here in Richmond."

Betsy scowled. "Some folks like to tell everyone else in the world how to live their lives rather than focusing on their own backyard."

"Not everyone treats their child workers as well as your husband," Evie said. Her mother had been keenly interested in child labor in factories. Although she had never been a member of the Society, her mother vehemently opposed children working in the cigarette factories. If what Betsy said was true, at least Marco was kind to some living creatures.

Betsy didn't respond. Julia looked back and forth between Evie and Betsy as though not sure whose side to choose. Sammy whined at Julia's feet, so she stooped down and scooped him into her arms. "I'd best take him outside for a walk around the block before it's time for the show. I'll see you both soon."

Evie watched Will remove Julia's props from the stage. Although his hands worked quickly to grab the dog's rings and mini chair, his bad leg hampered him. She heard the orchestra play a lively tune to cover the sound of his movements. She glanced down at her wristwatch. She still had some time before they would need to practice. She turned to Betsy. "Let's go grab a cup of coffee. My treat."

Betsy nodded. "Sounds good. I have no wish to watch Annie strut around onstage like an ostrich in a skirt."

At that moment, Annie appeared behind them and hissed, "Watch who you insult, Betsy, or one day you might find yourself out on your ear."

Betsy lifted her chin and pushed past Annie without responding. Annie looked down her nose at Evie and sauntered on the stage, shouting at Will to bring her props. Evie didn't wait around but raced after Betsy. She found her standing outside with a handkerchief in her hands to wipe away the hint of tears. Evie hesitated before putting a consoling hand on her shoulder. Betsy pulled away and waved her handkerchief at Evie.

"I'm fine. That awful woman doesn't realize that she is just the latest in a long line of Marco's women. Soon he'll cast her aside like the rest of them."

"Let's go get that cup of coffee. It'll give you a chance to get yourself together before we rehearse."

The two of them walked down the street to the coffee shop she had visited just days ago with Jack. This time of day, there were barely any customers, so Evie chose a table by the window so she could watch the people pass by. They gave the waiter their order, and soon the two women sat sipping their coffee without speaking. After the tension of the theater, Evie felt relief at the clatter of dishes and chatter from the other diners.

"Annie's a horrible person. Usually, I don't let her get me riled, but for the past few weeks, I've been so emotional. I don't know what's wrong with me," Betsy said. She set her cup down. "I know you think I'm a fool for tolerating Marco's indiscretions, but you strike me as someone who has never wondered where their next meal will come from or if they have enough pennies to buy a bed in a flophouse. I refuse to live that way again. Unfortunately, it comes at a price."

Evie didn't know what it was like. While her family wasn't wealthy, they had a pleasant home and neither she nor Peter had ever wanted for anything. She couldn't fathom trading her body and freedom for a bite to eat and a place to sleep. A marriage like Betsy and Marco's was just a more respectable form of prostitution, she realized. Her parents built their marriage on friendship and love. Evie knew if she couldn't have the same, then she wanted no part of purported domestic bliss.

"I guess I don't understand why Annie wouldn't realize what

Marco is like," Evie said. "How long has she been with the show?"

Betsy took a sip of her coffee before answering. "About three years. Strange as it may sound, she and I used to be friends. I would tell her things in confidence. Who knew she would use that information to wheedle her way into my marriage bed. I don't want to talk about it anymore. Tell me about you. No beau waiting in the wings?"

Shaking her head, Evie laughed. "No one even interested, I'm afraid. Since my mother… I mean, since my parents died, I've kept to myself. I'd go out with friends in a group, but to be honest, I haven't wanted to go anywhere or do anything. It wasn't until I heard there was an opening with the show that I got a wild hair and tried out."

Betsy arched a brow. "Thing is, no one knew we needed a new assistant. Annie filled in when Flora disappeared. Then suddenly you show up and ask for a job saying a friend told you about it. What gives?"

She considered playing dumb, but Evie knew that Betsy was too smart to be fooled. Instead, she said, "You'll think I'm a terrible person, but I eavesdropped on some men. I heard one of them say his sister disappeared from the show. He must have been talking about Flora. I saw an opportunity, and I seized it. Until I joined the show, I moped around my aunt's house all day and had no life. Aunt Dorcas is great, but I needed to get back to living. This seemed just the thing."

Betsy still looked suspicious. "We're just a lark for you?"

"At first, maybe. But now, I love it," Evie said, excitement in her voice. "The first time I looked out at the theater and imagined the audience watching and waiting for the next magic trick, I was hooked." She looked down at her hands and blushed. "You probably think that's silly, but it's true."

Instead of laughing at her, Betsy said, "You've been bit by the bug. Good. We need an assistant that will stick with the show. Felix goes through them like water through a sieve."

Evie considered Betsy's words. He was charming and affable, if a little intense. "Really? Why do they leave the show?"

Instead of answering, Betsy pulled out her purse and put a dollar on the table. When she spoke, Betsy failed to meet Evie's eyes. "I know you said you'd treat, but the coffee is on me. You got me out of there before I said something nasty to Annie that would have set off a row. We'd best get back before Marco realizes we're gone. He's definitely someone you don't want to make angry."

Chapter Nineteen

The orchestra played the opening notes for the magic act. Evie steeled herself for her entrance, knowing her father and Aunt Dorcas watched from a balcony seat. She listened to Felix engage the audience with his opening patter and sensed the audience's anticipation as he performed his opening trick with his top hat and its never-ending stream of scarves. When the audience's laughter died down, Felix introduced Evie. She took a deep breath and stepped onto the brightly lit stage. Smiling as she turned to face the audience, Evie knew she was made to perform. Her nerves calmed. The first tricks flowed without incident.

After they finished the sawed lady illusion, Will, dressed in a black suit, wheeled the box offstage. Next, Felix and Evie performed the Chinese linking rings act. After a flawless trick, it was finally time for the disappearing cabinet. Will rolled it onstage, and the last illusion began. Evie stepped into the box and as soon as Felix pulled the curtains, she lifted the trapdoor and slipped down the ladder into the cellar.

As the trapdoor closed behind her, Felix's chatter faded away and darkness engulfed her. She stifled a gasp of fear. Will had failed to light the lanterns before the evening's performance. Evie wondered if it was a simple oversight or a deliberate act on his part. Her hands gripped the ladder, but Evie calmed herself and relaxed her grip. She knew the path was clear from one side of the cellar to the other. As long as she kept her wits about her, she could make her way across and escape this makeshift dungeon.

"You can do this," she whispered. Easing herself down, her foot found the next rung. She slowly climbed down. Her feet touched the ground and she let go of the breath she hadn't realized she'd been holding. "Now, straight across and you'll be out of here quick as a stitch."

With her hands stretched in front of her like a child playing Pin the Tail on the Donkey, Evie made her way across the cellar on foot. Rather than a nimble prance across the floor, she shuffled her feet, fearful of tripping and falling. After what felt like an hour, Evie's fingers found the brick wall. Her feet searched the bricks until she found the steps. She scrabbled up and pushed the door open. It relieved Evie to see the backstage lights and hear the click clack of the sewing machine. She walked to where Mary sat and flopped into a nearby chair.

"I could use a sip of your rheumatism medicine if you have any left," Evie said with a half-laugh, half sob.

Mary's foot stopped treadling as she glanced at Evie. "Lord, child. What's wrong?" She reached down into her sewing basket and pulled out a flask. Unscrewing the cap first, she handed it to Evie.

"Will forgot to light the lamps below the stage. It was pitch black down there." Evie took a sip of the whiskey and winced at the sharp taste.

Mary shook her head. "Not my Will. I watched him go down there before the show started. They were lit. I could see the glow when he came back up."

Evie was silent as she considered Mary's words. She was the only act who went below stage. Had someone blown out the lamps to frighten her, or did they have a much more sinister plan in mind? She shuddered.

"Were you here all evening during the performance?" Evie asked. Mary's work area had a partial view of the trapdoor.

"Yes," Mary said. "Well, no. I went outside to stretch my legs. I get stiff if I sit for too long. Maybe they were low on oil and went out by themselves."

Evie considered the idea, but immediately dismissed it. One lamp, even two, but all five lamps? The odds were against it. "I think someone blew them out intentionally."

Mary put her hands up. "It wasn't me. These hips wouldn't fit in that tight space. It's why I can't be a magician's assistant. I ain't as slim and lithe as the likes of you and Betsy." She laughed at her own self-deprecation.

"Did you notice anyone near the trapdoor?"

Mary didn't respond right away. "Not really, but like I said, I stepped outside for a bit. Plus, when I'm sewing, I don't always hear what's going on around me. Old Suzy here is a little loud." Mary patted her sewing machine.

"How long were you gone?" Evie asked.

Mary shrugged. "Maybe twenty minutes. I wasn't really paying attention. Listen. You're making a big deal out of a small thing. Many things could cause those lamps to blow out. Who knows? It may have been Felix's spirits," she said with a sly grin. But at Evie's look of dismay, she shook her head. "Sorry, love. I was only teasing. I wouldn't worry about the lamps. Strange things happen in every theater. Don't let it bother you."

Evie took another sip from Mary's flask before handing it back to her. "Thank you. You're probably right. It was just a breeze."

Mary tipped the flask and poured a healthy dose of the illegal whiskey into a chipped teacup. "Just a breeze," she said, parroting Evie.

Evie bid Mary a good evening and hurried to go to the curtain call. After her final curtsy, she went to change. Her hands shook as she unbuttoned the bodice of her costume. She hastily changed and ran her fingers through her bob. She had promised to meet Harry after the show. After such a fright, she just wanted to get out of the theater and away from people she didn't know if she could trust.

Ten minutes later, she slipped out the back entrance. Harry leaned against the opposite building with his disguise from yesterday back in place. Relief washed over Evie. If she had had to wait in the alleyway until the show was done and others left the theater, they would have invited her along for a post-performance drink. Now, she didn't have to reenter that den of wolves until the next performance.

"Good evening, Evie," Harry said, giving her his arm. She slipped her arm through his, and the two of them hurried out to the street where a car awaited.

"Gosh, am I ever happy to see your face. Well, er… some of your face," Evie said.

Harry peeled away the false mustache and removed the glasses that helped to conceal his identity. "You seem uneasy. What happened?"

Evie related her tale of the lights being extinguished below stage. When she was done, she shivered and clutched the collar of her coat closely. "It was intentional. Whether Will did it or someone else, I don't know. I could have been seriously hurt if I fell. There are wooden crates stacked in that space. I'm surprised Jake Wells allows the area for storage. It's awfully tight down there as it is."

Harry patted Evie's hand. "I'm glad you weren't hurt. Your father would have never forgiven me if anything had happened to you."

"Daddy! I forgot!" Evie exclaimed. "He came to the show tonight. I wonder what he thought."

"You'll find out shortly. He's meeting us for a late supper along with Dorcas and your friend Maeve."

Evie hoped her father approved of her performance. Not that she needed his approval, but it would be nice if he thought she had done well. She didn't share these thoughts with Harry, although she was dying to know what he thought, too.

"I've worked with Jake Wells in the past. He's fanatical about safety and runs a tight ship with all the shows on his circuit. I think it might behoove you to see if you can get a look into those crates," Harry said. "It may have nothing to do with Flora's death, but we should look into it."

"The theater is closed tomorrow." She hesitated, then said, "I could try to break in like I did on Thursday."

Harry sat back and looked at her closely. "You broke into the Bijou? You may have your mother's beauty, but there's a great deal of Dorcas in you. Full of spunk and not afraid of anything. Dare I ask how you got inside?"

Evie explained about gumming up the lock and he laughed. "I think it's time I give you a real lesson in lock picking, however, it will have to wait. We've arrived at the restaurant."

After Harry paid the taxi fare, he escorted Evie into a small restaurant whose only signage was a discreet black sign painted with the word *Tally's*. Evie had never been here, but she knew it catered to the wealthier residents of Richmond. The maitre d' must have recognized Houdini because if he could have genuflected without seeming ludicrous, Evie supposed he would have. He escorted them to a large round table covered with a white damask tablecloth and black napkins folded into elaborate fans.

"The rest of my party should be here shortly. In the meantime, if you could bring out a bottle of Chandon to celebrate Evie's outstanding performance this evening," Harry said. "Don't bother telling me it's not available because John Sullivan is not one to dump his best champagne due to some outrageous law."

After the maitre d' left, Harry turned to Evie, his eyes twinkling. "So how did you like the speakeasy last night?"

Evie's eyes widened. "How did you know?"

"My dear, don't believe for a moment that I didn't trail you. I made sure you arrived at your destination safely. You've been hanging out with too many scoundrels and deadbeats if you thought I wouldn't. A gentleman's word is his bond. I promised your father you would be safe."

A large hand clamped down on Evie's shoulder. "And it's a good thing, too, or else you would find yourself in the pokey without a way to escape. Hello, Evie." Her father leaned down and pecked her on the cheek.

"It was the most spectacular performance I've ever seen," Aunt Dorcas said, tapping her brother on his leg and nodding her chin towards the chair next to Evie.

"Erm… quite so. It was thoroughly entertaining," her father said as he pulled out a chair for his sister.

She handed George her cane, then turned towards Harry. "Harry, dear. You're looking well. How's Bess?"

"Bess is well. She's taking a much-deserved break from keeping me in check. I spoke to her this morning on the telephone. What an amazing age we live in. I can talk to my lovely wife whose clean across the country in Hollywood."

"I thought Maeve and Harold were coming?" Evie said, looking at the restaurant entrance.

"Maeve begged off. It seems her mother is suffering from another migraine, so she stayed home to care for the brood," George said. "Now enough chit chat. I want to know what you've discovered."

The appearance of a waiter with the chilled bottle of champagne and glasses saved Evie from an immediate answer. Harry waited until everyone's glass was full before he raised it. "A toast. To the intrepid and talented Evelyn Harris."

"To Evelyn," Dorcas said, raising her glass. Evie felt giddy with pleasure.

It was short-lived. Her father took a sip from his glass, then turned toward his daughter. "Tell us everything you've learned."

Evie swallowed and laid out the case. Aunt Dorcas knew most of it, but even she let out a gasp when she learned of Evie's time below stage earlier. When she finished her tale, she said, "I still don't know who killed Flora. It could have been any of them. I have to solve this case, or the murderer will get away. The show leaves for Norfolk in a week."

Chapter Twenty

Dinner had gone well the previous evening. Aunt Dorcas and Harry regaled the group with stories of their various exploits around the world. It was after midnight when they left the restaurant. Her father put aside his anger over Harry failing to stop her investigation, and by the end of the night, the two men had shared brandy and a laugh over a mutual acquaintance. Harry escorted Evie and Aunt Dorcas home, and despite the late hour insisted on showing Evie how to pick a lock. She now counted his lock picking kit he'd given her earlier as not only a prized possession, but a useful tool she could use.

The next morning, Evie and Aunt Dorcas arose before dawn. Although she rarely used it, Aunt Dorcas possessed a 1920 Nash Touring. She kept it in a small carriage house and only drove it during the summer months. Fortunately, the late winter cold weather was leaving, and the roads were dry for Evie's first driving lesson.

"First thing you need to learn to do is to make it go," Aunt Dorcas instructed Evie as soon as the two of them were seated.

Evie didn't doubt Aunt Dorcas's driving ability, but there was something she thought was even more important to learn first. "I think I need to learn how to stop before I need to know how to go," Evie said.

Aunt Dorcas suppressed a smile. "I suppose you're right."

After a few fits and starts and a stall that blocked the road for several minutes, Evie finally got the hang of learning how to ease the Nash out of the drive and into the road. Fortunately, there weren't many cars, although she had a near miss with a hay cart pulled by a mule once they reached the outskirts of the city.

"There's so much power beneath my hands," Evie said. She wished it was warmer so she could open the windows and feel the breeze on her hair. She wondered why she had waited so long to get behind the wheel of a motor car. She turned and grinned at her aunt.

"Slow down, Evie!" Aunt Dorcas exclaimed.

Evie returned her attention to the road just in time, for ahead was a long curve with a large truck lumbering toward them. She hadn't had to navigate past any other vehicle as yet since it was so early on a Sunday morning. She gripped the wheel and held her breath. If she thought it would have helped rather than hurt, she would have shut her eyes.

The other car passed dangerously close to the side of their vehicle as Evie turned the wheel to maneuver the curve. Evie felt the wheels shudder at they left the road and yanked the steering wheel to the left. The Nash swerved towards the opposite bank. Aunt Dorcas yelped in alarm.

Evie held tight and kept the Nash on the road without hitting the other vehicle or the small squirrel who had foolishly ventured out at the first sign of warmer weather. Once she expelled the breath she'd been holding, Evie decided that slower might be better. She eased off the throttle and kept her attention on the road ahead.

"Excellent job, Evie. Now if I survive this trip to Norfolk today, I expect you to continue with your driving lessons. There is no better way to independence than to leave and go where you want, when you want. I refuse to wait for a train, a trolley, or a man to go anywhere. I would like my niece to have the same attitude," Aunt Dorcas said.

"I do," Evie said. "I think I do. May I ask you an impertinent question?"

"Is there a better kind to ask?" Aunt Dorcas replied. "Fire away, girl. My life is an open book."

"Why didn't you get married and have a family?"

Aunt Dorcas was quiet for so long that Evie at first thought she hadn't heard her. She risked a momentary glance away from the road. Aunt Dorcas appeared lost in thought.

"Not that I didn't have opportunities," Aunt Dorcas began. "I had many a beau in my youth. I have many a beau now, but I gave my heart away a long time ago."

Evie knew her aunt was considered a beautiful woman, so it didn't surprise Evie to hear men clamored for her attention. What surprised her is that her aunt had only loved one man. "Who was he?"

Aunt Dorcas sighed. "His name was Bohai, and I met him when I was not much younger than you are now. He was a sailor on a ship that had docked in Norfolk. I was visiting your Great Aunt Sara."

"Bohai? That's an unusual name."

"He was an unusual man. He was from the Orient, and the most beautiful man I ever laid eyes upon." Her voice choked with emotion. "I'm sorry. I haven't thought of him in many years. It was a part of my life I boxed away in my mind."

"I'm surprised they allowed you to see him," Evie said.

"I wasn't. When Uncle Emmett discovered I was seeing a man and a foreigner to boot, he locked me in my bedroom. It was scandalous at the time for a girl to step out with a man without her family's permission, let alone someone who wasn't white."

"Did Daddy know?" Evie glanced at Aunt Dorcas from the corner of her eye. It was straight as far as she could see, but she dared not let her attention stray from the road.

"No, I don't think he did. He and your mother had just met, and the two of them only had eyes for each other. Besides, George and Rose were in Richmond that summer. Anyway, I knew Bohai's ship was scheduled to leave the next day, and I was determined to go with him. I dressed in a pair of my cousin John's trousers and shirt, then I shimmied down the big oak tree next to the house. I knew no one would question a man walking around the docks at that late hour. I made it to the shipyard and paid a boy to get a message to Bohai."

"Did he meet you?" Evie asked. The thought of her aunt's late-night assignation in disguise was both thrilling and romantic.

Her aunt gave a small bitter laugh. "No, he didn't. Uncle Emmett and his pack of men had taken care of what they considered a problem. I discovered they lynched Bohai. They left his body by his ship as a message to any other Chinese sailor who made the mistake of loving a white woman."

Evie slammed on the brake of the car, and the car shuddered to a stop. She turned to her Aunt Dorcas. "What? Why? I can't believe someone in our family would do such a horrible thing."

Aunt Dorcas pulled a handkerchief from her purse and dabbed at her eyes. She gave Evie a look. "I left that day with the few coins I had saved and got a job dressed as a man on a ship heading to Brazil. You might think I'm a horrible person, but when I learned of Emmett's death some years later, I was happy. I returned to America not long afterward."

"I'm so sorry that happened to you," Evie said. "I can't imagine anything more cruel. I'm glad I never met Uncle Emmett. I would have given him a piece of my mind."

Aunt Dorcas snorted. "Emmett Davis was the worst kind of bully. He was cruel to Aunt Sara and treated his hound dog better than his wife. That summer changed my entire outlook on men and marriage. I washed my hands of ever answering to a man that day."

"I suppose I don't have an excuse for not wanting to marry," Evie said. "I just want adventure and staying home to cook and clean for a man holds no appeal for me."

"You may change your mind if you meet the right person," Aunt Dorcas said. "There's nothing wrong with loving a man, Evie. My words of wisdom to you are to make sure it's a good man."

"Maybe."

Evie restarted the car and with a lurch continued down the road. They had two more hours until they reached their destination, so she didn't have time to sit beside the road processing the shock of Aunt Dorcas's former life. The two women were silent after that. Evie mulled over the clues to Flora's death and Aunt Dorcas's revelation. Aunt Dorcas seemed lost in her own memories as she gazed out the window at the passing fields. An hour later they saw more traffic as they got closer to Norfolk. Evie could have sworn she could smell the salt in the air from the bay. She rolled the window down an inch to allow the fresh air into the car.

"It's a mile or so more," Aunt Dorcas said. "Once we pass an old store that I hope is still standing, we turn down a side road that follows the Elizabeth River. My contact should be waiting for us."

Twenty minutes later, Aunt Dorcas instructed Evie to pull up to an old shack. Several fishing boats were dry docked next to it. They waited in the car until a grizzled old man with a cap pulled down low over his brow motioned for them to come in. Evie glanced around and saw there was no one else nearby. She hoped Aunt Dorcas knew what she was doing because Evie felt distinctly nervous. "How do you know this fella?"

"He was a sailor on that boat I took to Brazil all those years ago. He's good people."

The two women got out of the car and stretched their limbs for a moment. Evie's fingers were stiff from gripping the steering wheel so tightly. Despite the stress of driving, she had enjoyed the feel of the road beneath the wheels and the sense of freedom as fields zipped past them.

"Best not dilly dally. Teddy doesn't suffer fools or lolly gaggers lightly," Aunt Dorcas said before heading to the shack. She used her cane to brush a fish head out of her path.

Evie cringed at the remains of fish entrails littering the ground but followed behind her aunt without hesitation. If Aunt Dorcas trusted this Teddy character, then she knew she shouldn't worry. Despite her bravado, when Evie stepped into the gloomy shack with its windows covered by yellow newspapers, she had a momentary urge to dash back to the car.

"Hurry and shut the door before you let the flies in. A warm day like this, the buggers buzz at the first sign of spring," Teddy grumbled. He turned to Aunt Dorcas and grabbed her into a big bear hug. "Where've you been, you old nag? It's been too long."

Aunt Dorcas laughed and smacked him lightly on his arm. "Who are you calling old, you old buzzard? How long's it been? Ten years, I think."

"Bout that," Teddy said, a wide grin splitting his face to reveal a gold tooth. "This must be the niece. Teddy O'Sullivan, at your service."

"Evie Harris," Evie said. "It's a pleasure to meet you, Mr. O'Sullivan."

"Call me, Teddy. Everyone does. Now what can I do you for?" Teddy turned back to Aunt Dorcas. He grabbed a wooden chair that was relatively clean from the corner and set it next to her.

She settled into the seat with a grateful sigh. "This ankle is going to be the death of me. Are you still in the business?"

Teddy turned sharp eyes on her and narrowed them. "You thinking about getting in?"

Aunt Dorcas waved her hand at him. "Pshaw. I'm too old to get back into the game. Evie, show Teddy the code you found."

Evie reached into her pocketbook and pulled out the code she had copied from the book in Marco's office. She handed it to him. Teddy took it and without a word, pulled two more chairs of dubious cleanliness from the corner and indicated Evie should sit. He sat in the other and pulled out a cigarette case. After offering one to them both, which they declined, he lit his and pondered the piece of paper.

"What you have here is a list of drop-off points for illegal liquor. If I'm wrong, I'll eat my hat," Teddy said. "Look here."

Teddy leaned over to Evie, who had to hold her breath at the whiff of old fish emanating off of his clothes. He pointed to the YOU with 20g TW next to a date. "That 20g is 20 gallons and I would venture to say the BW is Black and White. That's a Scottish whisky. You've stumbled upon a bootlegger's diary."

Aunt Dorcas gave a satisfied snort. "As I suspected. I knew there was something suspicious going on in that theater."

"Where did you find this?" Teddy asked Evie.

She hesitated. She looked at Aunt Dorcas, who nodded before she answered him. "It was in a book kept by a man named Marco Croucher."

Teddy let out a roar of laughter and slapped his knee. "I knew it. I knew Marco was back and working the circuit. He's cut me out of the loop."

Evie leaned back in surprise. "You know Marco?"

"Damn right I do. Pardon the language, but Marco Croucher is well known around here," Teddy said.

"How?" Evie asked. "Marco isn't a fisherman. He runs the vaudeville show where I'm working as an assistant."

"Well, he's always had that as his cover." Teddy dropped his cigarette on the dirt floor and ground it out with his boot heel. "Let me tell you something about Marco Croucher. He's been using his brother's show to smuggle things into this country for years. I guess liquor is just his latest venture."

"Smuggling? I thought people made cheap gin in their bathtubs or moonshine in the woods," Evie said. "What else has Marco smuggled?"

Teddy shook his head. "You are too young and innocent to be mixed up with the likes of Marco Croucher. He's run guns for the Mexicans years ago. Silk, jewelry, people… you name it, and Marco has smuggled it. Now it appears he has his finger in the rum running business."

"People want real liquor, not the rotgut you young folks drink," Aunt Dorcas said. "From what I hear, the Brits run their smuggling operation using these bigger rivers along the coast. Folks offload under cover of night. They hide the liquor beneath real merchandise. Someone hauls it inland, and it changes hands from there. There's an entire network of criminal gangs who operate up and down the coast and into the Midwest."

The depth of her aunt's knowledge about smuggling and illegal liquor astounded Evie. After a moment, though, she realized her aunt had a separate life with people outside of Evie's ken. It guaranteed a ride home filled with plenty of questions.

Teddy snapped his fingers and pointed at Aunt Dorcas. "You are one smart cookie, Dorcas Harris. Me and the boys have been hopping down here, but in the past six months, some of our regular customers have been canceling orders. They said they had a new supplier. I'd venture to say it's Marco." He spat on the floor.

Grabbing her cane, Aunt Dorcas hoisted herself up. She hobbled over next to Evie. "I think this sheds a different light on our murder."

"Murder? Marco murdered someone?" Teddy looked at Aunt Dorcas in surprise. "He's oily, but I can't see him killing anyone. Marco cares about one thing and that's money."

"They found a girl who worked in the show murdered," Evie explained. "I'm wondering if her death had something to do with Marco's smuggling operation."

"Marco usually kept the women in his life under tight wraps and away from this side of the business. Unless this gal threatened to turn him into the revenuers, I can't see him killing anyone over a bit of whisky."

"Men have killed for less," Aunt Dorcas said with a grimace.

"True, but Marco is a small fish. Unless he's gotten involved with some families out of New York or Chicago, I doubt he has it in him," Teddy shook his head. He stood and walked toward the door. "You two ladies be careful heading home. And Evie, I wouldn't nose around Marco Croucher's business too much. He may not have it in him to kill anyone, but I know he's a mean cuss when it comes to laying hands on a woman."

Evie thought of Betsy's bruised face and knew Teddy was right. "I'll be careful. Thank you for your time, Mr. O'Sullivan. I mean, Teddy."

Teddy held the door open for them. "Anytime. Dorcas, don't be such a stranger. Gladys would love to see you. Next time you're down this way, you need to come for dinner at the house. We'll open up some of that sweet sherry you like so much, even if it tastes like syrup."

He clasped Aunt Dorcas's hands in his own before pulling her into a hug. "You stay safe, you old nag."

"You, too, you old buzzard."

Aunt Dorcas was teary-eyed as she turned away from the fishing shack. She allowed Evie to help her get her injured leg into the Nash. Evie tucked the travel rug around her aunt and took her place behind the wheel. She had learned a great deal during this driving lesson down to Norfolk.

Now, she knew what she had to do.

Chapter Twenty-one

Before Evie could get a word out, Aunt Dorcas said, "Head down this road for five miles. There's someplace I'd like to go. I can answer all those questions I imagine are brewing in your brain better on a full stomach than an empty one."

She started the Nash. This time, she eased out onto the road without quite as many starts and stops as before. Following her aunt's directions, she soon navigated the car in front of a restaurant—Aunt Sally's — which nestled on a small spit of land that jutted out into the water.

Fifteen minutes later, a hostess seated them at a small table with two glasses of sweet tea in front of them. A waitress had already taken their order for fried oysters. The restaurant was full of people dressed in their Sunday finest. The clatter of silverware and glasses filled the surrounding space. Evie spent a minute or two watching the people as they came and went at nearby tables. She mulled over everything she had learned and wanted to think before speaking for once.

"You're awfully quiet, Evie, and I can hear your mind working," Aunt Dorcas said. "You know you can ask me anything. Like I said before, my life is an open book, or it will be once I finally sit down to write my memoir. With your help, of course."

Evie took a sip of her tea. "Tell me more about Teddy O'Sullivan. He's a bootlegger and fisherman. I guess I'm surprised you know so much about the illegal liquor business. I'm waiting for you to tell me you know how to make moonshine."

"As a matter of fact—" Aunt Dorcas began, but she stopped when she saw Evie's expression of interest. "I'm joking. I've had adventures in my life, that's for certain. Not every country is as easy to get into and out of as America. Teddy and his crew were useful to me down in South America. Don't let his looks fool you. He has more money than King Midas."

At Evie's incredulous look, Aunt Dorcas continued. "He made a fortune smuggling Orientals across the border through El Paso so they could work on the railroads. A lot of men made their money in the 1890s that way. I don't agree with some of his choices, but he's honest, and he never mistreated any of his cargo, unlike a lot of his ilk. I've been known to bring extra jewels or a bar of gold or two with me when I return to the country, but it was more a bit of fun rather than a means to an end."

"I'm shocked, Aunt Dorcas. A nice, upstanding denizen of society stooping to such levels." Evie tried to keep a straight face but failed. She had to smile at the thought of her aunt stitching jewels into her undergarments.

"You jest, but trust me when I say, people smuggling is a horrible business. I'm glad Teddy appears to be sticking to liquor. He owns an enormous house in Yorktown. He keeps that shack and boatyard to escape from his wife and her expectations. Gladys spends most of her time proving that she's worthy of hobnobbing with old money."

Evie didn't know what to say in response to that. She couldn't reconcile grizzled and weather-beaten Teddy as a wealthy man with a huge mansion and a wife. She realized her life was much narrower than even she had realized. Would she have had enough gumption to jump on a ship to South America in defiance of her family? At one time, Evie would have said yes, but now she hesitated. She longed for adventure, but she and her father were all they had left. Could she leave home and start a new life on her own?

"A penny for your thoughts," Aunt Dorcas said, interrupting Evie's reverie.

She shook her head and gave her aunt a sad smile. "I don't think I'm as much of an adventuress as I thought I was. I could never leave Daddy on his own and jaunt to another country without a backward glance."

Aunt Dorcas stopped stirring the sugar into her tea and gave Evie a sharp look. "What makes you think I didn't look back? I missed my family terribly. Every single day. But I knew that if I went back, I would bend to their will and find myself married with a kid strapped to each hip before I knew what had happened. It would have broken me. It doesn't mean that you can't carve out your own path, Evie. You can have a life outside of marriage and family without hopping on a tramp steamer to foreign lands."

The arrival of their lunch saved her from answering. They made quick work of eating the pile of fried oysters with a side of collards. The two women sat silently save for the occasional sound of a fork hitting a plate or a clink of ice in the tea glass. Fifteen minutes later, Aunt Dorcas sat back with a satisfied groan.

"This place has always served the best clams and oysters on the east coast."

Evie placed her napkin beside her plate. "I don't think I could eat another bite. I was hoping for a slice of apple pie, but if I want to fit into my costume tomorrow, I'd best pass."

"I've been thinking about what Teddy said. If Marco Croucher is running liquor using the show as cover, he could stand to lose a great deal of money if someone grassed on him. Perhaps Flora discovered what he was doing and threatened to go to the authorities," Aunt Dorcas said.

Evie shook her head. "I don't know. From what I've learned, Flora liked to have a good time. I saw her myself at The Black Cat. She wasn't shy about the booze. I can't see someone like that having righteous indignation over a little rum running."

Aunt Dorcas inclined her head. "This is all supposition. I think you need to get a look into those crates. Perhaps Marco Croucher hauls more than hooch and some magic tricks on the circuit." She motioned the waitress over with a ten-dollar bill. "Let's get back to Richmond. You and I have a building to break into tonight."

Evie looked at her aunt's cane, which rested on the floor. "I don't know if you're the best cohort in crime for tonight."

"Every burglar needs a good lookout. Who better than a feeble woman with a cane to delay any potential onlooker?"

Evie admitted her aunt had a good point and dropped her objection. She would need to practice her newly gained lock picking skills once they were home. A thirty-minute lesson was great, but she was no expert. It wouldn't do for a foot patrolman to catch her in the alley next to the theater door.

The return trip to Richmond wasn't as fraught with tension as the drive to Norfolk had been. Evie felt much more comfortable behind the wheel and wondered why she hadn't asked her father to teach her to drive before. It was one of the only things he didn't object to a woman doing. Her own mother had learned to drive, although she had only ventured out with their car on rare occasions. Her mother had hated the rattles and bangs of the metal monster as she had called it. She preferred to walk or catch the trolley.

The sun had set, and stars appeared in the night sky by the time Evie pulled the Nash into the driveway in front of Aunt Dorcas's home. She wasn't confident enough to park inside of the old carriage house, and as Aunt Dorcas pointed out, they would need it if they had to make a quick getaway from the theater that evening.

Once home, Evie and Aunt Dorcas made a light supper of cheese on toast with cups of coffee. Evie felt the late evenings weighing her eyelids down as she contemplated another midnight excursion downtown. Rather than rest, she spent an hour jiggling a ball pick in one of her aunt's old, locked doors. After a few failed attempts, she performed the correct twist of her wrist and heard the desired *click*.

"I did it!" she exclaimed, startling her aunt from her chaise where she had been dozing.

Aunt Dorcas rubbed her eyes and glanced around the room, rapidly blinking her eyes, trying to wake up. "Did what? Oh. Good show! I knew you could do it. Now, I think a bit of my elixir to give us some courage is in order before we change clothes and head to the theater."

Evie tucked the lock pick set into the pocket of her skirt before pouring her aunt a healthy dose of her wine. She allowed herself enough of a splash to wet the bottom of the glass. She dared not risk drinking anymore since she needed to keep her wits about her later.

At eleven o'clock, Aunt Dorcas declared it was time to get ready. "Go into the trunk in the second bedroom down the hall from mine. You'll find just the right outfit for tonight's adventure."

In the bedroom, Evie opened a large wooden trunk with frayed leather straps. Inside, under a layer of scratchy wool blankets of an indeterminate gray, she found several pairs of men's pants and dark gray shirts made of broadcloth. A houndstooth Scully cap was tucked into the left corner, and Evie placed it on her head. She held the pants up to her slim frame and chose the pair most likely to fit her. Fortunately, there was a pair of leather suspenders attached.

Fifteen minutes later, Evie descended the stairs from her room where she had quickly transformed from budding flapper to a fresh-faced teenage boy. She had used some hair oil to slick her bob back and tucked it under the hat.

Aunt Dorcas clapped her hands in delight. "You could pass for a boy even with a second glance as long as you keep your head down. Now, go start the Nash and let's go break into the Bijou."

At five minutes after midnight, Aunt Dorcas linked her arm into Evie's and whispered, "Walk casually and slowly down the street. You're just a sweet, young man escorting his mother home from a late evening of playing bridge at her sister's house."

Evie pulled the brim of her cap down low and whistled an aimless tune. The cheese toast she had eaten earlier lay like a lump of lead in her stomach. The streets were dark and other than one old Model T, no cars or pedestrians were out. It was a typical Sunday night in Richmond's theater district.

When they arrived at the alley to the right of the Bijou, Evie peeled away from Aunt Dorcas's side and slipped into the dark. She had a small flashlight tucked into the generous pockets of the man's coat she wore but didn't want to use it in case it alerted anyone to her mission. She crouched on the ground in front of the door and offered a small prayer that she could do this by feel rather than sight. Using the same pick she had practiced with earlier, Evie slid it into the keyhole, but she immediately felt its forward movement stop. She pulled it out and using her fingers, found the rake pick and inserted it. She gave a sigh of relief as it slid easily into the hole. Holding her breath, she jiggled, turned, and listened like Harry had instructed. She had to suppress a whoop of delight when the pick found success. She grabbed the handle and turned. The door swung inward, and she slipped inside.

Once the door was closed, Evie felt safe to switch on her flashlight. The dull yellow circle of light did little to banish her fear, but she pushed it down and proceeded to the stage. Although she had been here with Maeve and Harold, that night had been filled with a sense of adventure. Those feelings were absent as Evie confronted the empty stage and the idea that she would climb down through the trapdoor into the coffin-cold space underneath the stage. Shivering, she closed her eyes and tried to calm her nerves.

"Quick as a flash down the steps, take a peek, then out," she said to herself. Walking purposefully across the stage, she stopped and leaned down to hook her finger into the small hole. Pulling up the trapdoor, she held the flashlight under her chin while she attempted to maneuver down the ladder rungs without dropping it.

A moment later, her feet touched the floor and she let go of the ladder, grateful to have not lost her flashlight. Evie trotted over to the wooden crates. The first one's lid was hammered tightly down and no amount of pushing or pulling on her part would budge it. She shone the light around, avoiding the dark brown stains in the corner. She spied one box with its lid slightly askew and hurried to it. Holding the light in her left hand, she lifted the lid with her right. Inside, nestled in sawdust, were dozens of bottles. She reached down and picked one up to read the label. In the dark, under the weak glow of the flashlight, she could make out *Kilvannon Old Irish Whiskey*.

Evie tucked the bottle into her trouser pocket, causing the waistband to slip down on her narrow hips. She moved it to her coat pocket. She considered leaving it behind in case someone noticed it missing, but immediately dismissed the thought. This was proof that there was illegal bootlegging going on at the theater. It could be the reason they murdered Flora. She didn't know for sure, but she knew it was important to have proof of her discovery. She didn't know how long these crates would remain here, so she couldn't take a chance. Moving the lid back into place, Evie hurried across to the other side of the cellar. She tucked the flashlight into her other pocket and used her hands to find her way up to the backstage area.

Evie eased the trapdoor closed. As she turned to retrace her path to the back exit, a bright light shined on her face and blinded her. She threw her hand up to shield her eyes. Frozen with fear, she stood stock still, praying that it was Betsy and not Marco who had discovered her.

"Evie?" The beam from the flashlight dropped to the floor. Evie lowered her hand and saw Will staring at her, mouth agape. "What in the blazes are you doing here? Why are you dressed as a man?"

"I—uh—I wanted to practice my routine?" Evie made it a question rather than a statement, giving her lie away.

Will walked to her and peered at her face, then scowled. "I might be less than a man with this bum leg of mine, but I'm not stupid, Evie. If

Marco had found you in here... well, I don't like to think about what he would have done to you."

Evie's eyes widened. Was Will admitting that Marco was dangerous? She scrambled to think of a valid reason for her to be inside of the theater in the dark of night. She opened her mouth but quickly shut it. She decided the best course was to go on the offensive. "Why are you here in the middle of the night?"

Will grabbed her by the arm and turned her toward the backstage area. Evie yanked her arm from his grasp and considered running. She could only pray that Aunt Dorcas had spotted Will and had gone for help.

"I run errands for Marco sometimes," Will said. "You need to leave here before he shows up."

Evie stopped. "What errand? Are you in trouble?"

He stopped trying to lead her from the theater. "I'm not in trouble. Marco likes to run a bit of liquor now and then. A little extra dough helps me take care of Ma. She's not well."

Evie saw her opportunity and pounced on it. "Did Flora find out about the bootlegging and try to stop it? Is that why she was killed?"

"Flora? Why would you say that? Flora didn't try to stop it. She asked Marco if she could get in on the act. He strung her along, but he had no intention of including her."

Will's revelation stunned Evie. Her theory was that Flora had stumbled on a rum running operation and had been killed because of a simple mistake. Now, she didn't know what to think. "Who would want to hurt Flora then?"

As she said the words aloud, she realized it was foolish of her to say this in front of Will. She tried to back away. Her face must have shown her fear because Will stepped back as if she had struck him. He held his hands up. "I didn't hurt Flora. I—I loved her." He ducked his head. "I would have done anything for her if she had only given me a second glance. She only had eyes for Croucher though."

Anything she could say died on her lips as the sound of the door rattling interrupted them.

"Quick!" Will hissed. "Get in the ladies dressing area!"

Evie didn't argue. Her fate was in Will's hands, and she could only hope that she could make it out of the theater alive. She ran to the dressing area and slid into one stall. It scared her to even breathe. She closed her eyes and tried to stop shaking. She had been foolish to come here tonight. She heard heavy footsteps stride across the floor, and then heard Will and Marco talking.

"Any problems meeting Frankie this evening?" Marco asked.

She couldn't make out Will's mumbled reply. She said a silent prayer that Will wouldn't reveal her hiding place. She eased forward to see if she had a clear path for escape but ducked back behind the curtain when she saw Marco. She gripped her hands tightly over her mouth to try to quell the sound of her teeth chattering from fear.

"We need to unload this shipment fast. Cops sniffing around here isn't good for business. It makes my suppliers nervous," Marco said.

"The cop who came by here asking about Flora didn't seem too concerned. It's a shame she's dead. She was a good-looking gal," Will said.

"Dames are a dime a dozen. She was a looker, but I knew she was trouble two minutes after I hired her. Her brother sniffing around, trying to convince her to come back home. For all we know, he's the one who killed her. Listen, I don't have time to chew the fat. Did Frankie pay you the full amount or did he try to haggle?"

"One hundred and eighty dollars. He said his friends are parched, so he had no problem handing over the cash," Will said. "Huh? I must have dropped the pouch of money when I went on the stage. I thought I heard a sound, but it turned out to be a bat."

"What are you waiting for? Go get it, and let's get the hell out of here."

Evie peeked out once again. She saw Will glance over his shoulder and give a quick jerk of his head. She nodded her understanding. As they left the backstage area, Evie slid out of her hiding spot and dashed to the door. She ran down the alley and around the corner before she stopped.

A shadow stepped from the building entrance across the street. Aunt Dorcas's silver-topped cane glinted from a streetlamp's pale glow. Evie rushed across the street to join her. Out of breath, she gasped, "Let's go."

Chapter Twenty-two

Evie told Aunt Dorcas everything as she drove them back to the house. It surprised her how well she navigated the empty streets of Richmond since her hands were still shaking from her close call. The Nash's headlamps pierced the fog that had crept over the city in the past hour.

"Did you believe Will when he said he had nothing to do with Flora's death?" Aunt Dorcas asked.

"My gut says he didn't hurt her. It sounded like he really loved her," Evie said. "I have to say, I'm surprised Flora wanted in on the bootlegging action. It's a dangerous business from everything I've read in the newspapers."

"I think you need to accept the fact that Flora may not have been the angel her family thought she was," Aunt Dorcas said. "Families have blinders on with their kin. No one likes to think their daughter likes to sip at the giggle juice and attend petting parties."

Evie's eyes widened. "Aunt Dorcas! How do you know about those kinds of things? Maeve and I thought we were modern gals. It appears my aunt knows more than most girls my age."

"Ha. I might be old, but that doesn't mean I don't have young friends. I know what goes on in the streets and alleys of Richmond. Regardless, if Flora had a little fun, who are we to judge? She was young and entitled to enjoy a little of life. Sadly, she won't have a chance."

Evie pulled the Nash into the drive next to the house and turned off the headlamps. As she did, a shadowy shape peeled away from the side of the house and moved toward them. For a moment, Evie thought one of Felix's shadow spirits was here to do them harm, but as it moved closer, she made out a homburg on a man's head. She realized it was Jack.

Evie allowed him to open the door of the automobile. "Jack! You gave me a fright! What are you doing here in the dead of night?"

Aunt Dorcas leaned across Evie and held out her hand. "I'm Dorcas, Evie's aunt. I've heard quite a bit about you, Jack Thompson. How about you come in the house and introduce yourself properly?"

Jack touched his hand to the brim of his hat and nodded. "Yes, ma'am."

He helped Evie out of the automobile before hurrying over to lend Aunt Dorcas his arm. They made their way slowly since Aunt Dorcas appeared to be limping more than usual. Evie felt a twinge of guilt at having her walk on the injured ankle.

Once inside, Jack settled Aunt Dorcas in front of the fire, which had died down to smoldering embers. Evie poured them each a finger's width of Aunt Dorcas's special recipe and sat down on the settee. Jack took a minute to stoke the fire. Once it was crackling and emitting a decent amount of warmth, he sat down on the hearth.

"I suppose it seemed odd to find me outside your home at such a late hour, and for that, I apologize, Miss… Mrs. Dorcas?"

"Dorcas is just fine. It's Miss Harris, but I prefer to go by my given name. Now, continue with why you were skulking around my front garden after midnight." Aunt Dorcas tried to sound gruff, but Evie noted a twinkle of mischief in her aunt's eyes.

"I got back from Pittsburgh early this morning." He turned to Evie. "I went straight to your father's house, and he advised me you were staying here. He gave me quite an earful. Fortunately, Harry had the forethought to telephone and let me know everything that transpired during my absence.

"I should have stayed to comfort my parents, but the thought of you risking your life to solve Flora's murder didn't sit right with me."

Evie felt herself bristle, but when she saw the exhaustion and grief etched onto Jack's face, she let go of her ire. "I appreciate your concern. I've been careful. Just like I promised when you left. How are your folks doing? It must be horrible for them."

"As well as expected." Jack shook his head. "I don't know if Mother will ever recover from the loss. She's taken to her bed and refuses to eat. I'm hoping with time, she'll recover. As they always say, time heals all wounds. I need to catch the man who killed my sister. Maybe it will bring Mother some peace of mind."

"I can tell you from experience that the pain never goes away. It's like a sharp, broken tooth your tongue always gravitates toward. A constant reminder. Over time, it wears down and may not be as painful, but it's always there." For a moment, Aunt Dorcas's face looked haunted, and she aged twenty years, but then she shook her head and the specter of grief disappeared.

Evie reached out and grasped her aunt's hand. Aunt Dorcas gave her a ghost of a smile. "So, young man, it still doesn't explain why you were waiting outside of the house."

Jack had the grace to look down and when he looked up, he glanced at Evie, and she could have sworn his face reddened. "I was worried about Evie. I stopped by here after I spoke to George. No one was here, so I went to check into the Jefferson Hotel with the plan to come see you this evening. When you were still gone, I'll be honest, my mind started imagining different scenarios and none were good. I went by the theater and saw it locked up tight. I finally went by your friend Maeve's, and she told me the two of you had driven down to Norfolk. I waited at the hotel, but I'm impatient, so I came here to wait for you."

"We went to Norfolk and learned about Marco Croucher. It appears he's rum running and using the show as cover," Evie said.

Jack snorted. "I'm not surprised. He's as crooked as a snake oil salesman and twice as dangerous."

"You must have missed us when we returned. We've been doing a little reconnaissance on the theater this evening looking for evidence to take to the police," Aunt Dorcas said. "That's why we're returning so late. Evie's become adept at picking locks."

Jack shook his head. "Harry's a horrible influence. They could have hurt you for breaking into the theater. What were you thinking? Does your father know you two were doing this?"

Evie wasn't sure if it was exhaustion or resignation that caused her to let out an exasperated sigh. "Mister Thompson, I'm an adult, and I don't need my father's permission. I'm not some wilting flower in need of your protection." She stood up and gestured towards the door. "Now, if you'll excuse us. It's been a long day, and I'm tired. I appreciate your concern, but I have rehearsal tomorrow and dark circles under my eyes might arouse suspicion."

Jack gave her a contrite smile. "You're right. I'm treating you like a child, and for that I apologize. I just… well, I just don't want anything to happen to you, Evie." He stood up and gripping his hat tightly in his hand said, "Can I call on you tomorrow evening?"

Aunt Dorcas looked from Evie to Jack, then back to Evie. She looked as if she wanted to say something, but she pursed her lips tightly together to suppress a smile that didn't escape Evie's notice.

"I suppose we need to compare notes," Evie said, her cheeks warming. "I have your sister's things. I hope you don't mind, but I picked them up from the boarding house."

"Thank you. It was business I dreaded doing, so I'm glad you've taken care of it. It's time I take my leave. Shall we meet tomorrow after your afternoon rehearsal?"

"Our rehearsal will be late tomorrow. They have an afternoon movie matinee until three. Will six o'clock work?" Evie asked. He nodded and she walked with Jack to the door. "I am being careful. I realized today that there are more moving pieces to Flora's death than I first realized."

Jack held her gaze for a moment, then leaned down and kissed her hard on the lips before grabbing the doorknob and strolling out the door. Evie wasn't sure, but she thought she could hear him whistle quietly as he walked down the drive towards the street.

Aunt Dorcas chuckled behind her. She whirled around and tried to glare at her aunt, but she found herself with a bemused look instead. "He's worried about me. I don't even like him. Well, not that much."

Aunt Dorcas pursed her lips. "He fancies you. Don't be so prickly, Evie. You don't have to fight the world every day. It exhausts a person after a while. I should know."

With that cryptic comment, her aunt thumped her way down the hallway and left Evie lost in thought, staring after her.

The next morning, Evie didn't awaken with the sunrise like she normally did. Instead, the smell of coffee wafted its way from the kitchen to her nose and pulled her from a restless sleep. She grabbed her dressing gown from a hook on the back of her door and hurried downstairs. The mantel clock showed it was ten-thirty, and that made her slow her steps. She wasn't due at the theater until three o'clock. It gave her several hours to consume enough coffee to make her pass for awake and wash away the exhaustion of the previous night.

"Good morning, sleepyhead," Aunt Dorcas said, placing a plate with slices of toast in the center of the kitchen table. She poured Evie a cup of coffee before settling into a chair. "You young people don't have the stamina for the late nights. Back when I was younger, I would play mahjong until dawn and still work all day on the boat."

Evie would have rolled her eyes, but now she knew her aunt's stories were mired in truth. "I need to help you with your memoirs, Aunt Dorcas. I would love to have even a quarter of the adventures you've experienced."

"You will." Aunt Dorcas clapped her hands onto her thighs and leaned forward. "So, what's your plan for today?"

Evie took a sip of her coffee and considered. "If Will hasn't squealed, I'll carry on with the matinee performance as usual. After last night, I feel like I can eliminate Will. Mary's rheumatism is so bad, she couldn't have made her way into the cellar. I think that's where Flora was killed. I'm still undecided about Felix. I don't think he would have intentionally hurt her, but sometimes he seems lost in another time and place. Perhaps in one of those moments, he hurt Flora. I know too much laudanum makes folks crazy. Perhaps Marco overdosed Felix by accident causing him to go wild."

"What about Marco's wife? What's her name… Belinda… Betty…"

"Betsy. I can't see her as the killer. She knows about Marco and Annie, so jealousy doesn't seem to be a factor. What other reason could she have to harm Flora?" Evie picked up a piece of toast from the plate and tore a corner of the crust off before popping it into her mouth.

"Women have other reasons than a man for murder, Evie. Money and greed are powerful motivators, too."

Evie swallowed her bite of toast. "I know, but my gut says this was personal."

Flora was flitting around Marco, which could have developed into more than a harmless flirtation. Evie would bet her eye teeth that Betsy was still in love with Felix, though. Now that she thought about it, perhaps she had been too hasty to strike Betsy from the list of murderers. If Felix had shown more than a passing interest in Flora… Evie shook her head. It didn't sit right with her. She believed Felix when he said he and Flora were only friends. It rang true.

She shook her head. "It's making my head hurt thinking of all these suspects. Marco makes a good villain, but this isn't one of my adventure magazines. Daddy always says to follow the evidence to catch the criminal. Marco is a criminal. He's hauling illegal liquor. He has the strongest motive to kill Flora."

Aunt Dorcas held up a finger. "But Will said that Flora wanted in on the bootlegging. That makes Marco a weaker suspect."

"Unless she asked for a cut to keep quiet," Evie countered. She looked down and realized she had torn her toast into shreds. "She was leaving the show. Did Marco turn her down, and she threatened to turn him in? We're going around in circles, and I've got to go get dressed."

Evie went upstairs to her bedroom with her spirit deflated and more confused than when she started investigating. As hot water filled the porcelain claw foot tub, Evie looked in the mirror above the sink. She wiped her hand across the surface to clear the moisture and gazed at her reflection. "Who killed you, Flora, and why?"

Chapter Twenty-three

"I can't believe that codfish is Julia's mother," Betsy said, a sour look marred her pretty face. She bent down and straightened her stockings.

When Evie arrived at the theater at a quarter 'til three, Will studiously avoided looking her in the eye. She had been nervous when she entered the dressing area, but the hubbub of the theater was the same as the previous week. It appeared no one else knew of her late-night adventure. Now, she and Betsy stood in the wings and watched Annie perform.

Betsy let out a loud cough which caused Annie to turn their way. The plate that had been spinning on the rod crashed to the ground, sending shards of china everywhere. Annie glared at them but finished her performance. Annie stomped across the stage. She looked down at the dainty wristwatch adorning her wrist. "It's my time on the stage. You two should scram. Maybe put a little more color on your cheeks. You're looking a little wan, Betsy. Marco likes his... performers healthy."

Evie stiffened and opened her mouth to defend Betsy, but she didn't need to say a word. Betsy stepped forward with a satisfied smile. "You're so right, Annie. I need to take care of myself and little Marco Junior. You're so considerate. I'll let Marco know how thoughtful you are."

Betsy spun on her heel and strutted away, leaving Annie gasping and looking like the codfish Betsy had called her only moments before. Annie's eyes narrowed and hardened. "What are you looking at, schoolgirl?" She touched the jade and silver necklace on her throat.

"Will! Come clean this mess up. I need to finish my rehearsal."

Betsy's pregnant! Evie headed to the dressing area to find Mary. She passed Will on the way with a broom and metal dustpan in his hands.

"Be careful of Annie," he whispered. "You don't want to get on her nasty side."

With that cryptic warning, Will lumbered to the stage with his bad leg thumping heavily on the wooden floor. Evie knew Annie wasn't the sort to run afoul of. Back in school there had been an occasional petty squabble over a guy, but the girls she grew up with were all on friendly terms. Annie had a brittle hardness to her personality that tarnished her good looks.

Evie found Mary seated on a chair with one leg propped up high on a stool. Mary squinted over a needle as she threaded it with a vibrant blue thread. Her nicotine-stained fingers expertly tied a knot.

"Leg bothering you?" Evie asked as she settled herself on a nearby chair.

"Ayuh," Mary mumbled around the pins she held tightly between her lips. She plucked them out one by one and used them to pin the edge of the costume. "A storm is coming. I guarantee it. The old knee likes to give me grief every time the weather turns. First, the cold bothers me. Now, I've got the spring damp. Give me sunshine, and I'll be happy." Mary leaned over and rubbed her propped knee before glancing sideways at Evie. "Heard you had a late night."

Evie looked around quickly to make sure no one was nearby. Mary let out a moist laugh that ended in a cough. "Oh, girlie, don't worry. Your secret's safe with me, but you might be careful meeting Felix here. His brother has a habit of popping in at all hours of the night."

"But I—" Evie protested but stopped. This was the perfect cover if someone said anything. She could say she had been looking for Felix. An eager assistant who developed a crush on the magician. "I suppose Will told you I was here. I'm so embarrassed. What must you think of me?"

Mary's eyes gleamed as she appraised her. "I admit when I first met you I thought you were a little too pure for show business. You're a little more streetwise than you appear to be. I suppose if you were going to make eyes at anyone, better Felix than Marco. The last gal made a fool of herself carrying on like she did."

"Flora chased after Marco?"

Mary chuckled. "Like a cat in heat, she was. Batting her eyelashes at Marco and cooing. Like any man, Marco lapped it up."

"What about Betsy? Didn't she mind?"

"Ha! Betsy looks out for Betsy. Her family helps Marco out in some of his nighttime activities. He should treat Betsy better, or he'll bite the hand that helps feed him." Mary bit the thread off she had been using to hem the skirt of the costume. "Listen to me nattering on and telling you things you don't need to know. My Will says it's a bad habit. He doesn't understand that his mother gets lonely for a bit of gossip and tea. You won't tell anyone what I said, will you? Marco would be angry that I spread his business."

Evie stayed silent while she digested what Mary had divulged. After a moment, she shook her head. "No… no, I won't say anything. Your secret's safe with me." She echoed Mary's own words. "I'd best get up front. Felix likes to start our rehearsal on time."

Annie had left the stage when Evie returned. She spotted Betsy on the other side of the stage, whispering with Marco. Evie wondered if Betsy was expecting or had said that to dig under Annie's skin. Her own skin was tingling as she considered all she had discovered over the past few days. There was something gnawing at the back of all those thoughts, but it wouldn't come to the forefront. Every time she thought she would remember, it would flit back into the deep recesses of her mind.

"Penny for your thoughts," Felix said, holding up a penny as he leaned against the wall next to her. "You were a million miles away, Evie. Are you okay?"

Evie smiled at him. "I'm fine. Thinking over the weekend's performance."

Felix straightened and stepped closer. "You were beautiful on stage. The way the light glinted off your costume. It made you look ethereal."

Evie snapped her fingers. "That's it! Now I remember!"

"Pardon?" Confusion marred Felix's handsome face.

She waved her hand. "You must think I'm loony. I was trying to remember something, and when you said that it jarred loose in my brain."

He shook his head. "No. I don't think you're loony. I sometimes wish I could erase my memories. They don't want to stay buried though."

"Felix, I—I wish I could help," Evie said. She laid her hand on his arm and squeezed.

"You're sweet," Felix said. For a moment, he deflated, and his youthful face appeared years older, but the moment was fleeting. "We're wasting precious time. Let's get on stage."

They rehearsed without incident. Evie felt her confidence grow with each trick. Betsy's timing had been off with the sawed lady, but Evie covered it with patter. As Felix twirled the box around and around, she spotted Marco watching them from the wings with his eyes fixed on them.

When they finished the act, Marco glided across the stage with barely a glance at Evie. She let out a breath she hadn't realized she'd been holding. Will still hadn't revealed her late-night escapade, or Marco would act differently. He helped Betsy down. "Are you sure you're up to rehearsal, love? You look a little green around the gills. I can get Annie to take your place. Maybe Julia can start training to assist."

Betsy's face did look pale. "I'm fine, darling. Don't fuss. I'd like to finish here at the Bijou, then perhaps take a rest. We must find a replacement, though. Soon I'll be too big to fit in any of these contraptions."

Felix scowled. "Is there something you need to tell me, Betsy?" He turned to his brother. "Marco?"

"We wanted to wait, but now is as good as ever. Betsy's expecting. I'm going to be a father." Marco crowed, ignorant to the stricken look that crossed Felix's face.

If Betsy's face was pale, Felix's own was ghost white. His jaw clenched, but he bit out a tight, "Congratulations."

"Yes, congratulations," Evie chimed in. She had thought Betsy was unhappy in her marriage, but now she positively beamed at her husband. The two of them held each other closer than a pair of high school sweethearts.

Felix spun towards Evie. "Darling, I think we should have dinner at Vano's tonight. I know how much you loved it last time."

"Yes," Evie stammered, but when she saw the desperation in Felix's eyes, she smiled and moved closer to him. "I loved it, and I want to hear more stories about when you were a boy."

Marco gave her an appraising look. "It seems our little chickadee has made an impression with more than just the audience. We should all go out and celebrate together. Make it an occasion."

Felix's lips thinned. "Perhaps another time, dear brother. Evie and I would like some alone time. I'm sure you understand. A beautiful woman is a treasure, don't you agree?"

Although Felix directed his words to Marco, his eyes held Betsy's. She had the grace to look away. "Yes, Marco. Let these two have their time. You and I can celebrate with them another time."

Marco clapped his hands together. "Another time, then. Brother, let's go to my office and talk before we close up for the night. We need to discuss the upcoming dates and make changes."

The two men walked away and left Betsy and Evie alone on the stage. Evie whirled towards Betsy. "Are you really pregnant? I thought you said that to upset Annie."

Betsy blushed and looked down. Her hand went to her belly. "I am. At first I didn't believe it, but it's true. All these weeks of me being weepy. It's the pregnancy."

"Aren't you worried that he'll hurt you or the baby?" Evie whispered. "I've seen the bruises, Betsy."

"No. He's not like that. I say things that upset him and it makes him hit me. He always apologizes and makes it up to me."

"What about Annie?"

"What about her?" Betsy said, her eyes hard. "I told Marco she needed to go. He agreed. He plans to give her notice today. He'll let her finish out this week, but after that she's on her own. Come on. I need to get changed out of this outfit. It's already getting too tight."

Evie trailed after Betsy as they walked to the dressing area. She worried that Betsy was making a huge mistake. Men like Marco didn't suddenly change their ways. Betsy and now the baby would be at Marco's mercy.

In the stall, she changed back into her street clothes and hung her costume on the wooden hanger. She fingered the buttons on the front of the costume. Mary had replaced the lost one, and it was like new. Had this costume been the last thing Flora had worn? Had she died in this? Evie shuddered at the thought. She would tell Jack everything, but she wouldn't return to the theater. Money and jealousy were intertwined so deeply that she couldn't pull the strands apart. After Marco's revelation, the only thing she could say with certainty was

Felix was no longer on her suspect list. The raw pain she had seen on his face told her that the only woman who held his heart was Betsy. He had no reason to hurt Flora. That realization didn't comfort her because now she knew who murdered Flora, but could she prove it?

Chapter Twenty-four

Evie wandered to the makeup and hair room. She wanted to wipe the exaggerated Cupid's bow from her lips before hopping on the trolley for home. Felix peeked his head into the dressing area. "I'm sorry I put you in that position, Evie. I'll take you to that dinner if you'd like," Felix said.

"Perhaps another time. I have plans for this evening."

Felix gave her a sorrowful look. "Another man? I don't blame you. A pretty gal like you needs to step out with someone who isn't mooning after someone he can't have."

"Felix." Evie hesitated. What could she say to him that would wipe away the pain Marco and Betsy's betrayal inflicted? Anything she said would be trite. "How about tomorrow evening? It's too late for me to cancel this evening, but I'd love to go to Vano's again with you."

Felix's face brightened. "That would be marvelous. I'll see you tomorrow then. And Evie?"

"Yes, Felix?"

"Thanks for helping me save face. The spirits said you were here to make things right, and I can see that they were correct." He walked away from her. Despite her misgivings about promising a dinner with him, she was happy to see a little jauntiness in his stride. Perhaps, one more day of rehearsal couldn't hurt.

Evie continued to the makeshift makeup room. She saw Betsy seated in front of the mirror, cold cream smeared across her face. She glanced at Evie's reflection. "Please don't say anything. Someone like you will never understand someone like me. We're from different worlds, you and me." She picked up a facecloth and scrubbed the kohl on her eyes.

"You're right. I don't understand. But what I understand is that you have value and someone like Marco doesn't see you as anything but merchandise. What happens when the newness of the Croucher heir wears off? What then?"

Betsy stopped and spun in her chair. "Like I said, you wouldn't understand. I'm happy. Marco is happy. Leave it alone."

Evie opened her mouth, then closed it. She had said all she could. It was up to Betsy to decide if this was the life she wanted. Evie realized how fortunate she was to have a choice. Many women didn't. Society relegated them to second-hand status— a possession, merchandise to use, abuse, and discard when their husband decided. Evie vowed no one would ever place her in a similar position.

Betsy stood. "We'd best be going. Marco wants to lock up and go home early. Are you ready?"

Forgetting that she wanted to clean her face, Evie nodded. "Yes, I'm ready."

The two women walked together in silence to the alley door where Marco stood waiting. He flipped a large switch and plunged the theater into darkness. "It's raining. You'd best hurry home, chickadee, before you get soaked."

Evie glanced out the door at the beginning of what promised to be a deluge. "Oh no! This downpour will ruin my cloak."

"I have an extra raincoat you're welcome to borrow. It's hanging on the rack with the costumes. Bring it back tomorrow."

Marco reached over and turned the lights to the backstage area on once more. "Go ahead. I've locked the door. Just be sure to pull it shut behind you. Be careful in the alley. A few Johnnies were hanging around earlier until Will scared them off."

"I will," Evie promised.

Marco and Betsy headed out into the rain with Marco holding an umbrella solicitously over Betsy. Evie hoped this new version of Marco would stick, but in her heart, she doubted he would. She hurried back to the costume room to find the coat. She checked the time. It was almost five-thirty, and she needed to rush home to meet Jack. The day had gone so quickly that she hadn't realized how late it was.

She spotted the raincoat and slipped into it. She knew she'd better hurry if she wanted to catch the trolley. The theater was eerily silent as she made her way back to the door. She felt a whisk of air causing her neck hair to rise. Had one of the men who Marco said hung around the alley made it into the theater?

"Hello? Is anyone there?" Evie waited. She shook her head. She was on edge after Betsy's revelation and Marco's warning.

The creaking of the floor should have warned her. Evie was thinking about her upcoming dinner with Jack and telling him she knew who had killed Flora. It wasn't until she felt the blow to the back of her head that she realized she wasn't alone.

"Hell's bells!" Evie exclaimed as unconsciousness claimed her.

***

When she opened her eyes, Evie couldn't quite see her surroundings. She tried to sit up. When she did, the room spun in a nauseating circle around her. She lay back down on the cold, damp floor. She stretched out her right hand and felt the dank bricks beneath her. She was under the stage.

"You're awake. About time. I thought I was going to have to slap you to bring you around. Not that I would have minded," Annie's voice said from somewhere nearby.

Evie attempted to sit up again and this time, the room carouseled a little slower. She rubbed the back of her head. Her hand came away sticky and wet. Blood.

"Annie. You killed Flora and dumped her in the river." Evie fought back the bile that rose in her throat.

Annie's chuckle echoed in the small, dark space. "Ah, schoolgirl is smarter than she looks."

"Because of Marco." Evie blinked her eyes in an attempt to get them to focus. There were two Annies in front of her.

"He promised to leave Betsy and start a life with me, and now it's all ruined," Annie cried. "I have no job, no home, nothing."

Evie tried to slide her body slowly across the ground. Her foot caught on something and gave her movement away.

"No, you don't," Annie said, and in a flash, she was behind her and wrenching Evie's hair. "I found this beauty in your pocketbook. Why is a nice gal like you carrying a pistol?"

Evie felt the cold steel as it touched her temple and froze. She thought fast. "I'm sorry Marco did that to you. A beautiful woman like you deserves better."

212

Annie yanked her head back, and her hot, sour breath washed over Evie. "You're sorry? I'm thirty-six. Past my prime in the theater. Marco was my last shot at a life where I didn't have to scrabble. I only wanted a taste of a better life. A little luxury or two."

Annie released Evie's hair and paced around the small space. "The money was coming in. This show's money was a pittance. Movies are nudging acts like ours out. Bookings are lower each season. Marco and I figured we could use the circuit to smuggle liquor. It was brilliant."

"You helped Marco with the booze and Flora wanted a cut of the action, didn't she?" Evie asked. She knew she had to keep Annie talking. Keep her distracted until Evie could figure a way out of this mess.

Annie dropped in front of her and shoved the pistol against her chest. Evie shrank back from the madness in her eyes. "She thought she could come in here and bat her eyes at Marco and he would give her everything we had worked so hard to build."

"That wasn't right of her," Evie said, her voice catching. "She didn't need it. Her family has plenty of money."

"More money than I've ever seen. We were just a game for Flora. A way for her to pass time until the next shiny thing caught her attention. This? This is all I have. Now it's gone." Annie let out a sob but stifled it.

"You took Flora's jade necklace."

"Seems I'm not the only one with secrets. You've been nosing around. It's a shame that you didn't heed my advice that first day and go back home. I tried to scare you off. The sandbag. The lights. You're like a mosquito that won't stop. You kept coming back after being swatted away."

"She never left the theater alive, did she?" Evie prayed someone would return to the theater. Will. Mary. Anyone. She had to keep Annie talking.

"Little titmouse that girl. When Marco refused to let her in on the action, she started yammering about leaving the show. She could have squealed to the revenuers." Annie stood up and paced across the floor. She waved the gun in the air. "I thought you were Betsy tonight. You were wearing her coat. It was supposed to be her."

"What I can't figure out is how you got her out of the theater?" Evie tried to sound confused and weak. She needed Annie to let down her guard. Her fingers crept along the ground, searching.

"Will and Marco leave their keys all the time. I pocketed Will's and when everyone was gone, it was easy to drag her out through the door under the stage. It leads right into the alley. Tiny scrap of a girl weighed less than an elephant's bale of hay. I got her out of her costume and drove to the river. I dumped her next to the docks. Figured cops would assume a sailor had done it. Shame they fished her out. I hoped her body would eventually drift towards the Atlantic."

Evie's hand closed around the object she'd been seeking. She decided to lure Annie closer. "You can't hurt Betsy. She's going to have Marco's baby."

Evie knew her words found their target in Annie's rage. Annie lifted the gun and pounced at Evie. She leaned down to grasp Evie's hair once again. When she did, Evie lifted her hand and brought the loose brick crashing down on Annie's head.

Annie yelped and stumbled back. The gun clattered to the floor. Evie seized her chance. She knew this space. She had gone over these bricks and dirt every day for the past ten days. Not hesitating, her feet found their way across the bricks. Evie didn't look behind her but trusted her feet to remember the way. When her hands hit the wall, she fumbled to her left until her fingers found the narrow wooden treads. Despite her dizziness, she hoisted herself up the steep steps. She clung to the railing and forced herself upward. She was so dizzy.

"You little—" Annie's hand grasped Evie's ankle. Evie kicked as hard as she could. Annie lost her grip. Evie heaved the trapdoor open and scurried through the opening. As soon as she was free, she slammed the door back down and pulled a nearby chair on top of it. She had to hurry. The chair would slow Annie down, but it wouldn't stop her. Evie ran towards the alley door. She heard the crash of the chair as it skittered across the floor. She was almost there when she heard Annie's feet pounding across the wooden floor. With a last burst of speed that came from somewhere deep within her, Evie reached the door and wrenched it open. She dashed out into the rain without a backward glance. She kept running until she reached the corner diner where she had drank coffee the first time with Jack. She burst through the door and startled the lone gentleman hunched over his dinner at the counter.

"I need the police," Evie gasped. "Someone call the police."
She collapsed into the nearest chair before oblivion reclaimed her.

Chapter Twenty-five

A week later, Evie was happily ensconced in front of a fire in Aunt Dorcas's living room, holding a glass of her aunt's famous elixir in one hand and a chocolate-covered cherry in the other. A gold box filled with several more of the delicious treats, courtesy of Jack Thompson, lay on a table nearby.

"How did you know it was Annie?" Maeve asked. She sat close to Harold, a beautiful, new diamond ring glinting on the ring finger of her left hand.

"The necklace. Aunt Dorcas had said people kill for money or love. In Annie's case, it was a mix of both. She killed Flora and then took what she could from her room. She wanted a taste of what Flora's life was like. I think she was desperate to feel young and beautiful. Flora didn't want Marco. She wanted the thrill of bootlegging and tried to use her feminine wiles on Marco. When it didn't work, she decided it was time to move on to the next adventure. Unfortunately, Annie didn't realize Flora planned to leave and not say a word to anyone about the booze. She decided to take out the competition."

Maeve shook her head. "I'm just glad you're okay."

Evie's fingers reached up and touched the bandage on the back of her head. She had required five stitches and had sustained a concussion. At her insistence, they hadn't kept her in the hospital overnight. Instead, her father escorted her home and tucked her up in bed with a glass of warm milk like he had when she was a child. Mrs. Fortune had clucked over her like a worried hen with her chick and kept sending baskets of baked goods.

Her father was still in shock. He had wanted her to stay at their home, but Evie had insisted on returning to Aunt Dorcas's the next day. Now that she had a taste of independence, she was loathe to give it up. She had solved Flora's murder. Despite his worries, Evie had seen the pride in his eyes. She might not be his Peter, but she was definitely a Harris.

"You're lucky that madwoman didn't kill you," Harold said. He pulled Maeve a little closer to him, and Evie saw her friend's expression grow a little brighter. Despite her protestations that she was a career girl, Evie knew Maeve had found her happiness with Harold. Fortunately, Harold was a modern man. Evie just hoped he was up to being Maeve's husband. Evie had no doubt Maeve would keep him on his toes.

"I only hope they find Annie," Aunt Dorcas said. "The woman is a menace. I know I'll sleep easier once they catch up to her."

"Jack's on her trail. He'll find her," Evie said.

"How is the handsome and eligible Jack?" Maeve grinned.

Evie ignored Maeve's innuendo and sat a little straighter. "I'm sure he's busy tracking Annie. He left yesterday on the morning train. She had people out in Kansas, so he's headed that way."

"Poor Julia. To find out your mother is a murderess," Maeve shook her head.

"Mary said they'll take care of her. They really do operate like a little family," Evie said. "Mary and Will stopped by yesterday. The show closes down tomorrow. Felix's magic act fell a little flat without an assistant, but they'll regroup." She took another sip of the elixir then set it down. It really packed a wallop, and her head was still tender.

"I can't believe that they didn't find any liquor in the crates under the stage," Harold said. "Marco Croucher must have the luck of a leprechaun."

"Will made the delivery the night Aunt Dorcas and I broke into the theater. There was nothing left to find. Daddy said the revenuers will keep an eye out on him," Evie said. "To be honest, I hope he doesn't get caught. I don't like Marco, but I think Betsy deserves a little happiness, even if it's only for a short time. I don't think Marco will change his ways, but maybe eventually she'll get the courage to leave."

Aunt Dorcas shook her head. "I hope you're right, Evie, but I've seen too many women trapped by circumstance. Which is why, I'm still happily single."

Before Harold protested, there was a knock at the front door.

"I wonder who that could be? I'm not expecting any more visitors today."

"I'll get it," Harold offered. He reluctantly peeled himself away from Maeve's side.

A minute later, he returned with an enormous bouquet in his hands. He handed them to Evie.

"Who are they from?" Maeve asked.

Evie pulled the card and read it. Her brief frown was followed by a huge grin. "They're from Harry Houdini. He needs me to head to New York. He's got another case for me."

The End

* * *

Acknowledgements

This book would not have been possible without the support of my Sisters in Crime Central Virginia critique group. My heartfelt thanks to Heather Weidner, Frances Aylor, Catherine Brennan, Marjorie Bagby, Sandie Warwick, Susan Campbell, and Kellie Murphy. Their guidance and feedback throughout the writing of this book was invaluable. Many thanks to my friends Charlene Harris, Myra Cramer, Pat Lyttle, and Megan Upshaw. They listened to my opening chapters and provided opinions and encouragement. Thank you to my developmental editor, Eve Porinchak, for her gentle edits and rewrites. My gratitude to Deranged Doctor Design for my cover art. Thank you to Hannah Nystrom for her beautiful artwork for my website and her constant encouragement. Hannah, you are an amazing artist! And as always, much love to my husband and my two sons. They are my rock upon which I stand.